MW00529007

Daisy and the Crimson Rose:

A Pirate's Tale

Shoshana Louise

Copyright © 2019 by Shoshana Louise. All rights reserved. Printed in

the United States of America.

ISBN13: 978-1-7330050-0-5

MATURE AUDIENCE

This book is dedicated to my Papa,

Julian Joseph Sugarman.

For our shared passion for literature will keep us bonded forever.

May your soul rest in peace.

And to Jaris,

For your continued support

In all my endeavors.

Acknowledgements

I would like to thank my father for always being there to push me toward my greatest potential. My mother, for always being supportive of everything I do. And to my grandmother, for cheering me on and providing insightful feedback on this book. I would also like to thank my editor, Blair Bordelon and my book designer Alessia Casali on facebook @AC Graphics.

CHAPTER ONE

Springtime in Yorkston, Virginia was impeccable. A picturesque view of flowers in full bloom lined the outside walls of the Clark family home. Daisy proudly admired the blooming beauties she planted soon after the last bit of snow melted away. Her garden was the one thing that brought meaning to her life. It allowed her peace and serenity with a short escape away from her troubles.

The gift of cultivation was passed on to her by her mother. She remembered how her mother worked vigorously day after day to keep her garden vibrant. "If you give them some water, some sun, and a little bit of love," her mother would say as she tapped her daughter's button nose leaving behind a smudge of dirt, "they will brighten your life and help you forget about all of your worries."

Daisy did not understand her mother's words until she grew older. Life was hard, something she knew nothing of as a carefree child, sheltered by loving parents. But as she aged, she found comfort in the calming nature of the beautiful garden.

Daisy briefly remembered her mother's face as she would lean over her delicate flowers, ensuring each one received the same amount of care. She remembered how her eyes glistened as the sun's rays struck her bright blue irises. She remembered how pink her smile looked as the lilies' glow radiated back toward her face. She remembered the beads of sweat from her mother's forehead dripping into the garden like a token of her love. And she remembered the proud look on her face when she would gaze lovingly at her young, beautiful daughter helping her tend to her magnificent garden.

Today was a particularly lovely day. The flowers appeared to be in full bloom under the bright, sun-lit sky. Clouds were sparse, but the ones that remained were as white as freshly fallen snow. The blue sky was almost entirely in view as Daisy watched a flock of birds playfully frolic overhead. As she knelt by her garden, Daisy sat back onto her knees and closed her eyes to listen to the soft humming of the bumble bees enjoying the sweet, succulent nectar. She inhaled deeply to appreciate the assortment of fragrances that intertwined into an aroma of pure bliss. With her head tilted backward, she smiled graciously toward the bright, blue sky and soaked up the sun's rays into the porcelain-like skin of her face.

"Excuse me miss." Daisy jolted at the unexpected salutation.

"I am so sorry, my lady, I did not intend to frighten thee."

Daisy turned to see an unexpected guest standing behind her.

"No, no," she replied while gazing at the exceedingly handsome intruder. "It is no problem at all. I was merely tending to the garden. It was just unexpected to have a guest arrive at this time of day," Daisy lied, knowing they rarely had any guests at all.

The tall, handsome stranger reached out to help Daisy up. Daisy blushed as she took hold of his strong, masculine hand and pulled herself to her feet. She dusted off her dress, and as she met him face to face, she could no longer find her words.

"My name is Nathaniel Alexander," the man said with a grin, acknowledging Daisy's bashfulness.

"I am Daisy Flynn," she stuttered, glancing at his incredibly attractive physique. Nathaniel was tall and slender. Charming, really. His hairless face was accentuated by his high cheekbones and strong jaw line. His blonde hair was combed backward into a neat bob of waves that slightly curled upward at the edge of his ears, resting at the nape of his neck. Daisy had to shade her eyes when she glanced up toward his face, for his slightly tanned complexion seemed to radiate in the sun.

"What a beautiful name," Nathaniel replied.

"Yes, thank you, my mother named me after her favorite flower. She had a strong interest in gardening and loved the beauty in nature."

"Ah, how lovely. It seemed she had an eye for beauty and named what she knew to be true."

Daisy felt her face grow hot once more, knowing she turned as crimson as the roses in her garden. "How kind of you, sir," she replied bashfully. "But what brings you to our humble abode?" Daisy asked in pure curiosity.

"I am here to speak with Mr. Abner Clark; that is your husband I presume?"

"Oh no," Daisy replied quickly to clear up any misconception. "Mr. Clark is merely the man who raised me once my parents passed. He is more of," Daisy hesitated, "a father figure, I suppose."

Nathaniel looked relieved as he grinned more deeply. "I am sorry for the passing of your parents. You seem to have been quite close with your mother, as I can see you partake in similar pastimes." Nathaniel then gestured by wiping his own cheek. "You have a little, um, may I?"

Daisy froze and nodded subtly as Nathaniel reached over and brushed the dirt from her smooth cheek. She found herself smiling as his strong hand touched her face with such care. He smiled in response then said, "good as new. Is Mr. Clark in the home?"

"No, he is more than likely at the tavern just a short distance up the road if you'd like to meet him there."

Nathaniel looked displeased with her response, so Daisy ventured, "or, you are more than welcome to join me for a cup of tea until he returns."

She watched as Nathaniel's face lit up. "Yes," he replied, "I would definitely fancy a cup of tea."

Inside the double-storied, white-paneled home, Daisy pointed to a chair in the kitchen and welcomed Nathaniel to sit. She frantically attempted to tidy up the kitchen a bit as she filled a kettle with water and hung it in the already lit hearth. Once the tea was boiled, she poured a cup for herself and for Nathaniel and she sat down adjacent to him at the round, dining room table. He stared admiringly at her as he sipped his tea.

After a couple hours of innocent chatting, Nathaniel said without any apprehension, "I'm sorry, my lady, I cannot help but gaze at you. You are the most beautiful woman I have ever seen. Surely, you must have some gentlemen courters."

Daisy smirked. "Thank you, Mr. Alexander, you are too kind, but no, I do not get out of this house very often to even find that opportunity."

"Please," Nathaniel responded, "call me Nathaniel."

Daisy grinned. "It's a beautiful spring time day outside, don't you think?"

"Why yes, it is. But I am not very interested in the weather at the moment. I would much more like to know about you. It's bizarre, I know many of the women in this town and yet, I have not until now had the pleasure of making your acquaintance. Surely, you have come into the market square at one point in time or another?"

Daisey quickly interjected to change the subject. "Ah, so you know many of the women in town?"

Nathaniel chuckled. "Ah, yes, but not in the way you are thinking, my lady. And if you are interested in knowing, none of whom have seemed to catch my attention as much as thee."

Daisy blushed. "You seem to be a well-groomed man with some sort of status I'm sure. Why, might I ask have you not yet been wedded?

"I have been waiting patiently for the perfect woman to become my bride. And here you have been all along."

"You know nothing of me," Daisy snapped as she stood up from the table and made her way over to the basin to wash out her tea cup. She scrubbed the cup vigorously as she dealt with her frustration.

Nathaniel sat silently, ashamed of his forwardness. Then he said, "please, my lady, do not take offense. My intention is not malicious." He then stood and approached her from behind. He gently placed his hand on her arm to turn her around. He waited for a response, to see if she would object to his touch. When she stilled, seemingly accepting his gesture, he spun her around and gazed lovingly into her eyes. He was astounded by her long, flowing, honey locks with soft waves like the gentle current of the river. He felt as if he could lose himself in her deep, chocolate colored eyes. He then said, "I can see you, and I feel like I have known you for longer than just these few short hours we have spent together."

He moved closer and reached out to touch her soft, delicate face. Daisy grabbed his hand as it landed upon her face and shifted in discomfort, although she strangely accepted this gesture and trembled with the anticipation of his body moving closer to hers. Nathaniel stepped closer, and slowly drawing her face toward his own, kissed her luscious, pink lips ever so gently.

Daisy felt tears run down her face as she was confronted with such conflicting emotions. She was slightly uncomfortable being this close to a stranger. Yet she was overwhelmed with feelings she had never felt before. She yearned for his body to be even closer to hers,

6

for him to caress her skin with his strong hands and cover her with passionate kisses from his soft, satiable lips.

Suddenly, the door in the kitchen swung open and collided loudly with the wall. Daisy's lips detached from Nathaniel's as she moved away from him so hastily that she almost lost her balance. She swiftly wiped the tears from her cheeks as she was greeted by the daughters of Mr. Clark. "Well hello, Miss Daisy." Helen sneered. "What do we have here?"

Nathaniel held out his hand and introduced himself to the two women who had entered the home so obscenely.

"My name is Helen Clark," the older of the two said. "And this is my sister, Elizabeth," she explained pointing at a shorter, rounder girl that was giggling uncontrollably as if she were a child. "I see you have met the help, Miss Daisy. I hope she was treating you well," Helen smirked. "Would you like to stay for supper, kind sir?" Helen batted her eyelashes toward Nathaniel as she waited in anticipation for an answer from the handsome intruder.

Nathaniel gazed at Daisy with a baffled look, mouth fixed open and then replied, "no thank you, Miss. I have to be going now."

Helen appeared displeased and said, "Daisy, be a dear and start making our supper. It seems you have been too preoccupied here to do anything productive, as I see it is obviously going to be late. I will escort this fine gentleman out."

Daisy stood ashamed in the middle of the kitchen, too embarrassed to defend herself against Helen's false description of her role. Nathaniel walked toward the door and nodded his head at the women as he left the house with Helen. Daisy closed her eyes and took in a deep breath. She then proceeded to slice the potatoes angrily. "Oh my goodness, he is so handsome!" Elizabeth squealed in excitement. "Who is he? Is he trying to court you?"

"No, Elizabeth," Daisy said. "He was just a man in pursuit of your father."

"Well, what did he want from him?"

Daisy stopped slicing potatoes and hesitated in deep thought. What was he there for, she thought to herself. They had never gotten to that matter.

Before she could respond, Helen came storming back into the kitchen. "What in goodness's name do you think you are doing?" Elizabeth sighed and rolled her eyes. "I know, there is no possible way you could even fathom the thought that a man like that would want anything to do with you."

Daisy continued slicing potatoes as she faced the wall. She remained humble and kept a stern face as she knew that any discussion of the events that occurred would cause utter chaos in the home.

"You know I will have to tell my father what you have done, trying to seduce the governor's son and all."

Daisy stopped slicing the potatoes and looked at Helen in bewilderment. "What are you saying, Helen? I had no idea he was the governor's son. And never did I attempt to seduce a man in my life! Please do not tell your father of this matter. I promise, I will not speak with that man again."

"Of course you won't," Helen sneered. "He is to return tomorrow, and I will assure you that my father and I will be here to ensure that I get more acquainted with him. After all, it is my father who he requests to speak with."

"Why do you have to be so evil?" Elizabeth chimed in.

"Pipe down, Elizabeth!" Helen demanded. "This is none of your business. I don't know why you always take Daisy's side anyway. She is just an intrusion in our family!"

"Then I will leave, Helen, if that's how you feel. I have no shame in going on my own. I hope you enjoy cooking and cleaning for yourself. You know how your father demands the daily chores to be done before you can leave the house." Daisy dropped the knife and potato and walked out of the room.

Helen thought for a moment that without Daisy in the home, she wouldn't be able to live her carefree life, socializing daily in the town square and attempting to entice the many available men. She chased after Daisy.

"Fine, Daisy, I will not report your shenanigans to my father. Just don't let it happen again." Daisy grinned and climbed the stairs to her bedroom, smiling to herself for having finally stood up to her sworn adversary.

***

That night, Daisy lay quietly, awake in her bed. She felt the cool breeze blowing through the bedroom window as it whispered sweet songs into her ears. She lay in conflict with her thoughts. She was finally able to feel a sense of desire. How she yearned to be with

9

Nathaniel. However, she was now unsure of how he felt. The governor's son could never want a woman like her. A man of his status could never court "the help." It was unheard of. Moreover, she truly believed that she was undesirable. Her body had been defiled and her love for a man had been tainted.

She shivered in reminiscence of her destructive beginning as a woman. She remembered the event that led to almost nightly incidents that traumatized her soul. When she was just twelve years of age, she was left under the care of Mr. Abner Clark. He was a husky man, about five-foot-nine inches tall, who had just lost his wife. She remembered the night he came home, drunk from ale, stumbling into the girls' bedroom. At just twelve years of age, she knew nothing of the poisons of alcohol nor the horrifying act that was about to occur.

Although Mr. Clark was never the kindest of men, he was quiet and aloof. But that night was different. Mr. Clark was different. He was loud and unkempt and walked with an off-balanced gait. When he reached Daisy's bed, he grabbed her tightly by the arm and covered her mouth with his rough, filthy hand. He dragged her out of the room and into the courtyard, demanding that his daughters go back to sleep, assuring them that everything was okay. But it wasn't okay. It was horrifying. It was revolting. It was malicious.

Mr. Clark dragged Daisy into the courtyard and threw her small, frail body down into the mud, flopping her down like a rag doll. With his rough, filthy hand covering her mouth, he lifted her gown and heaved his incredibly heavy body on top of hers. She remembered when he thrust himself inside of her, a searing pain

10

where she had not felt pain before, shot between her legs, like she was being sliced in half by a sharpened dagger.

She tried to scream but his hands were far too large to allow a word to escape. Instead, she felt her throat tighten as her vocal cords struggled to produce a shrieking cry for help. Her eyes protruded with shock, and tears drained down her face and onto Mr. Clark's rough, filthy hand. She remembered the heavy, bitter stench of Mr. Clark's breath as he groaned deeply into her face. His gray, disheveled beard felt like insects crawling on her neck. Daisy's attempts to fight were weakened by this new existing pain that she was overcome with.

When the horrifying act was over, Mr. Clark whispered into Daisy's ear, "if you tell anyone what we did, they will burn you alive at the stake. You are being punished. You were a bad girl today because you did not listen to me. Do not let it happen again." He then proceeded to stumble back into the house, leaving Daisy to lie in a mixture of mud and deep red blood, under the moon-lit, black, silent night sky.

As Daisy recollected the events that she had endured, she did not shed a tear. Over the years, she became immune to the frequent nights of horror that stole her youth and tarnished her fragile body. She anesthetized herself with soothing thoughts of her mother in that beautiful, peaceful garden. She forced her private areas to become numb along with her feelings of shame, fear, and worthlessness. As she grew older, the events slowed down and eventually stopped. But the fear of "being punished" remained with Daisy. And so, she remained silent, always doing what she was told.

Helen made her life no better. Daisy remembered, as a child, the two of them would enjoy their days frolicking together in the courtyard. But, after the death of Daisy's parents and Helen's mother, things changed dramatically. It was almost as if Helen lived every day in envy of Daisy. It was Helen's mother's dying wish that her family continue to treat Daisy like a Clark, just as she had done. Instead, both Mr. Clark and Helen seemed to project the blame of Mrs. Clark's death onto Daisy.

In the days following Mrs. Clark's death, life became unbearable for Daisy. She began to be treated as a servant and no longer as a member of the family as she had when Mrs. Clark was alive and nurturing her like she was her own daughter. She cooked, and cleaned, and remained in the home. The only way Daisy maintained her sanity was by creating a luscious garden that provided her with serenity to drown out the pain of her devastating life.

And so, Daisy lay quietly, eyes flooding with a feeling of heaviness as she fought her sleep, dreading the horrid memories she knew would haunt her dreams. She could feel her eyelids working hard to close. And so, she finally succumbed to the harmonious chirping of the crickets that filled her ears with melodious songs and drifted off into a restless sleep that would lead to a much-anticipated day on the morrow.

CHAPTER TWO

Daisy was awakened at dawn by the vexatious howling of the rooster's call. She stretched her arms over her head and dressed herself before heading down the stairs and outside to gather eggs from the chickens. Daisy gazed upward at the sky and once again, inhaled deeply to appreciate the pleasant fragrances of her blossoms combined with the fresh scent of morning dew that draped each blade of grass.

The vast sky was breathtaking, painted brightly in shades of tangerine and plum. Daisy spent a few moments appreciating the aesthetic beauty of the world around her, before she busied herself with the tedious tasks of her daily life. She sighed deeply and then proceeded to the hen house, shooing the nesting mothers from their perches before reaching in to collect the freshly laid eggs. She then returned to the house where she began to cook breakfast for the entire Clark family.

13

"Good morning, Daisy," Elizabeth yawned as she sat down to enjoy a hearty breakfast, once again, prepared by Daisy. "Thank you so much for cooking this morning. This looks delicious!"

"It looks okay," Helen sneered from across the room. "Hope you slept well. Today is a big day for me. I need you to help me get dressed for our honorary guest."

"We don't even know what business he brings," Daisy responded. "What makes you think he is coming here for you?"

"Excuse me, Daisy! How dare you speak to me like that!"

Elizabeth tried hard not to chuckle.

"And what exactly are you so cheerful about, Elizabeth?"

"Oh nothing, but it appeared that Mr. Alexander had some interest in Daisy?" Elizabeth dared to speak.

Daisy chuckled.

"Nonsense!" Helen shouted. "Why don't you just worry about your own pleasantly plump figure and what you will need to do to find a man desperate enough to take even one look at you!"

"Helen, that is enough!" Daisy snapped. "It is one thing when you say unkind things to me as nothing that you say will ever trouble me. But your sister looks up to you. You should never treat her with contempt."

Helen sighed in annoyance and continued to finish her breakfast, watching as Mr. Clark came stumbling into the kitchen and plopped down into the seat across from Daisy.

"Papa," Helen began, "you remember what we discussed last night, right?"

14

"Of course I do," Mr. Clark replied. "You think a little whiskey could make me forget that my daughter may finally find herself a rich husband to take us out of this bloody hell hole?"

"Papa, please don't be so obscene. Oh, and we need to get you cleaned up." Helen looked worried as her father had not been sober in years, let alone clean. His tangled hair intertwined with his long, disheveled beard. His filthy clothes reeked of urine and booze. Daisy continued to stare into her plate as she ate her eggs and potatoes in silence.

"And you, Daisy. You make my daughter look like you. Tie her corset up a bit tighter. Make her pathetic excuse for breasts appear more," he paused, "just, bigger." He looked at his daughter, then back down at his plate, shaking his head. "My lord, you sure did get your unsightly looks from your mother."

"Father!" Helen shouted. "That is enough!"

"Alright, alright," Mr. Clark responded. "Just go, do something! Daisy go help her, and Elizabeth, clean up this mess." Mr. Clark, as usual, gave orders all around.

"Papa!" Helen scowled, "Sober up!"

With that, she grabbed Daisy by the hand like a child claiming a new friend and dragged her up the stairs.

In her bed chambers, Helen paced the room frantically. "The gown needs to be perfect," she snapped, unsympathetic to the fact that Daisy was there to help her.

Helen's poor treatment of Daisy seemed to reside in pure envy. Daisy was far more beautiful than Helen, and Helen seemed to know that. She was twenty-six years of age, the same as Daisy, but far less appealing. She had a boyish figure that didn't seem to fill out her dress quite as nicely as Daisy's did, and because of that, Helen refused to allow Daisy around when Nathaniel arrived.

Daisy picked out a suitable dress for Helen and began to brush her long, straggly, dark brown hair. "Pin it up for me, Daisy," Helen insisted. She knew that if it were pinned up, Nathaniel would not be able to perceive that it was not as full-bodied and flowing as Daisy's. "I think I need a veil, or something to hide my eyes a bit," Helen said. She was not incredibly content with her eyes as they were sunken and closely set together. "I need to look my absolute best for my future husband."

Daisy sighed as she continued to brush Helen's hair.

"What is the matter, Daisy? Aren't you having fun?"

Daisy looked at Helen through the mirror and responded, "What do you think, Helen? What happened to you? What happened to us? We used to be the best of friends."

Helen looked up, baffled at Daisy's remark. "Just hurry up. He will be here very soon."

Daisy continued fixing Helen's hair in silence, patiently waiting for a response to her question, but it never came.

***

A couple hours past noon, a rapping came at the door. Daisy proceeded to answer it, but Mr. Clark interrupted her. "Daisy, what do you think you are doing?" Mr. Clark questioned.

"I am simply answering the door, Mr. Clark, as I always do."

16

"This, Daisy, is not like any other time. In fact, you mustn't be here at all. It is prudent that I find my daughter a husband that will take care of her, and a man of his prominence is hard to pass up. Do you understand?"

"Yes sir," Daisy said. She was amazed to see Mr. Clark as sober as he was. This was, undoubtedly, a rare occasion. In fact, Daisy hadn't seen Mr. Clark sober since the day his wife had passed, so this was obviously important for him. But Daisy couldn't help but feel the injustice in the matter. She never yearned for any man as much as she yearned for Nathaniel. Her body was filled with desire. A feeling so new yet surprisingly welcomed. Nevertheless, she obediently left the room and headed upstairs to where she would be unseen for the entirety of their meeting.

Mr. Clark smoothed his blouse, cleared his throat, and then answered the door.

"Good day, Mr. Clark, I am Nathaniel Alexander and I am very pleased to meet you."

"Yes sir, the pleasure is all mine," Mr. Clark responded. "Please, do come in." Mr. Clark gestured for Nathaniel to enter the home. "Please, have a seat. Would you like a cup of tea?"

"No, thank you," Nathaniel responded as he sat down in a chair that Mr. Clark led him to.

After he sat, Mr. Clark rushed to inquire about the nature of his visit. "I hear you have business for me? What may I ask, is it that brings a fine gentleman, such as yourself, to my home?"

"Well sir, word around town has it that you provide the finest craftsmanship of all the timepieces in Yorkston."

"Well yes, sir," Mr. Clark stuttered, "but I haven't worked my craft in quite some time. You see, since my wife passed, I have lost all interest in my work."

"Ah yes, I am sorry to hear that. However, I am to be headed back to England in a couple of months to show some of the finest watches in my collection. You see, I am an avid collector. I have watches made from all types of fine material, jewels and gems. Watches from all over the world. However, I have not had one made in my own town, especially by such a fine craftsman as yourself. It would be an honor to possess a watch by Mr. Abner Clark himself. I would, of course, provide you with the gem stones I desire and gold if so necessary. What is your price for such a piece?"

Mr. Clark's face suddenly lit up. "The price, good sir, will not cost you any gold. In fact, it will not cost you any silver. What I would truly desire for a price for the best timepiece this town has ever seen, would be for you to take my daughter's hand in marriage."

Nathaniel was happily surprised as he thought back to the day before when he had experienced such a passionate kiss from the most beautiful woman he had ever seen. A woman that he wished nothing more than to wake up to every single morning for the rest of his life. But in that moment of reverie, he had forgotten the nature of their conversation. So, in his lack of clarity in that moment, he graciously accepted the offer.

"Wonderful!" Mr. Clark shouted. "Let me go and retrieve my daughter for your meeting."

Nathaniel stood in anticipation of seeing the woman he had fallen for with just one kiss. He could hardly contain his excitement as he smiled wildly with eagerness to see her once again.

"Mr. Alexander," Mr. Clark stated proudly as he emerged from the next room, "I am pleased to introduce to you, my daughter, Helen."

Helen curtsied and replied, "I am pleased to meet you more formally, Mr. Alexander."

Nathaniel's smile suddenly disappeared, and his face turned completely ashen. "Yes, the pleasure is all mine," Nathaniel stuttered, desperately looking around the home to find the woman of his fantasy. "Wasn't there another sister here, yesterday?" Nathaniel asked boldly. Helen's face turned scarlet with infuriation.

"Well, yes," Mr. Clark stated, a bit on the confused side, "but she is three years Helen's junior and likely far too plump for your liking."

"Ah yes, but what about your daughter, Daisy?" Nathaniel finally blurted out, without intention of causing any trouble.

"Daisy?" Mr. Clark asked in pure disgust. "Oh no, sir, you are mistaken. She is not in any way kin to me. She is merely the servant, and not a very good one at that. She is, in fact, no longer with us. We have sent her down to Carolina to help with my ill brother's estate."

19

Nathaniel looked perplexed. "I apologize to you sir, but I mistakenly thought you were speaking of a different woman."

Mr. Clark looked angry. "Mr. Alexander, I assure you, my daughter would make just as good, if not better, a wife than Daisy. She can cook and clean and weave clothes. She will take care of all of your needs." Helen clenched her lips tightly and struggled not to erupt in her envious rage. "With all due respect, kind sir, you are the governor's son, and I know for certain it would be unacceptable for you to go back on your word."

Nathaniel appeared astounded. He felt he had been fooled, yet he knew he mustn't disrespect his father by voiding an agreement. Furthermore, the woman of his dreams had gone away, and he knew he might never find a woman as perfect as she again. "Okay, Mr. Clark, I will follow through with my concord so long as you hold up your end of the bargain. I will give you one month to create the timepiece out of the finest material you can find, and the timepiece must then be credentialed by the town. Should it be deemed fine craftmanship, then I will graciously accept your offer."

Mr. Clark smirked eagerly, as he was confident that his work was, in fact, the best in town. "Then it is a deal," he replied as he shook Nathaniel's hand.

"Good day to you Mr. Clark. Helen," Nathaniel nodded graciously toward them both before turning to the door and walking out, bewildered and fuming with resentment and anger at the trickery he had endured.

No sooner did Nathaniel leave their home when Helen
exploded in fury. "Father, in what world does it make sense for a man
of his status to want to be with someone like Daisy? She better not
ruin this for me! We have been nothing but loyal to her, allowing her
to share our home, to eat our food, and to spend unthinkable amounts
of time procrastinating in that ridiculous garden of hers!"

"Don't you worry, sweet Helen. There is no way I will allow
her to get in the way of your happiness."

"But Father, she still lives in this home. Surely, he will see
her at one time or another, and when he does, he will realize that you
were dishonest with him. Then he will for sure make your agreement
null and void!"

"Well, that will not be happening!" Mr. Clark raced up the
creaky wooden flight of stairs to the top floor and into the girls'
shared bedroom. "How dare you attempt to steal a man that was so
clearly meant for Helen! What makes you think he had come here for
you?"

Daisy looked up from her bed that was situated on the wall
adjacent to the door, just opposite the wall where Elizabeth's bed lay
and adjacent to Helen's. She had been alone in the room, knitting to
keep herself busy; an attempt to drown out her disappointment.

"I apologize, Mr. Clark, that was never my intention. I was
merely in the garden when he arrived. It was unexpected, especially
for me, to have a visitor at that time of day." Mr. Clark's face turned
purple with rage as he marched into her room, roughly grabbing her
arm. "You are nothing more than a house whore, and so that is how I

shall treat you!" Just as Mr. Clark had pushed Daisy over onto her abdomen across her bed, with one hand on the back of her neck and the other readying itself to pull down his trousers, Elizabeth stormed into the room. She looked to the left where she saw her father assaulting Daisy on her bed.

"Father! What in heaven's name are you doing?"

Mr. Clark released Daisy's neck in a harsh, swift movement, dropping her to the floor, and turned to find his youngest daughter standing in the doorway, ashen with disgust.

"Nothing at all, sweet Elizabeth. Daisy, here, did something inappropriate and must be punished for it."

"But Father! What on earth has she done to deserve to be physically assaulted?"

Without a word, Mr. Clark proceeded out of the door, brushing his arm angrily against his youngest daughter who stood her ground defending her sister. Daisy remained on the ground with tears drenching her face as she inhaled and exhaled deeply, attempting to gain a whiff of her cherished blossoms that would calm her mind and numb her soul.

Mr. Clark slammed the outside door. Elizabeth helped Daisy to her feet as they peered out of the window and watched Mr. Clark head down the road in the direction of the tavern.

"Now look what you have done!" Helen reprimanded as she stood in the doorway with her arms folded across her chest.

DAISY AND THE CRIMSON ROSE

"I have done nothing," Daisy replied with regained composure. "Your father is nothing but a drunk, it wasn't long before he would be back to consuming his precious poison.

"Oh, you ungrateful little tramp!" Helen shouted. First, you steal my mother, taking up all her time before she died, and then you try to steal my soon-to-be husband?"

Daisy looked at Helen, apologetically. She remembered all the time she spent with Mrs. Clark who comforted her after her parents passed away. She remembered Helen's tantrums as she begged for attention from her mother, only to be rejected at a time when Daisy was in greater need for love and affection. "Helen," Daisy responded, "I did not intend to take your mother's time nor love away from you, and I am certainly not to blame for her death."

"She died soon after your parents did, catching that disgusting disease from them!"

"Certainly, you cannot believe that. Your mother fell ill long after my parents were dead."

"Nonsense!" Helen shouted. "You and your disease-ridden parents destroyed our family!" Helen stormed out of the room.

Elizabeth wrapped her arms around Daisy and spoke through tears, "I am so sorry for Helen's treatment of you and for my father, that despicable drunk. I always suspected my father was doing such horrid things to you, now I know it to be true."

"Do not cry, dear Elizabeth. I am fine. It hasn't happened in quite some time, and I hope to be gone soon."

"But you mustn't leave until you find a man to take care of you."

Daisy laughed. "Yes, dear Elizabeth, that had always been the thought. But how am I to meet a man when I am stuck in this house? That is no longer an option, I must seek a different way to make ends meet to care for myself financially."

"But Mr. Alexander, he certainly fancies you far more than he does Helen. He did not even take one look at her."

"Oh Elizabeth, a man like that would never have a woman like me."

"How can you say that?" Elizabeth shouted. "You are kind and beautiful and loving. Any man would be happy to have you."

"How sweet of you, Elizabeth. You have been the most kind to me. I hope the evil nature of your father and sister do not persuade your kind heart."

"Do not worry, Daisy, I will never allow that to happen. I will always be here for you if needed."

The two women held each other for a few more moments until Elizabeth rose to her feet, leaving the room, quietly shutting the door behind her.

CHAPTER THREE

The next day, Daisy was surprised to see Mr. Clark organizing the workspace in his barn. She couldn't remember the last time she saw him working. She slowly strode into the barn, hoping to remain unnoticed. She sat down on the stool next to their goat and placed a pail underneath it. She began tugging at its udders. The clangor of the milk hitting the bottom of the pail grabbed Mr. Clark's attention. As he walked toward Daisy, she straightened up and said, "good morning, Mr. Clark."

"Daisy, I need you to make yourself scarce the next couple of months."

"And, how do you propose I do that, Mr. Clark?"

Mr. Clark seemed to be struggling with his thoughts. "You need to stay inside. And if Mr. Alexander comes to the house, you need not answer the door. You need to stay in your room. You cannot let him see you."

"And if I do that, Mr. Clark, who will be responsible for collecting the eggs from the hen house in the morning? Who will be

SHOSHANA LOUISE

responsible for milking the goats so that we have something to drink? Who will be responsible for tending to the garden so that we have food in the house to cook and eat? And who will be responsible for feeding the hogs, so they do not die of starvation?"

Mr. Clark appeared to be growing frustrated. "I will have Elizabeth work in the yard. You just stay in the home."

"But what about Elizabeth's quilting? Without her work, the money that she and Helen bring in surely will not be enough."

Again, Mr. Clark appeared to be in deep thought. After Mrs. Clark passed away, and Mr. Clark began to take heavily to the tavern, the girls were left to make ends meet on their own. While Daisy was forced to stay in the home to take care of the daily chores, Helen and Elizabeth had to do something for financial gain. They were both skillful in the art of quilting. They learned from their mother when she was alive. So, they began to quilt and took them to the market square to sell. This allowed for them to engage in a strong social life, and their popularity allowed their business to thrive. Whether it was pity from the town for the girls whose mother passed away and whose father was a drunk, or their quilts were truly the best, they earned enough with their craft to survive all those years following Mrs. Clark's death.

Finally, Mr. Clark responded, "Then you will do the quilting, and she will do the work outside."

"But what about."

Mr. Clark interrupted her and shouted, "enough! You will do as I say. Nothing more, nothing less. Do you understand?"

26

Daisy remained silent.

"Do you?" Mr. Clark shouted in anger.

"Yes, I understand," Daisy muttered through her teeth.

Mr. Clark returned to his workspace where he began tinkering with clock parts. It wasn't long before Daisy noticed that he was beginning to tremble. She watched as he wiped the perspiration from his forehead. She continued to milk the goat, noticing as he became more restless. Suddenly, he threw his tools down and stormed out of the barn. After a few moments, Daisy rose and rushed to the barn entrance. She watched as Mr. Clark trudged down the road in the direction of the tavern.

Daisy smiled to herself. She knew it wouldn't be long before he would return to his precious poison. She then grabbed the metal pail and returned to the house where she poured the milk into three mugs. She quickly drank the first and then brought the other two into the room just off the kitchen, where Helen and Elizabeth were working on their quilts. Without speaking, she handed the mugs to the women. Helen took the mug and drank it without acknowledging Daisy. Elizabeth took the mug and thanked her.

Just as Daisy began to turn and leave, Elizabeth said, "Daisy, would you be a dear and help me with something upstairs?"

"Of course, Elizabeth."

Helen sighed and rolled her eyes as she remained in the chair working on her quilt. Daisy accompanied Elizabeth up the stairs and into their shared bedroom. Elizabeth sat down on her bed and gestured for Daisy to sit on it with her. When she sat, Elizabeth threw

27

her arms around her. Daisy couldn't help but feel as though her plumpness reminded her of Mrs. Clark's warm embrace. It comforted Daisy. Then, Elizabeth sat back and stated, "Daisy, I cannot help but feel awful for my father's behavior. And for Helen's poor treatment of you. I have tried to discuss it with her, but she refuses to listen to me."

"Dear Elizabeth, this is not your problem. You need not let it bother you so."

"But it does. I care for you, Daisy. I care for you like a sister. You have been nothing but kind to me and my entire family for years. What can I do to help you?"

"I fear there is nothing you can do, sweet Elizabeth."

"But there must be something I can do."

"All I ask is that you stay as sweet as you are."

"But what are you going to do? You said you wanted to leave."

"I am not sure just yet. But I need you to support me, for whatever I decide."

"Yes, of course," Elizabeth smiled.

Suddenly, the harshness of Helen's voice rang from the bottom of the steps. "Elizabeth, I am finished with this quilt. We need to go to the market to set up before we lose a descent spot."

Elizabeth hugged Daisy and then left the house with her sister.

Daisy sighed. She walked over to the window and watched as the two girls headed down the dirt path, quilts in hand. She then descended the stairs, and despite Mr. Clark's threats, she left the home and went out to her garden. She lay down on the grass and stared up at the sky, tears trickling down her face. She felt trapped. What was she to do? She wanted desperately to leave Mr. Clark's home. She wanted to find refuge. A place to escape the threatening nature of her life. She closed her eyes and allowed the sun's rays to drape across her body, warming her entire being. She hoped for a way out, praying for a miracle.

After a few moments in silent meditation, a dark shadow interrupted the wave of heat that draped her body. She squinted her eyes open to gaze up at a now familiar face.

Daisy sat up and said in a stern voice, "Helen is not home."

Nathaniel smiled and shook his head apologetically. "I am not here for Helen," he responded, "I am here for you."

"But why?"

"I needed to see if it were true that you had left for Carolina."

"What for? You didn't seem so interested when you left the house once Helen informed you of my role here."

"I left because the situation seemed tense, I did not wish to cause any harm. But how is it that you have not gone to Carolina as Mr. Clark reported?"

"Why do you suppose? He was clearly being dishonest in hopes of you marrying his beloved daughter."

Nathaniel hesitated, a pondering look fell upon his face. "Come with me," he demanded as he held out his hand.

"Where to?" Daisy questioned.

"Must you be so quizzical? Some things are meant to be unanswered."

"Unanswered, what for?" Daisy asked unsurely.

"For the joy of a surprise."

"Some surprises are not joyful, Mr. Alexander," Daisy replied ominously.

"Trust me, this one is," Nathaniel said with a wink as he continued to hold out his hand. "Just give me one hour of your time, and I promise it will be worth your while."

Daisy was hesitant. She knew that leaving the home would be a direct violation of Mr. Clark's orders. But she was tired of this life. She needed a way out, or at the very least, some adventure. She smiled and reached up to grasp Nathaniel's hand, pulling herself to her feet and headed down the dirt path to where he had left his beautiful, dark-chocolate colored horse.

"Her name is Aphrodite, after the Greek goddess of love," Nathaniel smiled as he stroked the horse's mane.

"Aphrodite," Daisy repeated, "how lovely."

Nathaniel climbed atop the horse then reached down to help Daisy up. She hesitated.

"What is the matter?" Nathaniel asked.

"I have never ridden a horse before," Daisy responded, seemingly ashamed.

Nathaniel laughed. "There is nothing to fear, let me help you." After he pulled Daisy up and she was seated in his rear, he instructed her to hold on tightly to his waist. After trotting along for a few moments, Nathaniel said, "What do you mean you have never ridden a horse before? How have you been getting to town? By foot?"

"I haven't gone into town," Daisy replied, ashamed.

"You have never left Mr. Clark's home?"

"No, I have not been permitted to do so."

"Permitted? Daisy, you are an adult woman. Surely you do not need permission to leave the home. Please tell me how you got into such a horrid predicament."

"It is a long story," Daisy responded.

"Well then, let us stop somewhere and you can tell me the whole thing."

They continued down the road in silence until Nathaniel urged his horse to go off-road and into a green meadow speckled with bright yellow dandelions. There was a small pond adorned with lily pads. Nathaniel climbed off the horse and extended his hand to help Daisy down. He left Aphrodite to graze in the meadow as he guided Daisy over to a large oak tree shading the pond. They sat down underneath the tree.

"This place is beautiful," Daisy smiled.

"Not as beautiful as you," Nathaniel responded, making Daisy blush, once again.

"So, tell me, what is your story? How did you end up with such manipulative people?"

Daisy shifted uncomfortably. "It's really not an impressive story."

"I have no interest in the impressiveness of the story, I just want to know more about you. I need to know why the life of such an enchanting woman has turned out the way it has."

Daisy looked down in mortification. "It all began when I was just eleven years of age. Both my mother and my father fell ill with Typhoid."

"What a shame, but how did you end up with Mr. Clark?"

"Well, when my parents fell ill, they knew that their time on this land was nearing an end, and so, they wanted to find a suitable family that would care for me as their own child. They worried about what might happen to me if they didn't. So, they left me with our neighbors, the Clark family."

"I do not understand how they could do that. Surely they knew how the Clark family would treat you?"

"Well, despite how you know Mr. Clark to be, Mrs. Clark was wholly opposite in nature. She was kind. She was loving. She was nurturing. She and my mother were quite close. My father passed first, but my mother died soon after. I remember the day my mother passed; I was devastated. I lay down in her garden for hours, watering the beautiful blossoms with my tears. It wasn't until later that evening when Mrs. Clark found me under the rose bushes, close to being stuck by a thorn. She scooped me up in her soft arms and brought me into her chest. Her enormous bosoms just swallowed me up." Daisy giggled. "Her reassuring embrace caused my tears to cease. And when I looked up, her face was glowing. It was almost as if a bit of my mother's soul was left within this woman."

"So, was your mother right about her, did she care for you as her own daughter?"

"Yes, very much so. But unfortunately, she too fell ill about a year later. Her passing affected Mr. Clark more than one could know. He began to take strongly to the tavern, often coming home in a drunken rage."

"And he took his anger out on you?"

"Yes, unfortunately I became the scapegoat of the family." Daisy sat in a brief moment of silence.

"Did he harm you?"

Daisy looked away and said nothing. Nathaniel placed a comforting arm around her shoulder.

"I feel so very apologetic to be sharing this all with you. I have never actually disclosed any of this information before," Daisy said.

"No, Daisy, please. Do not apologize for your story. I want nothing more than to know you. You are an incredible woman." Nathaniel leaned in and kissed Daisy gently on the lips. She felt her stomach turn in knots as this new, lustful feeling grew inside her.

"Shall we continue?" Nathaniel asked.

"There's more?" Daisy giggled in wonderment.

"Of course, don't you want to see what else is out there?"

Daisy nodded as she stood and followed Nathaniel back to the horse that stood alone in the broad pasture.

***

They arrived in the town square just a short while later. The market was bustling with more people than Daisy had ever seen in her life. Plump women in beautiful, flowing gowns with children clinging tightly to their legs picked through barrels of fruits and vegetables in exchange for coins. Men bartered at the various carts loaded with furs, tools, and tobacco. Donkeys and goats relaxed in the shade of the tall, stone buildings to hide from the beaming rays of the springtime sun. And a couple older men lounged in chairs, surrounded by a flock of chickens pecking through the dirt, playing a melodious tune on their fiddles.

"Oh my word," Daisy uttered in pure wonder, "this is the most incredible thing I have ever seen."

Nathaniel chuckled. "This is but a normality of daily life. Come, let us make some purchases."

Daisy grabbed Nathaniel's outstretched hand and hopped down from the horse once again. They wandered through crowds of people to a cart at the opposite end of the market. Daisy looked down at the table and was amazed by the beautiful assortment of jewelry. There were necklaces, bracelets and rings made from pearls and all types of metals and precious jewels.

"Which one is your favorite?" Nathaniel asked.

"Hmm," Daisy thought. "I think I really favor this one." She pointed to a simple long, gold chain with a rose engraved medallion.

"Beautiful," Nathaniel responded. "I'll take it," he proclaimed to the woman behind the cart.

Daisy looked astounded. "For me?" She asked.

"Of course," he snickered as he placed the necklace over her head and pulled her thick, honey-golden hair out to drape it behind the chain.

Daisy smiled and said, "it is so beautiful. Thank you so kindly."

"My pleasure. Are you hungry?"

"Yes, I haven't had lunch."

"Then, will you accompany me at my home for a meal?"

Daisy looked unsure. "I think I should be getting back."

"Nonsense," Nathaniel replied. "Surely you must have some food before you go."

Daisy thought for a moment. This was the most adventure she had ever had. A few moments more couldn't hurt. She smiled in agreement as they wandered back through the bustling crowds of townspeople toward Aphrodite that had been left tied up next to four other horses. They headed just a short distance up the road to one of the biggest homes Daisy had ever seen.

The house was made of charming, rusty colored bricks with six large, white pillars adorning the front of the home. Surrounding the house was a tall, wrought-iron gate where two guards stood holding rifles. A long, gravel path led from the gate to the large door that adorned the front of the home, standing between two pillars. Eight windows lined the two stories of the house with dark oak window panes, opened to let the sun shine into the enormous home. The second floor had a large balcony that wrapped around the entirety of the structure. It was something out of a fantasy for Daisy. It was much larger than the dark, log cabin that she had, for so many years, unfortunately called home.

"This is where you live?" Daisy gulped.

"Yes, would you please join me for some lunch?"

The guards opened the gate without uttering a word as Nathaniel directed his horse through. At the front of the home, Nathaniel hopped down from Aphrodite and once again held out his hand for Daisy to take hold of. He led her through the tall, double doors and into the home. "Alice?" he shouted. "Is lunch prepared?"

A woman with dark skin dressed in a black frock with a white apron appeared from the next room. "Yes sir. Shall I set the table for two?"

"Please," Nathaniel responded. "Will my father be joining us?"

"No, sir," Alice replied. "He is off at a meeting out of the home."

"Very well," Nathaniel responded as he led Daisy into the next room. "Have a seat, my fair lady," he said, gesturing to the seat he pulled out from underneath a large, rectangular wooden table. The table was set with the finest silverware Daisy had ever seen. She looked around the spacious room in pure amazement and sat down at the table.

Alice set a plate down in front of the two. The plate contained a six-inch piece of steak that oozed pink juice when Daisy cut into it. It was accompanied by the most colorful array of all vegetables. Colors of green, orange, red and yellow ornamented the plate. It was far different than the potatoes and corn with the occasional chicken or duck that Daisy was accustomed to.

"This food looks lovely Miss Alice," Daisy stated in gratitude.

"Thank you kindly," Alice replied, then she disappeared into the kitchen.

"Is she a slave?" Daisy asked hesitantly. She waited tensely for an answer. She was kind-hearted and had never agreed with the concept of slavery. She heard horrifying stories about slaves and desperately hoped the man of her dreams wasn't guilty of such sins.

Nathaniel laughed. "In a sense, she is. We purchased her from a slaveowner in Carolina who has a reputation of being one of the cruelest men in all the country. However, my father and I do not agree with owning people, nor the poor treatment of negros in this country, which is why my father works adamantly to amend the slave law. Anyway, that very man was traveling through our town and we caught glimpse of him beating that poor woman with a whip. And so, we offered him a price he could not refuse. We wanted to help her, give her a way out. However, we could not just purchase her and set her free, for some other person would snatch her up and treat her the same. But we needed a servant, at the time, to help tend to the household duties. So, we allowed her to stay in our home, but as part of the staff. We pay Alice and even give her a room here. She is treated with the same respect we treat all our staff."

Daisy's lips grew into a smile. Nathaniel was, without a doubt, a man she could see herself wedding. He was kind, he was debonair, and he had power. She hoped he had enough power to take her away from Mr. Clark. For she knew he would not let her go without a fight.

"Please, enjoy," Nathaniel stated.

As the two of them ate their lavish meal in silence, Daisy was lost in thought about how fortunate she felt in that moment. Finally, Nathaniel broke the silence by uttering, "I think that you are the woman meant to marry me."

Daisy choked. "But Nathaniel, how could you be so sure? We have only just met."

"I am sure. I can feel it."

Daisy beamed. She had never had a man fancy her the way he did, and this man was the most eligible in town. Any woman in Yorkston would only dream of the opportunity to be in Daisy's position, and yet, she was the one there. He chose her. Out of all the beautiful, young, single women in Yorkston, Virginia, Nathaniel chose her.

"Your father, he is the governor?" Daisy finally grew the courage to ask.

"Yes, he is. You were unaware?"

"I was when we first met, until Helen informed me upon your leaving our home."

"And how do you feel about that?" Nathaniel asked.

"I feel no differently, I suppose. I mean, you are the same man I met. Your position is not intimidating to me." She hesitated. "I worry about your accord with Mr. Clark, however. What of that?"

38

"I will find my way around that. Don't you worry, my lady."

After the two finished their meal, Nathaniel politely took Daisy by horse back to Mr. Clark's home. When they arrived, he helped her down from Aphrodite and said "Well, my lady, it was a pleasure having you join me for lunch."

"The pleasure was all mine."

She curtsied and Nathaniel kissed her on the cheek, bidding her adieu. As Daisy watched the horse travel down the long, dirt path and disappear into the distance, she felt her lips grow into a smile of pure happiness, something she had not felt in many years. She turned and skipped gleefully back into the dingy, small Clark family home.

Her gleeful moment, however, was interrupted by the nasty tone of Helen's voice as soon as she entered the house. "Daisy you foul woman! What in bloody hell do you think you are doing?" Helen was standing in the hallway entrance to the home with her arms folded, huffing and puffing with irritation.

"What in heaven's name are you talking about, Helen?" Daisy asked as she walked into the home, taking a defensive stance at the base of the staircase.

"I saw you get off that horse. It was Nathaniel, wasn't it?"

"Of course not, Helen, you are mistaken, you must have been imagining it."

"Poppycock! I know what mine eyes saw, you ridiculous tramp!"

"I was with a man, yes, but it was not Nathaniel," Daisy lied.

"I don't believe you," Helen shouted. "You know of no other man! How could you? You do not ever leave this house."

"Well, I happened to leave today," Daisy said confidently.

"You are soon to be wedded to the governor's son. Why can I not find a suitable husband for myself?"

"Because." Helen pondered for a moment, searching her thoughts for a suitable response. But her envy prevented any truly rational answer and so she replied, "you do not deserve to be loved! You are a disgusting whore! I watched you seduce my father all those years!"

Daisy gasped. She was stunned by Helen's foul accusation coupled with the new knowledge that Helen witnessed Daisy's torture all those years and did nothing to help her.

"How could you possibly think that I would want that vulgar man touching me the way he did?" Daisy shouted in rage.

"Don't you speak of my father that way," Helen said defensively. "The only one vulgar in this home is you!"

Such harsh words rang through Daisy's ears like a tea kettle reaching its boiling point. She couldn't believe that Helen had lost her temper the way she had. Her voice had never gotten to that volume, that unforgettable, painful screeching. All the rage that had built up inside throughout the years was finally pouring out through her lips. Disgusting, offensive words were slipping out of Helen's mouth like a sailor. But despite the anger that Daisy felt, she composed herself. She knew that she needed to control herself just a little longer before she could safely leave the Clark home with a definite place to go.

She walked past Helen toward the steps to her bedroom without uttering another word. Suddenly, she felt herself losing her balance, and she fell backward as Helen dragged her by her hair to the floor. Daisy held onto the back of her head to stabilize her hair as she plunged to the ground. Helen stepped back, eyes wide, almost as if she, too, were surprised by her actions.

Daisy crawled to her feet and peered at Helen in her reddened face with a devilish smile and spoke in the most confident tone that Helen had ever heard coming from Daisy. "Helen, what is the matter with you? You are going insane simply because a man does not want you. He wants me. He wants to marry me. Not you. You will never find a man as good as Nathaniel, nor will you ever be worthy of such a grand romance."

Helen gasped. "You take that back!"

"Never," Daisy said gracefully.

Daisy watched as silent tears trickled out the corners of Helen's eyes. She then turned and stomped out the front door of the Clark family home and disappeared down the dirt path in the direction of the tavern. Daisy took a deep breath and prepared herself for whatever was coming her way. She climbed the steps to her bedroom to gather what little belongings she had to escape with, if the time would come to do so.

CHAPTER FOUR

Dusk was upon the small, sea-port town of Yorkston Virginia, and trouble was now approaching. The sound of disorderly shouting of several different men flooded through Daisy's bedroom. The uproar was growing louder by the second, and as Daisy peered out of her second-floor window, she saw Mr. Clark leading a group of five men up the pathway toward the house. The men were disheveled and moving about the path with uncoordinated gaits. They passed around a bottle filled with brown liquid, each stopping to take a swig before moving on.

Daisy's heart began to race. What had Helen done? What was she to do? She raced to her bedroom door and slammed it shut. She locked the door, praying that Mr. Clark wouldn't find the key in his drunken state. She pushed Elizabeth's bed against the door, hoping it would keep the door from opening should the lock be broken. She froze, eyes fixated on the door knob as she waited for danger to arrive. She heard the voices grow louder, the wooden panels of the floor creaking as the half-dozen, over-weight men neared her bedroom door. Suddenly she heard an uncoordinated hushing and the voices turned to whispers. Shortly after, the whispers stopped. She watched with wide eyes as the doorknob turned.

"Oh Daisy," Mr. Clark sang in a taunting chant. "'Tis only I, your father. Don't you want to come out and spend some time with me?"

She heard the uncontrollable laughter of feeble-minded men coming from behind her bedroom door. Then a hushing and more silence.

"Daisy, don't be scared, we won't hurt you."

More laughing and then pounding on the old, wooden door that rocked it in its hinges. Mr. Clark's voice quickly changed from amused to angry. "Daisy, you better open this bloody door before we have to break it down!"

Continued pounding on the bedroom door loosened the hinges even more. Daisy knew, for sure, that it was going to come down. She frantically raced over to the bedroom window. She peered down at the long drop to the ground. She knew this would be her only exit. There was no way she would get past all those men. Her mind was racing, searching for answers. She looked down at her mattress, it looked as if it would fit through her window if she folded it. She shoved her blanket and pillow onto the floor and lifted the mattress to the window. The door was now creaked open as the hinges had slightly loosened, although it still clung desperately to the frame. She folded the mattress vertically and pushed it through the small window. It landed on the ground below with a thud. She hesitated and waited to see if the men heard or if they even suspected her escape. As the men continued to pound on the door, she realized that they hadn't. The door was now just barely holding on at the hinges. Daisy knew that if she didn't jump then, she would be brutally attacked by six very intoxicated men.

So, she braced herself and inhaled deeply as she attempted to calm her racing heart. She climbed out backward, dangling her legs to the ground as she held onto the window frame, lowering herself as close to the ground as possible. When she had steadied her rocking body, she dropped herself to the ground. The mattress certainly softened her fall. She assessed her body and found no injuries. So, without another wasted moment, she stood and raced down the dirt path to the main road where she headed in the direction of the town square.

As she approached the market place, she realized that the milieu was different from earlier in the day when the sun was shining, and women and children frolicked about. There were no women. There were no children. Darkness filled the streets. The only souls around were a few drunken men staggering about the road.

Daisy slowed her stroll and walked closer to the buildings rather than in the center of the road, attempting to be discreet and avoid any recognition. But her light-pink dress contrasted greatly in the dark streets of the night, creating a spotlight around her. She tried to steady her nervous shaking. She was terrified. Walking alone, in the streets of Yorkton, at night. No one around to help her should danger ensue.

When the streets fell silent as the sounds of drunken men diminished, Daisy exhaled and allowed her tight chest to loosen. But just as she thought she had evaded all danger, she felt a strong grasping hand around her arm, causing her tension to come back just as quickly as it left. "Well, well, well. What do we have here?" said a tall, thin man with unkempt hair tied partially back, slurring his words as he continued, "What is such a pretty lady like yourself doing out here in these cold streets alone at nightfall?"

"That is none of your concern," Daisy uttered sternly, "Now, unhand me at once!" She jerked her arm backward in an attempt to escape. But it only caused the man to firm up his grasp.

The man snickered wildly. "Now that is no way to talk to a fine gentleman like myself, nightwalker! What is your price?"

"I have no price. I am not a prostitute!" Daisy shouted.

"Then I will just help myself for free." The man laughed as he began to pull Daisy closer. He pushed her into a dark alley between two brick buildings. The alley reeked of urine and fish. She tripped and fell backward. The man quickly climbed on top of her and pushed her all the way onto her back. Daisy squirmed underneath, sucking in the stench of his hot, toxic breath. The man had her arms stretched out above her head, holding them together with one large hand, while he used the other to loosen his trousers. She tried to yank her arms away from his hand, but he was far too strong.

"This is not going to happen again." Daisy thought to herself, confidently. She paused for a moment, then lifted her hips off the ground as swiftly as she could, causing the drunken man to lose his balance and tip over to his left side, loosening his grip on her arms as he tried to hold his balance. She quickly pulled her arms free and began smacking the man in his eye sockets. As he rushed his hands to his scratched corneas, writhing in overwhelming pain, Daisy quickly pushed him the rest of the way off and began to run back down the road.

This time, she did not slow. Daisy ran the rest of the way through the town and down the road that led to the enormous, brick home that belonged to the governor. When she arrived, she was completely out of breath. Her body was drenched in perspiration. Alice caught sight of the distraught woman from the kitchen window and quietly unhinged the lock from the front door as not to awaken the governor. She then alerted the guards to allow Daisy through, and they, sleepily opened the gate for Daisy to enter. When she finally reached the doorway to the governor's home, Daisy dropped to her knees, gasping for air. Alice approached Daisy and helped her to her feet.

"Ms. Flynn, I pray thee, quiet yourself at once. We do not wish to wake the governor. What has happened to you?"

Daisy was tearful, unable to express herself with words.

Alice brought Daisy's head into her chest and caressed her shoulders as to comfort her. Her nurturing touch calmed Daisy. She thought of her mother, and how she would swallow her up in her arms whenever Daisy was upset, assuring her that everything would be okay.

"Would you please come in out of the cold, quietly? Let me fetch Mr. Alexander for you." Alice was initially hesitant as she did not wish to cause any trouble. She feared waking Nathaniel in the middle of the night. However, she saw the way he looked at Daisy during lunch, and she knew that much more than lust was brewing in his heart.

Alice left Daisy standing in the large atrium that welcomed people into their home as she went to fetch Nathaniel. When he appeared at the top of the steps wearing nothing but bottom undergarments, Daisy felt a little embarrassed. But Nathaniel thought nothing of it. Instead, he appeared extremely concerned. He raced down the stairs and threw his arms around Daisy to comfort her. Daisy hesitated, but then returned the gesture with her arms encompassing his topless chest. She was surprised by the smooth, warm, slightly moistened way his back felt against her arms.

"Are you alright, my lady?" Nathaniel questioned empathetically.

Daisy shook her head no, still unable to find words.

"What on earth happened?"

She took a few deep breaths and allowed her tears to dry before stating, "Helen knows about us. And now, too, does her father."

Nathaniel fell silent, held Daisy in his arms and kissed her forehead. After stroking her back for a few moments to bring her more comfort, he said, "My, my you are soaked. Have you run the whole way here?"

"Yes, I have. I ran into some trouble along the way."

"What sort of trouble?" Nathaniel asked angrily.

"Nothing I couldn't handle," Daisy responded proudly.

Nathaniel sighed. "Let me get you a change of clothes. My mother should have some gowns your size." Then he looked at Alice, "Alice, would you be so kind as to prepare Miss Daisy a bath?"

"Certainly," Alice responded as she disappeared from the darkened entranceway to the kitchen where she heated water under the hearth.

When Nathaniel returned, he offered Daisy a beautiful, rose-pink gown. It was a slightly darker pink than the one she was currently wearing. A white, lacy trim adorned the bottom of the dress. Nathaniel led her to the washroom where a warm bath was already waiting, and then he disappeared into the next room.

Daisy felt overwhelmed by the events that had occurred that night, but even more so by the kind treatment she was receiving. She was unsure of how to respond. When she was finished bathing, she dressed herself and left the washroom. She followed the flickering of the candlelight into the dining room. Nathaniel looked at her as if he was seeing her for the first time.

"Enchanting," he said. "I just cannot believe such a beautiful woman has come into my life." Daisy blushed, then he asked, "Would you care for a glass of wine?"

Daisy hesitantly accepted, knowing that she had never tasted the bitter existence of alcohol. She brought the glass to her perfectly plump lips and tasted the bitter yet somewhat sweet liquid. It swam on her tongue and slid down the back of her throat with ease. After just one glass, she felt a rushing sensation of warmth tear through every vessel in her body. Her vision became hazy, and her mind seemed to explode with thoughts and feelings of desire.

Nathaniel leaned in closer to Daisy. The flickering shadows of his face created by the lit candle highlighted his striking bone structure. Daisy's level of desire reached heights she was unfamiliar with. Nathaniel leaned in even closer and pressed his lips passionately against hers as he caressed the silky skin of her delicate face. She welcomed the kiss. He could feel the tension in her body relax. He then stood and lifted Daisy into his arms, cradling her as he carried her up the stairs and into a dimly lit room.

Nathaniel placed Daisy ever so gently down on the bed. Then, he stood back and gazed sensually at her hour-glass shaped body. Daisy felt a tingling, throbbing sensation between her legs. This feeling was so new, but so wanted. She bit her bottom lip in anticipation and strong desire for the man that stood before her. As he stood topless in front of her, Daisy finally had the courage to gaze away from his face and moved her eyes across his torso that was seemingly sculpted from gold.

Nathaniel lay down beside Daisy as he gently drew her hand away from her side and placed it onto his chest. Her body was shaking, nervous, anxious. Exhilarated by lust. She hesitantly traced her fingers down each firm bulge that lined his abdomen like a washboard. Nathaniel rested his lips upon Daisy's neck and moved slowly and sensually downward to the top of her chest.

"May I remove your gown?" He inquired more than politely.

Daisy nodded timidly as he began deliberately untying the knotted strings in the back of her dress. As he drew her dress away from her chest, her body shivered with desire. Nathaniel grasped Daisy's supple breast with the palm of his hand as he lovingly kissed the other, leaving no amount of skin untouched. He then floated his lips down Daisy's stomach, to her thighs, to her feet, to her toes. Then he moved back up until he reached her succulent, pink lips.

Daisy was bursting with desire. Her body was screaming for pleasurable attention. She felt the insides of her thighs moisten with warm beads of liquid like sweet nectar dripping down the petals of a flower in full bloom. She hungered for his manhood to penetrate her, to feel every bit of his engorged shaft grow inside of her. And so, she drew him closer, on top of her curvaceous, bare body, until she felt his member encounter her garden, and enter it smoothly with a gentle thrusting of his seamlessly sculpted hips.

For every moment that he was inside her, every second he kissed her lips, Daisy felt the center of her femininity explode with gratification. She was drowning in pure pleasure and didn't want to emerge for air. She wanted nothing more than to linger in this sexual bliss forever.

But even after the passionate activities ceased, Daisy's moment of ecstasy continued to flourish throughout the night. She felt an enormous amount of pleasure even as Nathaniel simply embraced her warm, satisfied body into his own. She lay with her backside tucked snuggly against his groin, delighted in the feeling of

Nathaniel's soft hands gently stroking her hair. She smiled at the comfort in feeling protected as she rested in Nathaniel's arms, and breathed calmly until together, they drifted off into a sensual dream.

CHAPTER FIVE

It wasn't long after Nathaniel and Daisy fell asleep that they were awaken by a loud rapping at the door. It was hours before dawn, the sky was still black, and the moon was still bright. An angry voice followed the loud rapping.

"Son, open this door immediately! We have come for the girl."

Nathaniel looked baffled at Daisy who was now sitting up in the bed, draping her breasts with the sheets. Her face was ashen. "Oh no," she whispered. "What has he done?"

"Dress hastily and hide in the closet," Nathaniel demanded as he handed Daisy the rose-pink dress.

Nathaniel put on his trousers and unlocked his chamber door. "What is the meaning of this, Father?" he asked sternly. Behind the door stood the governor accompanied by Mr. Abner Clark and two constables.

"Son, where is the girl? We know she is here with you."

Nathaniel looked at Mr. Clark whose face was red with infuriation. "How dare you betray me and abolish our agreement," Mr. Clark growled.

"Mr. Clark, you were not only dishonest with me about sending Daisy away to Carolina, but you left that poor, innocent woman fearing for her life."

"Ha, innocent! Over my dead body is that atrocious woman innocent!" Mr. Clark exclaimed.

"What crime has she committed?" Nathaniel demanded to know.

"Ms. Flynn has been accused of committing witchery," his father interrupted. "She has been using it to seduce you to help her flee the home of Mr. Clark. She is an indentured servant and has a debt to pay off. Son, she was merely using you as a pawn to help her escape her servitude."

Nathaniel lowered his eyebrows in confusion.

"Kind sir, my intentions were only to protect you by being dishonest about Daisy's whereabouts," Mr. Clark interrupted. "You see, my daughter, Helen, would make an excellent wife, but when Daisy heard of your plans to marry her, she flooded our home with rage, summoning an evil entity as a large gust of wind swept through our home! I saw her do it with my very own eyes! She began chanting your name toward the window. Her eyes rolled backward into her head as if the devil himself had possessed her!"

"Nonsense!" Nathaniel shouted.

"On the contrary," the governor chimed in. "She was using her witchcraft to make you see her as a beautiful maiden. She made you blind to her true self."

"I do not believe it! I will not believe it! Daisy is a beautiful woman, both inside and out."

"This is what she has been tricking you into believing. She is powerful, Son, who knows what else she is capable of. Where is she?" the governor demanded.

"I do not know. She is not here with me. I last saw her at noon."

"He's lying!" Mr. Clark muttered.

"Kind sir," the governor turned to face Mr. Clark. "I know that you are upset but I assure you, my son is an honest gentleman. I find it incredibly discourteous of you to speak to my son in that fashion."

"Then look for her yourself; prove me erroneous," Mr. Clark resumed.

The governor gestured to the two constables to search the room. Nathaniel appeared panicked. If the officers found Daisy hiding in his closet, they would for sure have her head.

"Father, this is absurd. I cannot believe you would think I'd be dishonest with you."

"I would never accuse you of acting out of character," the governor replied. "Son, you are simply under the enchantment of a powerful witch. Your actions cannot be held against you at present."

"Check in the closet!" Mr. Clark shouted through the doorway.

Nathaniel's breathing stopped. He felt beads of sweat dripping down his forehead. The first officer swung the door to the closet open and peered inside. The room grew silent in anticipation. The officer turned around, "'Tis empty, Sir."

"Good," the governor replied. "Thank you for cooperating."

The men regrouped and left the room, slamming Nathaniel's door behind them. Nathaniel placed his hands over his face in disbelief. He began to wonder if Daisy was truly a witch. He knew he did not imagine the beautiful, sensual experience they had that night, holding her warm, silky body close to his. He knew he instructed her to hide in the closet, but where had she gone? Had she used magic to disappear from the closet? Had she used her witchcraft to become invisible from the officers? Had she truly blinded him from the truth?

Nathaniel deliberately walked toward the closet. With one foot in front of the other, he felt his heart beating through his chest. He placed his hand on the door knob, and once again, his breathing stopped.

He sluggishly opened the door and peered inside. It was true. Daisy had simply disappeared from the closet. "D-Daisy?" he stuttered. The room was silent. Nathaniel's heart sank. He believed now more than ever that she truly was a witch. How could this beautiful, sensual, kind woman who he thought he loved betray him? He began to believe the stories he was told. It all made sense now. This woman had been estranged from her parents, left behind to pay off a debt. Mr. Clark was only doing his moral duty to protect the public from her sorcery, keeping her hidden within his home. But she was so beautiful. How could a witch have so much beauty?

He then remembered his father's words. Was she using witchcraft to blind him from her true self? Was he even able to see how she truly looked? Was it possible that she was truly hideous, and her spell made him see what he wanted, the most beautiful woman alive? Perhaps this was the reason Mr. Clark snapped at him in disgust when he asked about Daisy, instead of Helen. Perhaps the spell even made Helen unattractive to Nathaniel, forcing him to favor Daisy over her.

Before Nathaniel's thoughts become too erratic to control, he heard a tapping on the wall within the closet. Suddenly, a wooden panel from the back of the closet wall began turning around, and Daisy slipped through the small opening, cheeks moistened with salty tears. Nathaniel was astonished. "Daisy, how on earth did you do that?"

"I was so afraid, Nathaniel, I thought for sure they were going to find me. So, I began pushing on all the walls. When I was a child, my mother had a trick wall in our closet. She told me that it was there in case we had to hide from something awful. I was unsure if it would be in here, but I prayed that it would. And sure enough, there was one panel that pushed open, leading to this hidden room."

Nathaniel peered into the small, dark room, barely large enough for two people. He snickered in relief, but then regained his seriousness. "Is this true, Daisy, what they are saying about you. Are you a witch? Please be honest with me."

"Of course not! That is absurd. If that were the truth, I would have fled long ago."

Although Nathaniel had been pondering the idea, her logic along with her bright brown, honest eyes was reassuring to him.

"I believe you, my love."

Daisy smiled. "But what am I to do? They will for sure come and find me. What will they do to me?"

"I do not know. I feel responsible for this."

"No, Nathaniel. Do not blame yourself. There was no way Mr. Clark would ever have allowed me to leave without a fight, whether you were involved or not."

"Well, you now have your fight. You must leave town. He will surely be relentless regarding your capture."

"Leave town? But where will I go?" Daisy asked uncertainly. "I have never been anywhere until just now. I know nothing of the world outside the Clark home."

Nathaniel was lost in thought for a few moments. Daisy watched as the skin of the corners of his eyes wrinkled in concentration. Apprehension was spread across his face. It was almost as if he had a plan that he was not entirely sure of but thought that it was their only option. "Daisy, this may sound frightening, but you must do exactly as I say, any error may lead to your discovery."

Daisy looked up in anticipation.

"You must travel through the forest behind our home headed east until you reach the shipping docks. Once you arrive, I will have a ship waiting for you."

"A ship!" Daisy gasped. "You mean I will be leaving Virginia entirely? I fear I do not know how I will manage on my own."

"You will be just fine. Trust me Daisy, you are strong. You have dealt with all you have for so long, and you have not been broken."

Daisy pondered that thought, she had never thought of herself as being strong. Nathaniel believed in her. She knew she needed to believe in herself also. She then uttered more confidently, "How will I know which ship will take me?"

"Don't worry; they will find you," Nathaniel answered.

"But will I ever see you again?"

"Yes, my love. I will be sure of it. One day, we will be together. I promise."

Nathaniel pulled Daisy's face to his and once again, pressed his lips tightly against hers as they shared the most passionate kiss, as if this was the last kiss they would ever have.

"You must go now, before the sun rises. It will take you until night falls to get there. Once there, the ship will be waiting."

"But what ship sets sail at night?"

Nathaniel laughed. "Trust me, Daisy, I will call in a special favor for you."

Daisy smiled and kissed Nathaniel once more. She then tied her shoes as tightly as she could and followed Nathaniel quietly through the house and out the back door facing a dense forest.

"I will make sure the men are distracted so that they will not come looking for you right away. But believe me Daisy, they will come looking. You must be vigilant."

Daisy sighed, "I will."

She swiftly moved to the entrance of the forest, peered back toward Nathaniel who was standing helplessly in the doorway, and turned away as she disappeared into the timbers on that chilled, Virginia night.

CHAPTER SIX

Daisy ran for her life, faster than she had ever run before. She felt the wind wisp through her hair, entangling it with each desperate leap. Branches from all directions scratched up the smooth skin of her face. She felt agonizing pain as her ankles rolled upon uneven ground. Her heart was pounding, her breathing was heavy, her mind was racing. Racing with thoughts of being discovered and punished beyond anything she knew. Racing with thoughts of Nathaniel and his masculine body on top of hers. Racing with thoughts of the fear of leaving behind everything she had ever known. Her thoughts were chaotic. Her body was screaming with discomfort. And yet, she kept on running, desperate for her eyes to fall upon the sea.

Soon, her body surrendered to the agony, and she could no longer run. Her heart was pleading for a rest, crying out with each thump pounding against her chest. Her lungs were starving for air, craving the deep inhalation of pure, clean oxygen. Her mind begged for a pause, ceasing all her troubling thoughts. And her body wanted nothing more than for a cool breeze to encompass her being, allowing for ultimate relief.

She sat down with her back against a large oak tree, its abundant leaves draping above her. She placed her face in both hands and let her tears form a pool within them. Even when she thought her life could not get any worse, it had. Not only was she alone, separated from the world that she knew, but she was running from what she thought was a terrible nightmare, trying desperately to escape her past and, even worse, her present. The future that she had prayed for was slowly seeping away from her imagination. She was beginning to lose hope for a better time.

Daisy tried to still her racing thoughts as an attempt to cease her tears. She deliberately slowed her breathing and tried to take in the pleasurable fragrances of the forest, something she had done for so many years to help her cope with her abhorrent life. And so, she breathed in the bitter-sweet fragrance of the pine needles of the vast evergreens that surrounded her.

Daisy smiled as she took in the calming effect of the nature. Her tears stopped flowing and she wiped the moisture away from her cheeks. She felt safe. Nothing could hurt her while she was there, she decided. No one would find her in such a flourishing forest. She was hidden within the brush, camouflaged by nature, and she trusted it to keep her identity a secret.

As her dependable coping mechanisms enabled her to relax, and the rush of adrenaline flowing through her veins wore off, Daisy began to feel a searing pain coming from her right calf. When she reached down to stroke her leg, her hand returned with a thick, crimson liquid. She turned her ankle outward to view an unnoticed wound that was now causing her excruciating pain. The gash extended from just below her knee to the middle of her lower leg. Blood was gushing profusely from the opening, and the bottom of her gown had now changed from rose-pink to a deep, crimson red.

"Oh no," she muttered to herself. She tore off a bit of cloth from the bottom of her gown and tied it tightly around her leg. She remembered watching her mother do the same thing to her father when she was a little girl. Her father came home late one night after a long day at work, and his arm, too, was gushing blood. Daisy remembered how upset it made her to see that, but her mother did not panic. They could not afford a doctor, so her mother learned how to nurse over the years. She immediately took an old rag and tied it tightly around the wound. Her mother was brave and never showed signs of fear. She was a strong woman, despite all that was against them.

Daisy knew that she had to continue with her journey. "No more tears," she told herself. It was time to be strong and brave, like her mother had been. She knew that her mother would be disappointed in her had she known she was allowing feelings of discouragement to overcome her. She refused to give up. She needed to keep moving.

And so, Daisy stood up, tilted her head back to the sky, and smiled bravely upward, inhaling and exhaling deeply until she felt strong enough to move on. She picked up a large staff to help her walk with the nearly unbearable pain in her leg and began her trek once again.

The sun was high in the sky, so Daisy knew she had miles to go before reaching the sea port. She used nature to entertain her as she carried on her journey. A couple of feisty squirrels fighting over an acorn made her giggle. A mother bird feeding her baby on a tree branch high above her gave her a sense of hope. And a few deer, off in the distance, extending their necks and pointing their ears when they heard branches cracking below her feet, reminded her that she needed to stay alert.

Daisy continued her journey. Hours passed, and she watched as the sun made its way across the horizon, beginning to lower itself in the west. Nightfall was coming, and she knew she would be close to her much-anticipated destination. She kept trudging through the brush. Her entire body was dampened with perspiration. Her hair was disheveled into an entangled web of sticks and leaves. Her face was grayed with the dirt of the forest floor.

After hours of the most torturous journey she had ever experienced, nightfall was finally upon her, and Daisy stopped once more. She tilted her head back toward the sky and inhaled deeply. She finally smelled the fishy aroma lingering in the air around her. She could hear the sound of waves gently crashing into the shore and the rustling of the leaves produced by the ocean zephyr. She smiled eagerly, knowing that her moment of freedom had finally come. Her body was shaking in anticipation of this new adventure. And so, she began once more. The finish line was in plain sight; she was ready to be liberated from her melancholy existence.

But suddenly, the peaceful melody of the sea was interrupted by the uncoordinated howling of a pack of dogs. As the barking grew louder, Daisy heard the chattering voices of several different men. With the clamor came flickering orange flames between the trees. Her heart stopped. She instinctively turned around and raced back through the forest where she came. The barking grew louder, and she could hear something moving hastily through the bushes behind her.

Without warning, Daisy tripped over a large tree root that was growing upward through the ground and was trampled by an army of dogs. As she fell, she hit her head on a large rock and her vision went black. Through the darkness, she heard muffled echoes of barking dogs followed by the voice of two men that sounded like they were miles away. But soon she saw a bright, white light like the illumination of the moon shine in her mind as her eyes opened sluggishly. She felt the right side of her head throbbing uncontrollably, but her body was floating.

When her consciousness fully returned, she realized that she was in the custody of two men in uniform. They were carrying her limp body like a ragdoll, one man at her head, the other at her feet. Fearful, she began thrashing her body between the two men.

"Let me go!" she demanded.

"Stop this behavior!" one of the men shouted. "You are a wanted woman."

64

"I am guilty of nothing!" Daisy shouted as she continued thrashing about in a desperate attempt at freeing herself.

"This is foolish," the second man remarked. "Tie her up as we discussed before."

Daisy wanted to break free, but she knew that the fighting was only making it worse. Her limbs were tired; her body felt ready to give up. The men lowered Daisy to the ground and tied her arms together behind her back. They pulled her to her feet and walked her toward the seaport as she limped deeply between the two men.

When they arrived, the governor was waiting with a crew of three more men in uniform. He began a slow applause as they grew closer to him.

"Well, well, well. I see you have gotten quite far since you have left my son this morning. Quite a journey for a petite young woman like yourself."

"I do not know what you are speaking of, sir," Daisy squeaked.

"Ha!" The governor exploded. "I know what you are, and I know what you have done."

"You know nothing!" Daisy proclaimed.

"Well, with the evidence, it seems plausible that witchery is your specialty."

"And what evidence might that be?" Daisy asked quizzically.

"Well, not only do we have testimony by the town's most honest clockmaker and his kind daughter but look where you have turned up. You are attempting to flee the state, perhaps even the country. If you ask me, you made yourself appear guilty as charged."

Daisy said nothing more. The men proceeded to place Daisy into a horse-drawn carriage and headed down the road. Daisy peered back toward the sea and saw many ships docked in the port, none of which appeared to have any activity. Where was her rescue ship? Where was her rescue crew? It seemed no one was around.

Daisy wondered if Nathaniel was dishonest with her. Had he made her walk all that way only to have officials arrest her when she reached her destination? Did he inform the men of her whereabouts? Did this man truly love her, or had he used her body as Mr. Clark had, defiling her, only to throw her away like unwanted trash. She could not be certain of any answers at this time. All she could do was wait. Wait, and pray for another miracle.

CHAPTER SEVEN

Daisy spent the night on the dirt floor of a five-by-seven-foot cell in the dimly lit quarters of the jailhouse. She did not sleep. She sat with her back against the wall, holding her knees tightly to her chest. She spent the entire night alert, keeping her eye on the constable who was meant to secure the jail and prevent an attempted escape. Instead, he frequently dozed off, leaving Daisy unsupervised in her cell.

Soon, the morning sun rose in the sky, and Daisy knew she would be facing an unknown consequence. Suddenly, she heard a pounding at the door to the jailhouse, waking the officer as he jolted in his chair. Drowsily, he walked toward the door and peered out the tiny window. Daisy watched as he stretched his arms over his head and yawned. He then tugged at his trousers, attempting to pull them up over his protruding belly, and opened the door leisurely.

"Ah good morrow, Mr. Alexander. What can I do for you?" the officer questioned.

"I want to see the girl," Nathaniel demanded.

"I cannot let you do that, sir. I was given direct order from your father not to let anyone in here, especially you."

"You do understand, kind sir, that my father will not be governor forever? And when he leaves, and I am elected, the first person to lose his job will be you if you do not allow me to speak with Miss Flynn!"

"Yes, sir," the officer replied, "but just for a few moments."

"Very well. Please, give us our privacy."

The officer stepped outside as Nathaniel rushed toward the cell. He reached through the bars and stroked Daisy's hair.

"Oh, my word," he began, "I am so very sorry this has happened."

"What have you done, Nathaniel?" Daisy shouted, crying relentlessly.

"I have done nothing to be disloyal to you. You must believe me."

"Then how did they know where I would be?"

"Mr. Clark suggested it. He thought you might try to flee."

"But the ship, my rescue ship, it wasn't even there!"

"You made it all the way to the sea port? My goodness, no wonder you look as you do. The ship was there, I assure you of that. They are always there when called upon. But look at your leg. It is dripping with blood."

"I know. I will be fine."

"We must get you out of here!"

Nathaniel began frantically searching the room in desperate pursuit of the key. "What are they going to do to me, Nathaniel?" Daisy questioned in an uneasy voice.

"I do not know, my love," Nathaniel sounded apprehensive. "Let us just focus on getting you out of here."

"I know what they will do to her," a second voice sounded unexpectedly from the front of the jailhouse. The governor appeared in the doorway, accompanied by the overweight constable.

"Father, let her go, she has done nothing."

"On the contrary, son. You know what she has done. She is to report to trial immediately! We will determine her fate there. Guard, remove Ms. Flynn from the cell and arrest my son until the trial is over." Nathaniel shouted in protest, but as he attempted to fight the guard, his father pulled his sword from the sheathe on his hip and pointed it directly toward Nathaniel's face. "Son, I love you, but this is for your own good."

Nathaniel stood still, anger written across his face. He peered at the tip of the sharp, silver blade just in front of his eyes as he gritted his teeth and spoke between them, "You should be ashamed of yourself. If only mother were here to see how you behave toward your one and only son."

"Well, she is not here, and as I have mentioned before, this is for your own protection." The governor removed Daisy from the cell himself and chained her wrists. He then shoved his son into the cell and instructed the officer to lock it. As the two of them left the jailhouse, they heard Nathaniel's voice shouting through the walls.

But his voice was lost with the galloping of the horses that took them away.

When they arrived at the courthouse, Daisy was placed on the stand completely disheveled. Her dress was filthy and torn with bloody stains covering the hem. Her hair was intertwined with sticks and leaves, and her face remained greyed with dirt. Her appearance alone caused the jury to chatter amongst themselves. She heard the word "witch" being passed along from person to person.

"Good jury of the court," the governor began, "the woman presented before you is Ms. Daisy Flynn, daughter of the deceased Sarah and Soloman Flynn. As you all may recall, Sarah Flynn was quite the gardener, oftentimes spending numerous hours every single day tending to that garden of hers. But what was her obsession with that garden? Was she concocting magical potions with mysterious herbs that she would use with her witchcraft?"

The courtroom grew noisy with chatter. "Order in the court," the judge announced.

"After the death of her parents, Ms. Daisy Flynn was left in the custody of Mr. and Mrs. Clark. I am sure you all remember Mrs. Clark. A typical, kind, wholesome woman. But tragedy fell upon the house just a year after she agreed to take Ms. Daisy in. Coincidence or not?"

The governor's purposeful introduction left the courtroom with a biased opinion of who Daisy was. Daisy could see the look of contempt in all their faces.

70

"The first witness I shall call to the stand is Ms. Helen Clark." Helen stood up, curtsied to the jury, and stepped up to the stand. "Ms. Clark," the governor continued, "what is your relationship with Ms. Flynn?"

"Daisy was my neighbor when I was a child. We used to be the best of friends. After her parents died, my mother took her in. I loved Daisy like she was my own sister. We grew up together in my home."

"So, you would say that as close as sisters are, you are close enough to Ms. Flynn to know a lot about her?"

"Yes. I would say that is true."

"And how would you describe Ms. Flynn's behavior over the past few years?"

"Well, good sir, Daisy was never like any of the girls our age. She was strange, keeping to herself mostly. There were many times when I would ask her to dress up with me or do our hair together, as most girls our age do, but she never wanted to. Instead, she chose to spend most of her time in her garden."

"So, Ms. Flynn has a garden just like her mother had?"

"Yes," Helen replied.

"Has there been any occasion when you witnessed her bringing some of the plants into the house. Perhaps to create a concoction of some sort?"

"Now that I think of it, yes. I did see her bring in some flowers and herbs a few times and place them in boiling water."

71

"That's absurd!" Daisy shouted to defend herself. "That was only for a cup of tea!"

"Over ruled," the judge responded.

"Thank you, Ms. Clark, you may have a seat." Helen smiled at the jury and curtsied again as she walked over and sat down next to her father. The governor then continued to speak. "Will Mr. Abner Clark please report to the witness stand?"

Mr. Clark stood up and wobbled toward the witness stand. As he sat down, he glared at Daisy.

"Mr. Clark," the governor began, "can you please share with us the recent events that have occurred at your home?"

"Yes sir, I may. You see, your son reported to our house in search of me. He was in need of my services, to create a fine timepiece that he could add to his collection."

The governor interrupted. "If you do not know, Mr. Clark is one of our finest clockmakers here in town. Please continue, Mr. Clark."

"The day that Mr. Alexander arrived was the day that he met Daisy. We believe that on that day, Daisy cast a love spell on him, blinding him from seeing who she really was."

"And why do you feel she had done this to my son?" the governor questioned.

"Well, because the very next day when he returned, I introduced him to my beautiful daughter, Helen, and we agreed that my daughter's hand in marriage would be his payment for the timepiece I would generate. After the agreement was made, he broke

72

it, attempting to flee with Daisy instead. Because of his persistence in pursuing such an unkempt, atrocious woman," he pointed toward Daisy whose beauty was hidden beneath the dirt and blood from the night before, "I believe that the spell was so strong that this man would go to great lengths to do anything for her."

"And what did Ms. Flynn do once she found out that my son's heart was promised to another woman?"

"Oh, now this story is quite the frightening one." He turned to look back at the audience to alert those with children to cover their ears. "That night, we heard Daisy in her bedroom, howling out the window like a wild wolf. When we approached the room, her eyes were rolled to the back of her head with nothing but the whites of them showing. As she brought her arms outward, the wind blew hard through our entire home. The sky became dark, and lightning began striking. It was as if she called upon the devil himself to enter into our home."

The courtroom grew loud once more. Once the room was hushed by the judge, the governor continued.

"Thank you for your statement." The governor turned to face the jury. "Good jury, I would like to further express to you where we have found this woman after these events. She had been journeying by foot, through the forest, to the sea port. Was she attempting to flee because she was guilty of the accusation? Well, that is for you to decide." He ended his statement with a charming smile and sat down facing the judge.

"We will take a brief recess for the jury to decide on a verdict," announced the judge. "Please reassemble after thirty minutes."

***

Daisy sat for thirty minutes in pure disbelief. Hope for a better future was fading away with such haste. Time flew by quicker than she could imagine, and when the jury reassembled, she felt her heart racing.

"Order in the court," the judge demanded to once again hush the chattering crowd. "The verdict is in, and the jury finds Ms. Daisy Flynn," the judge paused long enough for Daisy to catch her breath, "guilty as charged." Daisy fell to the floor, her head spinning with the sounds of a ranting crowd. Never did she think that her life would end up in such a mess. She felt her body being lifted from the floor. Two guards stood beside her, each grasping one arm tightly. They faced her toward the judge to hear her punishment.

"Ms. Flynn, an act of witchery is unable to be controlled by mortal individuals through a typical prison sentence. Therefore, this offense is punishable by death. Your sentence is to be hanged by the neck until dead. Execution shall be carried out in the market square in one hour."

Daisy's legs gave out beneath her as the guards supported her weight. Her head was spinning, and all her senses were heightened. She began to feel the throbbing pain from the gash on her leg at an intensity unimaginable. She could almost make out each individual word that each person in the courtroom was speaking. All the words

74

were loud and clear; witch, devil, monster, evil. These were the words that rang through her ears like shrieking cats wandering the night.

The guards pushed Daisy toward a door behind the judge and into a darkened room. They threw her to the ground and left her locked in another tiny cell with chains tightly bound to her wrists. She didn't know what to do. The life that she had once dreamed of was coming to an end, and she could see how closely the end was to her. She no longer would be able to smell the sweet, succulent aroma of the roses in her garden. She would no longer be able to see the brilliant colors of her lilies. She would no longer be able to feel the cool breeze sweeping across her porcelain-like face. And she would no longer feel the gentle touch of Nathaniel's strong hands running through her beautiful, flowing hair.

The room was so dim, so quiet, and so alone. She felt defeated. The whole world was against her. She wanted so badly to close her eyes and open them back up to find out this was all just a bad dream. To be able to curl up and crawl into her mother's arms, rocking her like a baby, assuring her that everything would be alright. But when she opened her eyes after squeezing them tightly, she remained on the cold floor of that small, dark cell. She had nothing left to do, no more fight left in her. All she could do was pray. And so, Daisy got down onto her knees, formed prayer hands with chains draping from her wrists, and prayed the best that she knew how. Desperately pleading. Waiting for an answer.

CHAPTER EIGHT

Daisy's eyes squinted as sunlight seeped into the dark room through the now open door. Two guards walked in and approached Daisy, placing a brown, burlap sack over her head. Daisy began hyperventilating. She could feel her hot breath warming the inside of the bag. Her eyes began watering, moistening her cheeks with tears that streamed down to her neck. Her fear was unbearable. Where was the answer to her prayers? Where was her miracle?

As she grew closer to her destination, she heard the crowd growing louder and louder. How many people were there to witness her execution? She couldn't even imagine what the crowd would look like. Who would want to watch the life leave the eyes of an innocent, young woman? As she climbed up the steps to her worst possible fate and felt the noose being wrapped around her neck, all she could see was a bright darkness, caused by the sun's rays blasting through the fibers of the sack.

Daisy stood, shaking uncontrollably as she listened to the unruly crowd below her. Then she heard the voice of the governor hushing the crowd.

"Ladies and gentlemen of the good town of Yorkston, Virginia. You are all gathered here today to witness the hanging of Ms. Daisy Flynn, daughter of the late Sarah and Soloman Flynn. As many of you were not able to join us in the courtroom, I will expose the reasons behind this young woman's sentence to death."

The crowd was silent, hanging on to every word spoken by the governor.

"Ms. Daisy Flynn is sentenced to death by hanging, having been found guilty of committing witchcraft in the form of seducing my very own son, Sir Nathaniel Alexander. She is a threat to not only my son, but to every other resident in our lovely town, and as governor, I have vowed to keep all of you protected. Ms. Daisy Flynn is a witch, keeping her alive would put our entire society at risk. Therefore, it is my duty to cease her existence in order to keep all of you safe."

The crowd began cheering wildly in a sickening excitement over ending this woman's life.

"It is now my greatest honor, to present to you, Ms. Daisy Flynn."

The governor lifted the sack over Daisy's head, exposing her filthy face to the crowd. There stood hundreds of people; men, women, and children, all shouting obscenities toward Daisy. Daisy squinted over the crowd as the sun's rays stung her eyes. She felt the temperature in her body rising, her heart beat racing, and her breath catching as she managed one shaky inhale every few moments.

"And now, the time has come. Executioner, please join me." The governor shook hands with the man who had stepped up onto the lynching stage. The man was very tall and husky. His face was hidden by a black sack with two holes for his eyes. The governor then tipped his hat to the man and walked off the stage. The executioner walked over to Daisy and caressed her face. Daisy jerked away from his touch. The crowd went wild, cheering uncontrollably. He then walked over and placed his hand on a lever. No time was being wasted. This was it. The life that she lived, as disappointing as it was, was coming to an end. But despite all she had endured, she wanted to live so badly. Daisy closed her eyes and prayed with all her might. She needed a miracle; this was her last chance.

Suddenly, the crowd grew silent. Daisy thought she was dead. She no longer heard the howling crowd. Her end had come, and she was now entering into the quiet, lonely afterlife. But when she slowly opened her eyes, the crowd of people remained below her, yet they were no longer staring at her. Daisy followed their gaze and turned her head to see the executioner on his knees. When she focused her eyes better, she saw that both of his hands were grasping an arrow that had penetrated the center of his chest. A few moments passed, then a stream of crimson blood flowed out of the corner of his mouth. His body tipped forward as he tumbled off the stage and into the crowd below.

Four more guards, two on the right of the stage and two on the left, dropped to the ground, arrows protruding from the center of their chests. The crowd remained silent, staring in awe and confusion. Just then, an ear shattering thunderclap roared through the crowd, and everyone dispersed, racing madly in the opposite direction of the lynching stage like a stampede of cattle.

The governor looked panicked. He seemed to catch sight of something that spooked him as he ordered his guards to fight and then hopped on his horse and raced away. With four officers down, only eight remained. They stood waiting in anticipation for the next move, swords drawn, peering at every tree and building overlooking the stage.

Daisy attempted to loosen the chains around her wrists as she wanted desperately to remove the noose that was still wrapped around her neck. There were no signs of an enemy in sight, yet the evidence of five casualties remained lying on the grass beneath her. Suddenly, an army of twelve men strolled proudly toward the arena that was now only occupied by eight seemingly nervous guards. Daisy stood helplessly on the execution platform, an easy target for destruction.

Daisy squinted tightly to get a better view of the approaching army. The sun's rays, blasting her in the face, made it difficult to see. She watched the army move toward the stage, swords drawn. She thought that some of the soldiers appeared to be wearing gowns like hers. Were there women in this army? Why would these guards fear an army with women?

When the army drew closer, just below the lynching stage, Daisy could see that it was composed entirely of women. But they did not fight like women; they fought fiercely, like men. Daisy watched as the shimmering swords shone brightly in the sun as they swung over the heads of these women and sunk deeply into the chests of men in the governor's army. She watched men drop to the ground, blood flooding in a pool around their lifeless bodies. Beautiful women with long, flowing hair were fighting like men and defeating each one of the guards. She was flabbergasted by the strength they had coupled with their elegance. When all eight guards were dead, the women turned and strolled gracefully back through the market place where they came.

The market square was silent. No one was in sight. Daisy stood helplessly, peering over the casualties below her. Once again, she struggled to remove the tight chains from her wrists. Just as she was about to give up, she saw a fiery-haired woman approach from the distance in the direction that the army of women had left. When she arrived, she glided up the steps and onto the lynching stage. She was wearing a tight-fitted, brown leather corset that was tucked into her white trousers. She wore brown, leather boots Daisy had only ever seen men wear. Her enormous bosoms were protruding over of the top of her corset, caressed by the flowing waves of her bright red hair. She wore an oversized hat that shaded her gorgeous green eyes and protected the snowy white skin of her face from the sun.

The woman removed the noose from around Daisy's neck and gently grasping Daisy's arms, turned her around and placed her hands on the railing behind her. Daisy shivered at the touch of this beautiful, mysterious woman.

"Hold still," she demanded.

Daisy closed her eyes tightly when she saw the woman swing a large axe over her shoulder. She heard the clang of metallic striking and felt the chains from her wrists slip off and fall onto the ground. Daisy brought her arms around to her chest and held them tightly to her breasts.

"Apologies," the woman uttered. "It appears we were just a little late." She smirked. Daisy said nothing.

"Let's go." The woman grabbed Daisy by the hand and held on to her shaking body as she climbed down the steps of the lynching stage.

She led Daisy to one end of the platform, where a large horse had been abandoned by one of the panicked townspeople. "This horse will do, climb up." The woman instructed.

"Where are we going? And who are you?" Daisy finally gathered the courage to ask.

"Do you want to spend time chatting while the governor sends the rest of his army here, or do you want to get moving?" the woman replied sarcastically.

This silenced Daisy as she followed the instructions and climbed up onto the horse. The woman hopped on behind her and held onto the reigns leaning into Daisy's body.

When they reached the sea port, the fiery-haired woman led Daisy to a large ship. Daisy stared at the large vessel that rocked gently upon the ocean. She couldn't comprehend how such a large entity could float upon the water. She began to feel weak. Her heart was racing. She was overwhelmed with the new experience of sailing away on a ship and leaving her past and all she knew behind. But somehow, she felt that she could trust this unidentified woman, and so she followed her onto the ship.

After embarking, the woman began calling out orders: "All hands on deck! Raise the sails! Man the deck! Draw in the anchor! Cast off!" Daisy watched as the women aboard eagerly performed tasks she had only ever heard of men doing. The women were strong. She watched as their protruding biceps flexed as they prepared the ship to set sail. When all the sails were up, Daisy watched as one woman anchored a flag at the front of the ship. The flag was black with a white skull. Underneath the skull were two crimson roses crossing one another in an "X."

Daisy watched the land disappear as they glided through the water, away from the only home she had ever known. She was overwhelmed and befuddled at the events that had just taken place. Who were these women? Why did they come to help her? Was this just a coincidence or truly a miracle? Were her prayers finally answered? Daisy had so many questions. She sat at the stern of the ship, alone, waiting for answers to come.

After about thirty minutes of sailing, Daisy was approached by the fiery-haired woman who rescued her from her execution. Her beauty was striking, and her smile was mysterious.

"Ms. Flynn, how are you feeling?" she asked.

Daisy looked up surprised, "I'm a bit overwhelmed actually. How do you know my name?"

The woman laughed, "I know a lot of things, it is my job to know. My name is Captain Willie Spade, and, if you have not already noticed, this is my ship, and these beautiful, strong, sensational women you see, are my crew."

Daisy looked around. "Was I rescued purposefully?"

"Were you not headed to the seaport for a ship last night?" Willie asked as if she already knew the answer.

"Well, yes, but I did not see your ship."

"Well, the ship did see you, and that pack of bloody canines they sent on your rear!"

Daisy looked astonished, "You were summoned by Mr. Alexander?"

"Indeed, we were, Ms. Flynn."

"Please, call me Daisy."

"As you wish," Willie responded.

"Are you military? From another country perhaps?" Daisy asked.

Willie laughed once again, "No, no, my dear. Most of us are American, but not all."

"Well I can't imagine a group of women as fishermen, especially those who can fight like soldiers."

"'Tis true, we are not fishermen either."

"Then what is this ship for? What does your crew do?" Daisy asked in pure wonderment.

Willie laughed, "Ms. Daisy, you will have to open your eyes to a stronger truth. Your sheltered life has stunted your perception of how variable life can be. We are pirates, Ms. Daisy."

Daisy glared at Willie, wide-eyed, "Pirates?" she asked puzzled. "But from the stories I was told as a child, all pirates are men. Ugly men that have no compassion."

Once again, Willie laughed, "Again, life is not always as you may have been led to believe. We may not be as masculine as men, or as ugly as the pirates you have heard of, but we are just as strong, if not stronger, than the ones you have been told about through these tales. Come with me, I will introduce you to the ladies and show you around the ship."

Willie guided Daisy toward the front of the ship until they came across a group of women standing toward the sea, overlooking the edge. Daisy peered out over the vast ocean to find out what had caught their attention. Just below their ship was a pod of dolphins leaping playfully through the sea. Daisy stared in awe, "what are those beautiful creatures?" The women turned to look at her.

"They are called dolphins," one woman responded, chuckling in amusement. Daisy's face flushed in embarrassment. "Don't you worry, you will see a whole new world of things you have never seen before on this new adventure. My name is Tabatha, and I speak for all of us when I say that we are happy to have you aboard."

Willie interjected, "And this here is Margaret and Sarah."

"It's very nice meeting you ladies," Daisy curtsied, and the two of them moved on.

84

When they climbed down the steps, Willie led Daisy into a dimly lit room below deck. "All the ladies in the crew share sleeping quarters on the bottom deck. Unfortunately, there are no more cots left, so you will have to stay in the room that belonged to my previous first mate." Willie pointed to a door on the second floor and continued their tour. One more deck below, Willie pointed out one more room. "Here are the bathing quarters, I understand you have had a long day. Please, bathe yourself and join us for supper." Willie handed Daisy a clean gown and a bar of soap and left the room.

Daisy undressed herself and stepped into the bathing tub. She dumped a bucket of water over her head to wash away the debris from her journey through the woods. She sat down into the tub and let the tears pour from her eyes. She felt relieved, but at the same time very frightened to discover what the next part of her life would bring. She had never imagined a life of piracy. She was far too kind, genuine, and loving to think of committing any of the vicious crimes described to her through tales as a child. Would she be expected to behave as a pirate? Would she be expected to steal? Would she be expected to murder? She didn't know if she could.

Suddenly, the door to the bathing quarters swung open. Daisy grasped her knees in tightly as to hide her supple breasts. In walked a tall, beautiful, naked woman with a smooth, ebony complexion to her skin. Her hair was long and rope-like and swung behind her like a horse's tail. She looked at Daisy with dark, piercing eyes and asked, "Miss, what is it that you are tearful about?"

Daisy looked up with big eyes, "I'm sorry, I am just so distressed right now."

The woman squatted down beside her, "My dear, when life knocks you down, you get right back up and fight."

"But I'm afraid I don't know how to fight."

"The fight is inside of every woman who has been scorned, and I know that you have had a hard and painful life."

"How do you know that when we've only just met?"

"I can see it in your eyes."

Daisy took in what the woman was saying and then replied, "My name is Daisy, what is yours?"

"I am Zenobia, princess of Wagadugu."

"Where is Wagadugu?" Daisy felt embarrassed that she had no knowledge of the place.

"It is a village in Africa that has been taken over by the Portuguese and Dutch for access to our gold and our people."

"Your people?"

"Yes, the men who come capture our people and make us into slaves."

"I am so sorry to hear that, but what brings you to this ship?"

"Just like you, I needed an escape. And just like you, I was a warrior who fought for my freedom."

"But I am not like you, I have not fought, I gave up instead, I let them take me," Daisy began to cry again.

"Woman," Zenobia scolded, "wipe your tears. You must stay strong. Captain Willie Spade does not rescue the weak, we have all been chosen. She knows our true strength; she knows our inner warrior. You, Ms. Daisy, are a warrior; you must start believing that."

Daisy stopped crying and wiped the tears from her face. "I saw you earlier in the day. You were fighting for me, along with the others. Why?"

"Because we were all once in your position. We fight for one another. We stay true to ourselves and to our sisters. You will soon understand the importance of sisterhood and the bond that we all share." Zenobia handed the gown to Daisy and helped her to her feet. "Never forget, you are brave. You are a warrior. You have been chosen.

CHAPTER NINE

Supper time came and Daisy found herself apprehensive about meeting the rest of the crew. Would she fit in? Would they accept her? Was she truly a warrior as Zenobia insisted she was? She headed down the steps to the dining hall where a long, wooden table surrounded by eighteen women of all colors and sizes stood. The table was headed by Willie who gestured to Daisy to have a seat beside her.

"Ladies," Willie spoke.

"Aye!" The women shouted in a synchronized manner after they had a seat at the dining room table.

"Please join me in welcoming Ms. Daisy Flynn to our family."

Daisy timidly looked around the room at all the unfamiliar faces and began, "I just wanted to say how much I appreciate you all for rescuing me earlier today."

"Daisy, you are one of us now, you were born to be one of us. Most people consider pirates to be cutthroat, and that, we are. But only to those deserving. You see, we are different from the typical pirates you hear tales of. You might say we have more of a conscience that dwells in the nurturing manner that tends to be innate within women. But in reality, we have all been scorned. We have been beaten, we have been abused, and we have been kicked down over and over again. Our femininity has been perceived as weakness, but Ms. Daisy, I can assure you, we are far from weak. We are strong. We are brave. We do whatever it takes to get what we want and deserve. If you see something you want, you take it. And you never allow any man to weaken you or tell you that you cannot be as strong as they. Daisy, all of this can be yours, you just have to want it and accept it. But once you are in, you are in forever. There is no returning to your old life. The only way for you to leave us is by sinking to the bottom of the ocean. So, you must make the decision, whether you are in, or you are not. We will not hold you hostage. If your choice is to live a normal life, then we will let you off at the nearest port. You will be free, but think about what that means? Will you truly be free? Or will you continue to live the life that you had lived before; abused, disrespected, silent. As I have said, the choice is yours. You have twenty-four hours to make your decision."

Daisy glanced around the room. The women surrounding the table were glaring at her. The room was silent. The women were curious. Did Daisy truly have what it took to be a pirate, a sister aboard the Crimson Rose?

"Let us now eat," Willie commanded as the room grew loud with high-pitched chatter. The table was full of foods that Daisy had never eaten. Brightly-colored lobster and crab embellished the table. Whole fish with eyes gazing up at hungry faces were resting upon their plates. Bright yellow cobs of corn, orange yams with a pleasantly sweet odor, green beans, purple figs, and green pears lit up the room. There was more food on the table than she had ever seen in her life. Goblets of wine lined the center of the table, and the more they drank, the louder the room had become.

***

Later that evening, Daisy found herself feeling unwell as she lay in the cot within the privacy of her own room. Her body was trembling uncontrollably and sweat drained from every pore in her skin. She began seeing insects crawling around on the walls, but she couldn't bring herself to rise and squash them. She let out an agonizing moan which prompted the nearby captain to enter.

"Daisy," Willie began, "what is the matter with you?"

"I'm not sure, but I feel ill."

Willie glanced over Daisy's body until she caught site of her leg. "My goodness, look at this leg of yours." Daisy glanced down at her leg. The gash that was once saturated with crimson blood was now oozing with a yellow drainage, and Daisy was as pale as a ghost. Willie placed the back of her hand across Daisy's forehead. "You are burning like fire. I must take you to see the doctor at once."

"But I thought there were no men aboard this ship?" Daisy asked, concerned that she may not receive the care that she needed.

"There is not," Willie smiled.

90

Willie helped Daisy stand and then placed her arm around her hip to guide her into the doctor's den which was just below the dining hall.

When they entered the room, a pale woman with short brown hair that rested just below the nape of her neck stood to offer her assistance.

"What happened to Ms. Flynn, Captain?" the woman questioned.

"I'm not quite sure, it appears as if she has a wound on her leg and she feels very warm to the touch."

The dark-haired woman turned her hand over and placed it upon Daisy's forehead. Then she studied the opened gash on Daisy's shin. "Ms. Flynn," she said. "My name is Dr. Margaret Baynes, and I believe that you may be septic."

"Septic?" Daisy asked suspiciously, "What exactly does that mean?"

"It means that there is an infection in your leg that has now begun to travel throughout your blood stream. Is it painful?" Margaret asked.

"Yes, very much so."

"How did it happen?"

"I had been running through the woods, attempting to stay hidden from the men who were chasing me. I must have hit a tree branch or a rock on the forest floor. Am I going to die, Dr. Baynes?"

"Not if I can help it," Margaret smiled as she looked up at Daisy and then to Willie. "Captain, I will need to keep her here overnight for observation."

Willie nodded and left the room.

"Have you been treated for a wound like this in the past, Ms. Flynn?"

"No, I have not. Aside from the common winter-time illness, I have never been seriously ill."

"You have been lucky," Margaret smiled. "It is a blessing to have good health."

"Yes, I like to think so."

"Well, what I am going to do is clean the wound with some alcohol and then apply some medicine I have created."

Daisy nodded.

"It may cause minor pain." Margaret drowned the wound with rum from a nearby bottle. Daisy hissed like a snake. Then, Margaret reached across the room for a paste and slathered it over the wound followed by a cotton dressing. She then boiled some water over a small fire that rested within a stone-lined enclosure in the corner of the room and placed some roots and flowers within. "Here, drink this down."

Daisy drank the concoction. Her face wrinkled as the bitter flavor hit her tongue.

"We will continue this process for the next couple of days until it improves," Margaret said.

"Thank you, Dr. Baynes, but I don't have any money to pay you," Daisy sounded ashamed. She worried about the cost knowing that doctors were very expensive. She remembered that her parents saved up quite a bit of money to pay the doctor when they fell ill, but they didn't have enough to continue payments, which was why, Daisy believed, death ensued.

Margaret laughed, "I am the one and only doctor aboard the Crimson Rose, Ms. Flynn. This is my job; this is what makes me an active member of the crew. You do not need to pay me; we pay one another in our support. I'm sure you will be able to aid the Crimson Rose when it's needed."

"But I fear I have nothing to offer."

"Can you cook? Or clean?"

"Yes."

"Well, then you may be used in the kitchen one day. You will be trained to fight, I'm sure, and they will use you in battle."

Daisy appeared frightened.

"Do not worry, you will be well-prepared when the time comes. Most of the women here never even picked up a sword a day in their lives, let alone fought. And now, well, let us just say that we have one strong army."

Daisy relaxed a bit. "May I ask you a question, Dr. Baynes?"

"Of course, Ms. Flynn."

"How is it you have become a doctor. I thought that any education for a woman was illegal?"

Margaret laughed, "Yes, of course it is. My father trained me. He was a surgeon."

"That's very impressive."

"Well, thank you, Ms. Flynn. I have worked hard to reach this point. It wasn't an easy feat, and I faced a lot of obstacles along the way."

"Any doctor must be needed back in the colonies, what brought you to this ship?"

"Well, just as you were brought here, I too, was rescued by Captain Spade."

"What were you rescued from?"

"Prison."

Daisy hesitated to respond. "Is everyone on board. . . criminals?"

Margaret laughed, "On the contrary, my dear lady, none of us were criminals. Were you?"

"Pardon?"

"Well, from what I recall, we did rescue you from a lynching stage. To be hanged is typically the fate of a criminal, am I correct in saying so."

"Well, I was accused of witchery, but I assure you, I am very innocent."

"It doesn't appear that way," Margaret joked.

"Why, yes. You are right, it is difficult to believe my story."

"Nay, Ms. Flynn. Trust me when I say I, more than anyone, believe your story. None of us on this ship were criminals, although it may have appeared that way. Many of us were falsely imprisoned, some of us were slaves, some of us were beaten, some of us were simply disregarded as important members of society. Whatever the case was, we were all in need of a way out."

"So why were you in prison?"

"Just as you mentioned, Ms. Flynn, it is illegal for a woman to be educated, illegal for a woman to become a doctor."

"So, they imprisoned you for something that may help others."

"Of course, because it is something designated for a man, only. Don't you understand, Ms. Flynn, men's fear lies in the strength and power of a woman, so they try to keep us subordinate the best they know how."

"How long have you been aboard this ship?" Daisy asked.

"About three years."

"Do you have any regrets of becoming a pirate?"

"Not one. Life is better. I am respected. I have gained strength, or as Captain Spade has suggested, highlighted my inner strength that I've had all along. The captain does not just recruit any woman to this ship, we are individually selected as she sees fit. The captain is by far the strongest of us all; she is a great leader. But do not cross her, she is not as forgiving as she may seem. Now get some rest, that will help to fight the infection."

Daisy lay down on a cot that was set up in the room next to the wall. She watched Margaret sit on a chair underneath a desk and begin writing in a journal. Daisy tried to stay awake as she lay in a room with a woman she only just met, but her eyes surrendered as she drifted off to sleep through the flickering flame of the single, lit candle.

***

Daisy remained asleep for thirty-six hours, waking only to take her medicine and have some food that was brought to her in the doctor's den. Margaret remained by her side for the entirety of the time, monitoring her leg and changing the bandage every so often. When Daisy finally awoke, three days later, the gash on her leg had closed, leaving behind a reddened scab. She no longer felt ill and the color had returned to her face.

"How are you feeling?" Margaret asked.

"Much better, thank you so kindly."

"It was no problem at all. I hope you had contemplated your decision during your restful days, it is not often Captain Spade allows for more than twenty-four hours to pass."

"What decision?" Daisy asked, puzzled.

"You do not remember? You must decide on whether or not you wish to remain here with us, as a pirate aboard the Crimson Rose."

Daisy shuddered at the thought. She would need to learn how to fight. To kill a man? How could she? She never, in her wildest dreams, thought she would end up in this predicament.

"I suppose I hadn't thought much more on the topic," Daisy admitted.

"Well, you'd better think quickly; Captain Spade is expecting an answer tonight at supper."

***

Supper time came quickly. Daisy walked nervously toward the dining hall. She knew that this was the toughest decision she had ever made in her entire life, and she was dreading the thought of walking into a room with eighteen women expecting an answer so suddenly.

When she entered the room, she noticed that the dining table was already saturated with the women, surrounding another lavish meal. She inhaled the savory odors that oxygenated the room. Margaret walked in behind her, tapped her on the shoulder to alert her of her entrance and as Daisy stepped aside, she took her seat at the table.

Captain Spade, at the head of the table, spoke. "Ms. Flynn, won't you please have a seat beside me."

Daisy sat in the chair, frozen. All eyes were glued on her. The silence in the room was piercing.

"As you all know," Willie continued, "Ms. Flynn had an unfortunate illness fall upon her which was why this dinner has been delayed. Thankfully, our faithful, good doctor," she pointed to Margaret, "has healed Ms. Flynn."

Whispers grew loudly in the room, then ceased as Willie continued to speak.

"Ms. Flynn, we are happy to see that you are feeling better, but this ritual dinner that all the women have gone through must be honored, and your decision must be made. What is your decision in regards to remaining aboard the Crimson Rose and living the rest of your days as a pirate in the sisterhood we have created?"

Daisy felt her hands tremble. She removed them from the table and placed them in her lap, trying desperately to still them. She thought deeply, attempting to pull an answer deep within her core. Her entire being had been dictated by the force of being good. She thrived off her kind and loving character that her mother had helped shape her into. But now, the decision had come to change all of that. She heard the tales and she saw the women in battle. Pirates were cutthroat. They went after what they wanted, even if they had to use violence to get there. Could she ever allow herself the responsibility of taking another's life? She knew that murder and thievery were part of that life. Was she prepared for that? She looked across the table at Margaret's glimmering eyes, reminding her of their conversation just a few days before. A doctor was nothing more than a person designated to help others, and yet she had no regrets transitioning into her life as a pirate.

Daisy took a few more moments and pictured what her life would look like if she went back to Yorkston. Either she would be in hiding for the rest of her life, or she would be put to death. Her decision seemed to make itself. "I truly appreciate all of you for rescuing me from the worst possible fate. And I have nothing but the utmost gratitude to you, Dr. Baynes, for caring for me without expecting anything in return. That loyalty, which I have witnessed, is rare and genuine, and I would wish nothing more than to join the sisterhood of the Crimson Rose, to forever roam the seas in a life of pure adventure."

The sternness in Willie's face faded into satisfaction. "And so, it is done." Willie stood and instructed Daisy to do so as well as she held her clammy hand high in the air. The room became loud with applause and cheer. The women seemed genuinely pleased to be receiving another sister.

"Ladies," Willie interjected through the noise, "let us recite our mantra."

The women all held hands around the long, wooden table, now nineteen of them together, and recited in unity as Daisy listened intently:

"We are sisters upon this ship

Drink of the devil upon our lips

For hell on earth has brought us home

To our righteous place in which we roam

The seven seas in all its might

Should evil call, then we will fight

To secure the safety of one, of all

For hell shall rage if one should fall

And so, we live in this glorious tale

In dangerous waters, once we set sail

To stand strong and feared as the story goes

Aboard the ship of the Crimson Rose."

CHAPTER TEN

The next couple of weeks were challenging for Daisy. She had to learn the daily tasks of life on the sea. She had to learn how to fish and learn how to prepare the ship. Most importantly. She had to learn the basic skills of a pirate, and that included fighting.

Daisy always thought of herself as genuinely kind, and she was proud of that. She learned that from her mother, and from Mrs. Clark who so graciously accepted her as her own. She never, in her wildest dreams, would imagine herself fighting. That was, she thought, a skill meant for men. It was a skill meant for pirates. And so, she knew that her decision to become a pirate would force her to partake in activities that she was rather uncomfortable with.

When the time came for her to train, Zenobia brought her to the bottom deck where the weapons were stored. It was a large, open area. Weapons were stored on hooks that lined the wooden walls. Zenobia reached for a long, shiny sword and handed it to Daisy. Daisy's arm folded under the weight of the sword.

"You must keep your arm tight," Zenobia instructed, "like this." She demonstrated as she flexed her arm while holding the sword by the handle. Daisy did the same, although still a weak grip, she had gained a bit more control.

"Now," Zenobia said, "When you initiate a fight, you hold your arm straight and strong whilst staring your enemy in the eyes. This will instill your willingness to fight and prove your courageousness. However, in sudden combat when you are caught off guard, this step may be skipped over. Your stance must always be strong, your dominate foot must be grounded in front while your other foot placed behind. While you must stand strong enough to fight, you must be able to quickly and suddenly lighten your stance to move freely about. Standing in one spot will surely get you killed." She then demonstrated a fighting stance. Daisy took the same stance, but her glare was one based in fear, one based in uncertainty. The information was a lot to take in and she feared she might make a mistake that would cause her death.

Zenobia recognized her fearfulness and put her sword down. She walked over and took the sword out of Daisy's trembling hand. Then, she said, "the first rule is never to let anyone take your weapon." She smiled as she turned around, trying to hide her enjoyment.

Zenobia was a serious woman. She did not smile often, nor did she partake in celebrations as joyfully as the other women. Her fierceness was written across her face, and her physical strength was exposed by the rocky bulges that encompassed her body.

101

She set Daisy's sword on the ground, next to hers and turned back around toward Daisy who now hung her head low. "I think this may be an impossible task for me," Daisy whispered.

"Nay! 'Tis never a task impossible for any woman. But you must end your thoughts of being incapable. Because, my dear, those thoughts may be holding you back from achieving greatness."

Daisy nodded. Then, Zenobia said, "you may become a great warrior if you believe that you can. You will work hard and you will achieve. But you must be brave. Strength will come, have faith in yourself."

Daisy nodded again, this time more confidently.

"Then, shall we try again?"

Daisy smiled then bent down to pick up her sword. She held it straight out toward Zenobia's face. She stood in a fighting stance. She inhaled and exhaled deeply which helped to steady her shaking arm. Then, Zenobia picked up her sword, did the same, then swung it behind her and came back with such force that it knocked Daisy's sword from her hand.

Daisy looked stunned. Then, Zenobia said, "now, pick it up and do it again."

Zenobia repeated that over and over until Daisy was finally able to maintain her grasp of the sword as the sharp metal of Zenobia's came crashing into hers.

"Very good," Zenobia said. Now, I believe we are done for the day.

"But I hardly did any fighting. I merely just stood and allowed you to hit my sword with yours."

"You must learn to crawl before you can walk," Zenobia said as she replaced her sword on the wall and then walked out of the room. Daisy stood, relatively confused, but then replaced her sword on the wall as well and walked out.

The next day, Daisy met Zenobia again in the arms deck and said confidently, "I want to fight today."

"Very well. Zenobia said. We will do the same exercise as yesterday, only you will be the one hitting my sword. When you can knock it out of my hand, we will be done for the day."

Daisy nodded. She retrieved the sword from the wall, as did Zenobia, and pointed it directly at Zenobia's chin. She held her arm steady and took a fighting stance, strong but mobile. Zenobia did the same. Then, she swung the sword over her head with all her might and came smashing it upon Zenobia's sword. The sharp clanging of metal rang through the air, but Zenobia's sword did not budge. Her grip was tight and her biceps bulged as she held onto the sword's handle. "Again," she demanded.

Daisy continued to swing over and over but could not knock the sword from Zenobia's grip. Finally, Daisy said, "I fear you are a much stronger person than I, and there may not be any possibility that I can release you of your sword."

Zenobia lowered her sword, then said sternly, "do you think the men that you will be fighting have similar or less strength than you? Men have more physical strength than women, it is just the way it is by nature. But you may have more passion. It is that passion ignited within that will drive your force when you fight against men."

Daisy nodded. Then, she engaged initial contact with Zenobia once more. She closed her eyes and thought how badly she wanted it. How much she wanted to knock the sword out of Zenobia's hand. How much she wanted to defeat her enemy. She then opened her eyes and swung swiftly and strongly. Zenobia's sword broke contact with her fingers and flew into the air until it landed on the ground with a thud.

"Very good." Zenobia said. "But now, this leads me to the second rule: you must always keep your eyes on the enemy and on the sword."

Daisy stared at Zenobia wide-eyed, realizing that she had closed her eyes before she swung. She realized that in real combat, that would have been a fatal mistake. She nodded her head. "Are we done for the day?"

"Yes," Zenobia said as she replaced her sword on the wall and walked out of the room.

Daisy smiled. It was only day two and she felt that she was improving and becoming stronger after each session. A week had passed, and Daisy was beginning to learn how to fight and move at the same time. The third rule she had learned was that she must be quicker than her enemy. When her enemy draws their sword above their head, she should be coming back with hers. That technique, she learned, would give her more power.

Daisy practiced every day by herself, with Zenobia, and with others. She learned how to deviate from her own comforts to adapt to other styles of fighting. Zenobia taught her how to use a dagger. She taught her how to use a bow and arrow. And, she taught her how to load and shoot a pistol.

Daisy was beginning to gain confidence, but she still felt a bit uneasy about using her skills on another human being. She had never hurt anyone before, and she feared it may be difficult for her to do. But she tried to focus on Zenobia's advice; in a situation of life versus death, she must choose life and fight for it.

One night, while Daisy was preparing for sleep in her room, she heard a knock at the door. She was in her undergarments and reached for her gown. Then, she remembered that she was on a ship full of women who had no shame. So, she left the gown hanging and shouted for the intruder to enter.

Willie walked into her room and oddly she gazed admiringly at Daisy. Daisy stood to show respect. Willie sat down on the bed and Daisy did the same. "So, how do you feel your training is going?" Willie asked.

"I feel fairly confident in my skills, although I know that actual combat will be far more stressing."

"Yes," Willie laughed, "that it is. But I believe you will be a great warrior."

Daisy smiled.

"Ms. Flynn, how do you feel about life?"

Daisy was taken aback by the question. She had never given thought to such a deep explanation about what life is, and no one had engaged her in conversation on the subject. But she responded the best she knew how. "Well, I believe that you are given one life, and whatever happens in that life, you must accept who you are."

"Do you believe that you can change who you are?"

"I believe that you can change your behavior, but you can never change who you truly are."

Willie nodded. "That sounds like a perfect answer." She smiled, then said, "you have been working hard the past couple of weeks. Tomorrow, we go someplace where we can all have a rest. Good night Ms. Flynn."

"Good night."

CHAPTER ELEVEN

Port Royal, Jamaica: The wickedest city on earth. The place where pirates went to dine, drink, and behave as freely as they chose. Where laws did not exist, and common folk feared to go. Where promiscuous women roamed the streets, and nightly murders went unseen. For any pirate, the island was heaven on earth. For Willie and her crew, a place to rest freely ashore and briefly evade the vigorous waves of the maritime world.

Land was finally in sight after two weeks of experiencing nothing but the surrounding waters. Daisy longed for a steady ground beneath her feet. She had begun to forget what it was like to be planted firmly on a motionless ground, where one had total control.

The ocean was vast and dangerous. The Crimson Rose, although feared by many, was a pitiful vessel against the powerful maritime world. Mysterious creatures below the surface of the sea were larger than the ship itself. Daisy often peered overboard in the night, watching the superior shadow of a great whale illuminated by the moon's casted rays. She feared the strength of such creatures, but the beauty was what caught her attention. The graceful nature of the marine realm was calming to Daisy. It was, to her, something out of a fairy tale. But the reality was that with one erroneous move, the Crimson Rose, with all its members, could be swallowed up by the immense, perilous sea.

So, to see land was reassuring for Daisy. It allowed her to feel a sense of home, a sense of reality. But what was the purpose of this trip? As the ship docked in the port, Daisy focused her eyes on a sort of nature she had never seen before. The trees were different. Flowers were brighter with sweeter scents. The leaves of the trees were like large wings of an enormous bird providing a grand shade to all who walked below. The brush was a brighter green, mostly shades of lime and pear. The sky was a brightly colored azure, and the waters that caressed the shore were clearer than Daisy had ever seen. She was able to see straight to the bottom where the fluorescent colored fish swam below the surface of the sea.

Willie led the crew through the sandy beach and into a town that was bursting with noise. Men were chasing seemingly joyful women whose bosoms were bursting through the tops of their corsets. Women wore gowns that would be considered inappropriately colored back home. Shades of pink, red, yellow and lavender lit up the streets of the town. Taverns and brothels lined the roads with broken windows and cluttered yards. Glass bottles that had once supplied whiskey and rum were now shattered along their path.

The crew was led to a tavern where all the women dispersed throughout the room, joining in gleeful conversation with the men of the town. Daisy watched as some of the women flaunted their bodies around the men, some passionately kissing strange men they had never even known. Willie sat down at the bar and seeing Daisy's lost expression, gestured her to have a seat.

"Barkeep!" Willie shouted, "Bring us a couple of your finest rums."

Daisy smiled with relief as she had never learned how to order a drink at a tavern, but rum was not her first choice. Timidly, she stated, "Actually, I prefer to drink wine."

"Wine? Then wine it is. Barkeep, make that one rum and one glass of your finest wine."

Daisy smiled. "What is this place?" she asked Willie.

"This is the greatest place on earth, where pirates come to play." Willie laughed.

"I have never seen such plants and flowers before."

"This is a tropical island, the things that grow here can't grow up north. The weather stays hot all year round here. They never see any snow."

Daisy's face lit up, impressed with all the knowledge that Willie had. She was eager to learn more about the world. She never realized how naïve she was to anything outside of Virginia.

Suddenly, a man came up behind Willie, just barely caressing her body with his and whispered into her ear, "Well, if it isn't Wilhelmina Spade."

"That's Captain Spade to you," Willie replied confidently.

"To what do I owe this pleasure?"

109

"The pleasure is not yours," Willie replied, "I am here on business, none of which is with you."

The man looked disappointed. He was an extremely attractive man. Tall and muscular with a dark olive complexion to his skin. He had a scruffy face, not quite a beard yet not entirely clean and neat like Nathaniel's face had been. He carried a pistol on his hip, just as Willie had done. Daisy watched as the man continued to try to court Willie.

"And why, might I ask, have I not been able to meet your acquaintance yet? Trice, I have seen you upon this island and yet you continue to ignore my genuine attempts at winning over your precious, sweet, succulent fruit."

"How charming," Willie replied with the utmost sarcasm. "You truly know how to court a lady."

"Aye, but you are not a lady. You are nothing more than a prostitute with a pistol."

Willie turned to face the bar, took a swig of her rum, then smugly turned back to the man and punched him in the jaw upon which he fell to the floor.

Daisy gasped, shocked at the violent response to the verbal pestering.

"We do this every time," Willie turned to speak to Daisy and continued to drink her rum.

A few minutes later, once Willie had finished her drink, she turned to look at Daisy once more, "'Tis now the time to handle business. Care to join me?"

Daisy nodded as they stepped over the unconscious man on the floor and proceeded into a back room. The room was dark but not as crowded as the one before. When the two women entered the room, men that had been sitting at tables lining the walls looked up from their drinks.

"Aye, women! You have no business in here," one man shouted from across the room. "Women are bad luck in a room full of prosperous men conducting business. Now go back to your meaningless lives cooking for your men, I'll be over later to give you a taste of my spectacular cock." A roar of laughter filled the room.

Willie ceased in her steps, pulled out her pistol, and shot the man. "Anyone else have a spectacular cock?" Her question was followed by silence. A brave man shouted from a table in the corner, "Are you mad, woman?

To which Willie replied, "If you are asking if I am an angry person, then yes, I do have quite the rage residing in me. But if you are asking if I am mentally unstable, well then, yes, I would say I am a little of that as well. Now," she continued, "I am looking for Captain Santiago de la Cruz." Silence once again was among the men, until a tall man, more handsome than the one before, slowly walked into the room and glared at Willie.

The man walked toward the two of them with a stern face. Daisy felt her heart racing. This man would kill them for sure, she thought. She couldn't believe that Willie just shot a man for no good reason. Furthermore, she knew that Willie disrespected the men by shooting one of their own. She could feel her palms increase in moistness, heat rising to her face. But she had to maintain composure, just as Willie had done. When the man stopped just in front of them, Daisy was petrified. She feared having to use her training. She wasn't even sure if she was prepared, especially not to fight a room full of men when it was only her and her captain. Willie did not flinch. She was brave. The man asked in a subtle tone of voice, "You killed my carpenter?"

Willie looked over at the mess she had made, and simply said "He should have known who I was."

The room was tense. Men from all corners of the room had their eyes glued upon the intruding women with one hand on their glass, and the other on their pistol. "You should probably inform the rest of these fine gentleman who I am," Willie continued.

"I suppose you are right," the man stated. "Gentleman," he turned to face the rest of the room. "The lady that you see standing before you is not just any woman. This is Captain Willie Spade."

Chatter in the room became abundant. "You mean the Crimson Rose is real? It isn't just a wise man's tale?"

Santiago laughed. "'Tis true. The Crimson Rose is as real and as fierce as the stories proclaim."

One by one, the men stood and bowed down to Willie. Some men were astounded that the great Captain Willie Spade was a woman, others just impressed at the relationship between their captain and Willie. Daisy finally began to understand the level of respect that Willie had maintained over the seven seas. She was legendary in the eyes of these pirates. She had power, power Daisy had only ever known men to have.

"May we speak in private?" Willie asked Santiago.

"Yes of course," Santiago replied as he signaled the two women to follow him into yet another room. "It has been far too long, Wilhelmina," Santiago began when the three of them sat down in a small, private room in the back of the tavern.

"Yes, I know, but I have not come to reminisce on the time we have spent away from one another. I have come on business." Willie took another swig of her rum, the brown liquid sloshing around in her glass as she placed it back confidently on the table. "But first," she continued, "let me introduce to you Ms. Daisy Flynn. She is in training to become my first mate."

Daisy looked at Willie in astonishment but said nothing in response. "It is a pleasure to meet you," she said to Santiago as she extended her arm to him.

"Mucho gusto," he replied as he took her hand in his and kissed it seductively.

"So, what is this business you have come hither about?"

Willie hesitated, then leaned in and whispered to Santiago, "La Isla de las Sirenas."

Santiago turned ashen and peered at Willie with widened eyes. "No, Wilhelmina, you mustn't. I love you far too much to allow you to go."

Daisy was shocked at this expression of love, especially in Daisy's presence. Willie's behavior depicted that of a woman who despised all men, and yet a beautiful man before her was professing his love to her. Daisy was bewildered by all the new information she had gained, and she was beginning to become frustrated as she did not fully understand what was going on. She knew she had held her tongue long enough. She could no longer remain silent. Curiosity was bursting through her veins and she could no longer hold in her thoughts. She needed to fight her coyness and speak her mind. She needed to be brave, for she was in training to become the first mate. Boldly, she asked, "What is La Isla de las Sirenas?"

Willie and Santiago glared at Daisy as if she had just spoken for the first time in her life. Then Willie smiled and responded, "In English, it means The Island of the Sirens."

"What is a Siren?" Daisy asked, perplexed.

Santiago chimed in, "Sirens are legendary creatures spoke of by the Greek. They are half beautiful woman, half dangerous sea creature. Legend has it that they would lure sailors to their islands by singing their charming songs, only to have their ships crashing into the jagged rocks surrounding the island. Death by sharks or being impaled upon the rocks follow the shipwrecks. Those that make it to the island are made blind by their beauty, deaf by their songs, and then their bodies physically explode from the desire they have built up within."

"Where is this island?" Daisy asked.

"It is halfway between Greece and Egypt," Willie responded.

"And why do you wish to go?"

"Legend has it that Pharaoh Mostafan supplied an army of men to sail to the island and bury some of his most valued treasure with him in his tomb within a great temple. Gold and gems and diamonds, a treasure so vast that we would never have to commit piracy again."

"So why was it that those men were able to arrive onto the island when others have wrecked their ships?"

"The Egyptians had much smaller boats which were able to elude the rocks. Once they arrived at the island, the treasure was buried with their beloved Pharaoh, and they put in place a magical security system within the temple and throughout the island. Sirens were forced by an Egyptian curse to relocate from the pleasant Greek island in which they lived to that one in order to aid in primary defense.

"So, what makes you think our ship will not crash before we will even make it to the island?" Daisy asked.

"We are women, the songs of the Sirens will not affect us. The plan is to anchor our ship just outside the jagged rocks that lay beneath, lower our lifeboats, and take them to the island."

"Have you gone mad, Wilhelmina?" Santiago interjected. "The Sirens and the jagged rocks are just the first line of defense. Once you reach the island, who knows what you may encounter. This is outrageous. You mustn't attempt to go."

"I have not come here for your blessing, Santiago."

"Then what is it you have come for?"

"Coordinates," Willie replied confidently.

Santiago was silenced.

"What makes you think he would know the coordinates to such an island, if it did exist?" Daisy interjected boldly.

"Because he is a Spaniard," Willie replied staring coldly into Santiago's eyes. "There were a few men who have had contact with Sirens and have made it back alive. On this particular island, two men were able to do it. Marco Ortega arrived on the island with his hired musician, Luis Garcia. Marco was deaf, so he took a small boat to the island, while Luis remained on the ship, playing his lute loud enough to drown out the precious songs of the Sirens. When Marco arrived on the island, he stood face to face with a beautiful Siren and was immediately blinded at first glance. He was only able to retreat back to the ship as Luis caught sight of him struggling to return and swam to his boat, guiding him back to the ship. They lived to tell of the story, but Marco lived the rest of his life both blind and deaf, forcing Luis to become his caregiver. The coordinates, though, they remained a Spanish maritime secret, hidden from the rest of the world. Isn't that right, Santiago?"

"And what makes you so sure that you will be able to reach the island?" Santiago questioned. "You know how many people attempted this voyage. Even women have tried and failed."

"I have the only all-female crew ship in history. The Crimson Rose shall forever live in infamy once we excavate the treasure from the island and live to tell of it." Willie sounded confident in her plan.

Santiago smirked and said, "Wilhelmina, my dear, beautiful love, you never cease to amaze me. You are the greatest captain I will ever know, but I cannot supply you with the Spanish secret."

"Fine," Willie stood up and gestured Daisy to follow. "Come Daisy, we shall rest in this god forsaken island and set sail first thing in the morning."

***

As the crew exited the tavern to follow Willie to the inn, Daisy walked by Willie's side, feeling empowered. She was soon to be second in charge to this beautiful, strong army of women. She could not understand why she, of all people, was chosen for this position. But she decided to remain confidently by Willie's side, accepting whatever responsibilities would come with time.

When they arrived at the inn, some of the women following behind Willie had a man by their side. Others wobbled behind as drunk as sailors. Willie placed six gold coins on the table in front of the innkeeper and said, "Make my ladies comfortable." The innkeeper gave each woman a key of their own. Daisy watched as some of the women stumbled toward their room in a flirtatious manner with men that were just as intoxicated, by their side.

Daisy entered her room, alone, and lay down on the bed. She thought of the women preparing to fornicate with men they barely knew, and it reminded her of how much she yearned for Nathaniel and for his smooth, masculine body to be on top of hers. She missed his charming smile and wanted nothing more than to be by his side, living life in a sensual bliss. But the time had come for her to move on. She knew she needed to step up and take responsibility for the crew, her new family, her new life.

The inn was loud, filled with drunken laughter. Daisy could not sleep. She left her room and headed down the hall to Willie's sleeping quarters. She hesitated before she knocked on the door. "Who dares disturb me?" Willie shouted from within the room.

"It's me, Daisy," she responded with a stutter.

Willie swung open the door. There was a half-drunk bottle of rum lying on the floor. "Come on in," she ordered. "Can I help you Ms. Flynn?"

"I just wanted to talk to you about what you had mentioned earlier."

"Mentioned, of what?" Willie questioned.

"When you introduced me to Captain de la Cruz, you mentioned that I was training to be your first mate."

"Aye, yes." Willie placed her hand on Daisy's thigh, "My last first mate, god rest her soul, was a great warrior. She was beautiful and smart, and she truly knew how to handle the crew."

"What happened to her?" Daisy asked, concerned.

"I killed her." Willie picked up the bottle of rum lying in the center of the floor and took a swig.

Daisy looked astounded at Willie.

"She was manipulative. She was greedy. To her, gold and jewels came before the crew. She tried to take over my ship, tried to overthrow me and maintain the command. We don't function like that, Ms. Flynn. We are a team, a family. Life is fair. If you get out of

118

line, you are punished, but only by the honorary code. Josephine refused to live by the code. She wanted more, and she wanted everything for herself. So, she had to be stopped."

"So why on earth would you choose me as your first mate when you have a crew full of more suitable women."

"You are fresh. And besides, you are spoken highly of." Daisy's forehead wrinkled. How could the great Captain Willie Spade and poor, little Ms. Daisy Flynn have mutual acquaintances. Furthermore, who did Daisy know that would speak highly of her? "The rest of the crew, although most of them great warriors, were not meant for this job. You are honest. You are good. I can see it in your eyes. Those are qualities that I tend to be lacking. Therefore, you can help me lead more fairly. I need you as my better half, to keep me in my place and to help me lead as the best captain in the seven seas."

Daisy felt honored. She had never been spoken of in such a manner. "Now if you excuse me," Willie said, "I must go seduce a man into giving me coordinates." Willie stumbled out of the room, leaving Daisy alone.

Daisy went back to her room and lay down on the bed. She thought of Willie's words, so sure of Daisy, so confident in her character. She wondered what life would be like as a leader, how she would live a life at the top. As she continued to become lost in her thoughts, she finally succumbed to her fatigue and drifted off to sleep to the sounds of shattering glass, screaming women, and crying babies.

CHAPTER TWELVE

The scent of night lurked in the air. Willie stumbled out of the inn and down the dirt path to the main road where she began traveling west by foot. She walked near to an hour before coming across a small, tropical cottage buried by knee-high brush and heavily shaded by palm trees. Dark shadows cast by the moon portrayed an eerie appearance upon the solitary cottage.

Willie stopped for a moment, glaring at the house, giving second thought to her rather irrational behavior. Although she felt fairly confident that her decision to come was necessary, she realized that she needed the effects of the mind-poisoning rum to gather the courage to follow through. For days, she battled with her conscience to determine the right approach and ultimately decided that this was what was right. So, she took a deep breath, attempted to steady her spinning head, and walked up the stone path that led to the front door of the small, tropical cottage.

"Marisha?" Willie whispered loudly as she waited outside, expecting her soft voice to be heard. When no response came, she whispered the name a little louder, a rasp in her voice. Finally, the dark shadow of a woman appeared at the window.

"Wilhelmina!" the woman whispered back with surprise in her voice. "What are you doing here at this hour?"

"Don't, don't you act like that Marisha," Willie slurred. "Open this bloody door."

Marisha shook her head in disappointment, sensing the intoxication in Willie's voice. She closed the window and opened the door. She stepped outside, closing the door silently behind her.

"Look at you, beautiful!" Willie whispered.

"Keep your voice down, Wilhelmina. What are you doing here?" The woman demanded to know.

"Can I just come and see my beautiful, black butterfly?" Willie laughed.

Marisha sighed and shook her head. She was a beautiful woman with silky, smooth skin as dark as the night. She wore her long, dreaded hair on top of her head like a bird's nest, adorned sporadically with gold charms and colorful ribbon. A flamboyant necklace made from cowrie shells and colorful gems rested upon her voluptuous breasts as it shone brightly under the moon-lit sky.

Willie took notice of the necklace, "What a beautiful necklace you have there."

"What do you want, Wilhelmina?" Marisha asked again, noticing Willie's attention to the gift she had bestowed. "And at this time of night? The moon is still high in the sky, and you could not have chosen a more appropriate time?"

"'Tis never a time inappropriate to see a good friend."

"What is wrong with you, Wilhelmina? You have the poison in you, don't you?"

"Poison? Nay! But if you are speaking of the most wondrous beverage known to man, then yes, I have a little of that within my blood. Come now, Marisha, what's life without a little rum?"

Again, Marisha shook her head in disappointment and said, "I haven't the time for this, Wilhelmina. Spill it now, what have you come for?"

Willie frowned and pulled a brown bottle out from the satchel that hung at her waist. She took one more swig of her precious rum then reached back into the pouch. Marisha's arms were folded tightly underneath her chest as irritation swam across her face. Willie pulled out six gold coins and slurred, "Take the coins, I want to see the girl."

"For heaven's sake, Wilhelmina! Are you mad? You are boozed out of your mind!"

"I know, but I'm not, not really. To be boozed, what is the meaning of it anyway? Is it to be happy, because that, that I am, right now, ever so happy, and I want to see her, straight away. Retrieve her at once and bring her to me!" Willie rambled as she stood outside the door waiting to be let in.

"Wilhelmina, you know I love you," Marisha reached out and placed her hands upon Willie's shoulders as an attempt to steady her swaying. "But I cannot allow that, at least not now, come back at a more appropriate time, preferably when you are sober."

Willie leaned in and kissed the woman on the lips, "You are too kind, Marisha."

Marisha accepted the kiss, although did not return it. She folded her arms once more to show her seriousness.

Willie stumbled back down the stone pathway toward the dirt road, then turned back toward Marisha who was still standing with her back to the closed cottage door and shouted, "I will return to see my girl, first thing on the morrow!"

Marisha smiled, shaking her head with her arms folded tightly across her chest. Then she entered the small, tropical cottage and shut the door behind her, squeezing the gold coins tightly within her hand.

***

Willie trudged back down the road for yet another hour, sipping her bottle of rum intermittently until she reached the tavern. She placed the bottle back into her satchel and entered the tavern through the old, creaky door. She glided flirtatiously through the room, holding her body from stumbling about as much as she could, until she reached the man she came to see. She sat down on a bar stool next to Santiago and placed her hand on his chin. He glanced at her. His eyes following hers. She pulled his face closer to her and turned his head firmly until her lips met his ear. She whispered seductively, "'Tis been a long time, and I know you have been waiting for me."

Santiago peered into Willie's eyes, sitting in silence. Without verbal acknowledgement, he swallowed the last of his ale, rose from his seat and grabbed Willie aggressively by the waist, pulling her hip

123

close to his as he led her back to his inn room on the second floor of the tavern.

When they reached the room and entered it, Willie slammed the door shut behind her. Before she could turn around, she felt a strong hand grasp the back of her neck and then the sensation of a warm, moist tongue sliding smoothly between her earlobe and the base of her neck. Her breathing became heavy as he pressed her body against the door, ripping the laces from the back of her corset and forcefully pulling her boyish trousers from her curvy, feminine hips. She felt a rush of passion flourish through her veins as Santiago then turned her body around to face him.

There she stood. This fierce female pirate was now standing submissively bare in front of a much taller, muscular man. He deliberately removed his garments while pressing his mouth passionately against her lips, dominating her being as his body towered over hers. But Willie suddenly regained dominance as she lunged into Santiago's arms, forcing him backward onto the bed. "Ah, mi amor," he whispered affectionately in her ear as he ran his fingers through her fiery red hair. "I have missed you so much." Willie sucked on Santiago's ear and then ran her tongue smoothly down his neck until she bit down tenderly, causing him to moan in pure pleasure. She then caressed his strong chest, losing her fingers in the masculine hair that draped his enormous pectorals.

Willie slid her hand smoothly down Santiago's abdomen and then gripped his manhood firmly. He sat forward and held her bare body tightly against his as she straddled his waist, legs wrapped tightly around his back. Santiago lifted her body from underneath her thighs and directed her to glide smoothly onto his shaft. She bounced erotically up and down as she felt her body screaming with ecstasy. She dug her fingernails deep into his back as he moaned gratifyingly until his body exploded with passion and trembled with release.

Still inside of her, Santiago lay down on his back and pulled Willie chest to chest on top of him. He looked her deep in the eyes and gently stroked her hair. "My beautiful Wilhelmina. Te amo con todo mi corazón. You make me feel whole."

Willie smiled and kissed him on his lips. "If you truly love me, you will give me those numbers," she responded manipulatively.

Santiago's facial expression changed abruptly from one in pure happiness to one of disappointment. He pushed Willie off his chest and sat up on the bed. "Wilhelmina, you are not my whore, I will not give you payment to make love to you."

"Then be my partner." Willie stared at Santiago with a glimmer of hopefulness in her eyes. "Give me the coordinates and I will in turn share with you one fourth of the treasure."

"Wilhelmina, I cannot stand the thought of losing you. You are my one, true love. I want nothing more out of life than to settle down with you, start a family, and end this journey of piracy."

Willie sat in silent thought before responding. "Fine, once I retrieve the treasure from this island, I will retire as captain of the Crimson Rose, and we will settle down together."

Santiago thought for a moment and declined. "Woman, you are mad! You, like all the others who have tried will never make it.

And if you do make it to the island, you will never make it back alive."

Willie began to feel frustration. A rage built up inside of her. "Excuse me?" she exploded. "Do not undermine my expertise. I am the notorious Captain Willie Spade, and not only will I make it to that island, I will personally carry the treasure through whatever obstacles shall present themselves. I bring the fire to the forest. I bring the bullet to the pistol. Don't you, for one second, forget who I am, and most importantly, don't ever mistake my sexual submissiveness for weakness."

Willie was silent for just a moment to allow Santiago to speak. He said nothing, so she continued. "You must have forgotten who saved you and your entire crew in Liverpool."

Santiago thought back to one of the biggest attacks he had ever encountered by the British militia a few years prior when he had met Willie for the very first time. He had led his crew into the British town of Liverpool late one night expecting to gather supplies and raid the town. However, they were met with a surprise attack by the British militia who had prior knowledge of their arrival. Not far off the coast, Willie caught glimpse of the battle and decided to intervene. The Crimson Rose waited patiently at sea until the commotion settled and they were able to come forth and dock. Willie had not known Santiago at that time, but as an experienced and knowledgeable captain of a notorious pirate ship, she knew when her efforts to create an alliance with another pirate crew would be beneficial to her.

126

So, Willie and her crew docked their inconspicuous ship near to a market side where other ships had docked and awaited the morrow to come to start their trade. Once they disembarked the ship, the crew set forth toward the jail to set free all the pirates imprisoned by the British. Willie ordered her first mate, Josephine, to remain on the Crimson Rose to sail away when the time came. She then boarded Santiago's ship and silently murdered the two British soldiers who stood guard the commandeered vessel. She remained on his ship until he and his crew returned.

Santiago remembered how astonished he was to be released from jail by a crew of female pirates who murdered the constables in cold blood. Even more so, he remembered embarking his own ship only to see the most angelic woman with fiery red hair flowing in the wind, standing at his ship's wheel. He was impressed to see her take control as she instructed his crew to prepare the ship for sail, allowing Santiago to rest and time for his wounds to heal.

After all these thoughts, Santiago finally responded, "You cannot seriously consider using that experience to guilt me into giving you the coordinates."

Willie smiled wryly. "You owe me your life," she whispered.

Santiago finally gave in, knowing Willie would not cease to harass him until she got what she wanted. He reluctantly whispered the coordinates into her ear as he held onto her with his face close to hers, wetting it with his own tears. He begged her to be vigilant as he peered deep into her eyes.

"You know I am always cautious," she responded. "How do you think I got so good?" she smirked. "I will bid you farewell before we set sail, but I must now go and rest for I have some business to cater to in the morning."

Willie left the room and headed back to her inn to enjoy a restful night's sleep in preparation for the dangerous voyage that awaited her. She lay on her back with her eyes fixed on a crack in the ceiling as she thought about Santiago's tears of pure love, while she herself could not shed even one tear. Was she incapable of feeling the love he felt, she wondered? Had her troublesome past tainted her heart, making it unresponsive to any type of love? She refused to allow these thoughts to interrupt her sleep. She reached down to the almost empty bottle of rum and swallowed the last few drops, easing her mind so she could drift off into a restful sleep as dawn was biting into the horizon.

CHAPTER THIRTEEN

Willie was awoken by the bright rays of the Caribbean sun blasting into her small inn window. It was just a few hours after she drifted off to sleep, surely not enough time to detoxify her blood that had been saturated by the devil's rum the night before. She sat up on the edge of the bed and held her forehead with her palms to try to steady the alcohol-induced vertigo. She closed her eyes and inhaled deeply, taking in the strong mildew odor in the room. Her head was pounding. The sun made it worse, as if it was piercing her skull. But she knew she could not go back to sleep. Sleep was her enemy. She had things to do, and day time hours were limited. So, she rose from her bed and dressed in her typical attire consisting of a tight, leather corset tucked into her masculine trousers and leather boots upon her feet

Willie headed down the hall towards Daisy's sleeping quarters. When she arrived, Daisy opened her door, wide-eyed and ready to take on the day, for her alcohol intake was far less than that of the captain.

"Good morrow to you, Captain," Daisy proclaimed. "Are we ready to set sail?"

Willie held her eyes shut for a moment attempting to drown out the bright light blasting through Daisy's bedroom window. "Not quite," Willie explained. "I need to tend to one last matter before we set sail, but I need you to ready the crew."

Daisy was dumbfounded. She was unsure if she had the leadership qualities to carry out captain duties, and her lack of confidence erupted. "Me?" she stuttered. "Ready the crew? Do you not think Zenobia a more appropriate candidate for this type of endeavor?"

Willie appeared irritated. "Ms. Flynn, you are here for a reason. Had I not thought you suitable as a first mate, you would not be here. Now, are you going to follow my orders, or would you like out of this crew? Because I have no problem leaving you in this bloody excuse of a town."

Daisy was astonished by her response but realized that she needed to toughen up. This was a new life for her, and she needn't lose her opportunity at finding her true happiness. Already she had learned that although this life may be morally wrong, she had found a group of women who were deeply loyal toward one another, a feeling that she had never discovered before then.

With a brief hesitation, she gathered the courage to say, "I will gather the crew and ready the ship for departure, Captain."

"Thank you, Ms. Flynn."

"Captain, were you able to obtain the coordinates?" she asked.

Willie laughed, "Of course. If there is one thing you will learn about me, it is that I always get what I want."

Daisy smiled and watched Willie walk down the hallway and out into the tropical air. She peered out her window as Willie headed down the dirt path. Then, she began building up her own confidence to start giving orders to the rest of the crew.

***

After about an hour, Willie had finally reached her destination. When she arrived at the small tropical cottage where she had wandered drunkenly the night before, she knocked on the door and waited until she was greeted again by Marisha.

"So, you have found your wits and decided to return."

"Yes, my dear Marisha. Now please, let me see the girl."

"You have never thought it be a good idea for her to make your acquaintance, Wilhelmina. What makes you think differently now?"

"The timing is different, Marisha. I believe 'tis time for her to meet her proper mother."

"Wilhelmina, you are out of your mind, for what good might come from that, she is doing just fine. Why do you feel that now is the right time? She is already fifteen years of age and has done just fine with me raising her as my own."

"Marisha, please. I regret I cannot discuss the reasons for the matter. It is just absolutely prudent that she meet her proper mother before it is too late."

"Too late?" Marisha sounded worried. "Wilhelmina, dear, what have you planned? You have never a time been too concerned for your life, for the trust in your piracy skills has been too strong."

"This time is different, Marisha. I am attempting a voyage that no man has made out alive. I am leading the Crimson Rose to La Isla de las Sirenas."

"Are you mad?" Marisha shouted. While she had never been interested in piracy, tales of their perilous adventures were spread like wildfire throughout the small, seaport town. "How could you possibly attempt such a notoriously fatal voyage?"

"I am confident that my crew and I will make it to the island, past the perilous Sirens as we are a crew entirely of women. However, it is the danger in the unknown of the island that I may have minor concern about."

"Then why lead your crew into a potentially devastating expedition?"

"The conquering of this island, Marisha, will not only make my entire crew the richest of all pirates that sail the seven seas, but it will make me the most notorious captain that ever lived. The Crimson Rose will be the only pirate ship that has ever made it to and from that god forsaken island, a voyage so deadly that no man has ever attempted to go and succeeded."

Before Marisha could utter a response, an angelic young woman with flowing, fiery red hair tied back with a string of cowrie shells appeared at the edge of the brush. The young woman gazed perplexedly at this intruder who looked more like she than Marisha did. "Marisha," the young woman questioned, "who is this?"

Willie stood in silence, gazing lovingly at the young lady.

"Ella, my child, this is your birth mother."

Ella put her hand over her wide-open mouth as she stood staring in awe at the woman who stood before her. "My mother?" she asked in pure bewilderment. "I thought you said she was lost at sea?"

"She was," Marisha responded flatly.

Ella then ran over to Willie and threw her arms around her. Willie allowed the young woman to hold her tightly as her arms went flaccid at her sides. Cautiously, she raised her arms to return the hug. She found herself inhaling Ella's hair and shockingly allowed maternal tears to drip down her cheeks, the first tears she felt from her dry, cold eyes since she was Ella's age, fighting for her freedom. She wiped them before anyone could see and then said, "My dear, I have wanted nothing more than to see you for your entire life, but my career of choice is far too dangerous to bring you along. That said, I am thinking of retiring soon."

Marisha glanced at Willie in disbelief. "Your plan is to retire?" she questioned hopefully.

"Yes, after this final voyage I will have enough currency to live the rest of my life in utter luxury, and I will take care of the two of you as well."

"Will we live like the kings and queens?" Ella asked innocently.

"We will live even better than the kings and queens," Willie smiled as she responded to her beautiful daughter.

"Well what do you do that brings you such a large quantity of money?" Ella asked curiously.

Willie thought meticulously before responding. "My crew and I import expensive goods, mostly jewels and gold, items only the royalty can afford."

Ella gazed impressed at her seemingly remarkable mother.

Marisha finally stepped in and said, "Now Ella, give your mother a hug and run along. I need to speak to her before she leaves."

Ella once again wrapped her arms tightly around her birth mother and then disappeared into the cottage.

Marisha sighed deeply and said to Willie, "You mustn't make broken promises to that poor girl. Her life has been fine without you for the past fifteen years."

"On the contrary," Willie protested. "Her life has been fine with the gold I have come bearing, providing both you and her with a comfortable life, free from financial woe. And besides, this is not a broken promise, we will all be together once I complete this journey and come bearing the finest jewels you have ever seen. You will see."

Marisha sucked her teeth. "Fine, Wilhelmina, then when shall we expect to see you again?"

"Don't expect a time; just expect the time to come," Willie riddled as she turned and disappeared back down the dirt road through the thick, tropical forest.

***

When Willie arrived back at the seaport, the Crimson Rose was bustling with women hard at work preparing the ship for departure. Daisy was standing at the bow of the ship's deck, confidently calling out orders. Willie was pleased to see that the women of the crew responded well to her.

"I am impressed, Ms. Flynn," Willie said as she slowly strolled toward Daisy.

Daisy smiled. "I thought you had confidence that I could run this crew, Captain. Why now are you so surprised?"

"These women do not respond well to every first mate I have put in charge," Willie replied. "Yet they seem to sense leadership skills and respect those who have it. You have done well, Ms. Flynn, expressing traits of an excellent first mate. Now, I will take it from here."

When the ship was readied for the long voyage ahead of them, Willie took her post and began to sail the ship in the direction of La Isla de las Sirenas.

CHAPTER FOURTEEN

Seventy-two hours at sea and Willie was beginning to feel anticipation about their perilous journey, something she had never felt before. She was uncomfortable with the feelings she had of not being in control. She drowned away her fear with rum, swallowing it like it was the only way she could numb her mind.

The women at the table around her celebrated joyfully together, as they often did. Laughter was abundant, but Willie did not hear them. Her ears felt muffled as she drank her rum and let her meal sit untouched before her. No one noticed Willie sitting silently, battling her thoughts. No one noticed as she drowned out her thoughts with her rum. No one noticed, except for Daisy.

Willie left the dining room table before the rest of the women, as she often did. Nothing out of the ordinary. But Daisy felt that something was different about Willie that night. And so, she followed her back to her sleeping quarters.

When Daisy arrived shortly after Willie closed the door behind her, she boldly rapped on the chamber door. Willie answered and snapped at Daisy instinctively. "Why on earth have you followed me here. No one is to disturb me while I am in my sleeping chamber," she shouted in anger.

"Do not speak to me in such a way," Daisy shouted back boldly. "I am your first mate and I believe 'tis time you start treating me as such. You may be the captain of a notorious pirate ship, but you are still a lady, and you should act as one instead of relying on this brown poison to alter your behavior as a man would."

Willie was impressed by Daisy's assertiveness. Once a sweet, innocent woman who allowed many people to walk all over her, she was now courageous and strong. Willie did not say a word as she gestured for Daisy to enter.

Daisy looked around. The room was much different from the others. Her bed posts were made entirely of gold, and there was a vanity studded with diamonds surrounding a large mirror. On top the vanity were various expensive beauty products such as rouges, lip colors and perfumes. A bottle of brown rum sat in the center of these womanly products, tainting their existence.

"What have you come all the way to my sleeping chambers for, Ms. Flynn?" Willie frequently used Daisy's surname when she was irritated.

"Something is wrong. I can sense it."

"Nothing is the matter, Ms. Flynn, I assure you."

"No. I don't believe it. Something is the matter, and you refuse to let it out. Instead, you bottle it up and take to your precious poison instead. You need not keep your feelings hidden, especially from me. I can be here to support you, no matter what it is. While we are pirates, we are women first, and women care for one another and desire to mend broken feelings."

Willie sighed. "You sure are quite the empathetic one, Ms. Flynn. I fear, I am not the sharing type."

"I know that far too well, but you can change, just as I changed."

Willie inhaled deeply. "Ms. Flynn, I am simply worried about our journey to La Isla de las Sirenas, and I've never before been concerned for our safety."

"Then why attempt it? Isn't there treasure elsewhere that we may find."

"Yes, of course," Willie responded, "but the treasure is not what I am after on this voyage."

"Then what is?" Daisy questioned.

"The recognition. Daisy, don't you understand? Conquering this island and claiming Pharaoh Mostafan's loot will make me into the queen of the sea. My crew will be the most feared group of women in the entire world. For what woman does not desire the power that any man possesses? What woman does not desire the power of a king?"

"I understand," Daisy studied Willie's face and continued. "I believe that may not be the only of your troubles?"

Willie glanced back at Daisy and reached for the bottle of rum, placing it to her mouth and gulping it down to ease the uncomfortable feeling of sharing her thoughts. "I fear I have done something more terrible than I have ever done as captain of the Crimson Rose."

Daisy glanced at Willie, astonished, and allowed her to continue.

"I have not requested a vote on the matter of this journey."

"So, where does the crew think we are going?"

"They just think we are at sea, with no particular destination."

"And why have you not made mention yet to the crew?"

"They will not understand. They will not agree to put their lives in danger for this. But Daisy, you must understand. It is for their own good. They will thank me once this is all over, once we claim the treasure. This will make each one of them a very powerful woman. This will make their lives worth something. It will ensure they will never be tortured, humiliated, used, or degraded ever again." Willie paused. "I know your story, Ms. Flynn, I know where you came from. After the death of your parents, you were brutally raped night after night, and yet you stayed silent, powerless."

Daisy gasped. How could anyone ever know her truly unfathomable story? She had only ever told one person of the horrors she endured. But what bothered her the most was that she had never described what Mr. Clark had done to her in such a word. That word "rape" stung in her ears. It sickened her to describe what was done to her with that term.

"Well you know my story, Captain. What is yours?"

Willie looked at Daisy in disbelief. No one had ever attempted to ask her such a question, and she had not shared her story

139

with many people. She sighed, staring deeply into this woman's eyes who was clearly interested in knowing who she was. Willie opened a cabinet and pulled out a glass. She filled it with rum and handed it to Daisy.

Daisy stared at the dark liquid a moment before drinking it. Her face squinted as the heat of the rum burned the back of her throat. She was accustomed to the taste of wine, but rum was something new. "This is some strong beverage," she laughed.

"Aye," Willie responded, "a powerful drink for a powerful woman."

Daisy laughed and continued to sip on the rum as she waited for Willie to share her story.

"What exactly would you like to know, Ms. Flynn?" Willie asked.

"How did such a beautiful woman as yourself become such a cutthroat pirate? I have literally watched you take a man's life simply because he questioned your authority to enter a room."

Willie laughed, "I did do that, didn't I?"

Daisy giggled and continued to sip her drink.

"Well," she began, "I believe that my destiny was determined from birth. You see, my mother died during childbirth and my father, god rest his soul, had no one else to help raise me. He was a fisherman, and that was all he knew. So, in order to maintain his livelihood, he begged the captain to bring his baby boy aboard the ship as he continued to work as a fisherman."

"Baby boy?" Daisy asked, puzzled.

"Have you ever heard of any ship whether fisherman, merchant or military allowing a woman to travel aboard, Ms. Flynn?"

"No, I have not."

"And do you know why?"

"Not the slightest idea."

"Because women are considered bad luck on a ship. But you see, Ms. Flynn, there is no such thing as bad luck. Rather, we are distracting to these weak men who cannot contain their lustfulness. And so, the resulting factor is poor outcomes upon the ship. And of course, the blame is placed upon the woman. It is the very reason why women are made to believe we are inferior. The power that resonates from within the core of our femininity is far too strong for any man. And so, they limit our opportunities forcing us into submission so they may continue to maintain all the power in the world."

"And so, they believed it true you were a boy."

"Yes, my father raised me as a boy. Before my mother passed, she gave me the name of Wilhelmina, but my father called me Willie. He demanded I forget the name Wilhelmina and only ask to be called Willie. He dressed me in clothes meant for a boy and kept my hair cut short. It wasn't until I began developing breasts around the age of thirteen when they discovered my true gender."

"And what did they do when they found out."

"They murdered my father in cold blood, forcing me to watch while they slit his throat with a fillet knife."

Daisy gasped.

"But that was not where their inhumanity ended. All the men on the fisherman's ship believed they had been cursed. A woman had for years been upon their ship and they truly believed that my presence hexed the entire crew. They felt I needed a punishment far worse than simply watching the death of my father. Furthermore, these men were away from their wives for months and months at a time, and so temptation was too powerful for them to resist. And so, night after night, they had their way with me. One by one, until each fisherman filled my insides with their filthy penile fluid. To make matters worse, they locked me in a cage and fed me scraps of rotting fish, just enough to keep me alive."

"And how did you escape?"

"A boy, a sweet but courageous young boy helped me to escape."

"Who was he?"

"He was the cabin boy. His father was very wealthy and because the boy was born with a silver spoon in his mouth, he wanted his son to learn responsibility, how to behave as a man. And so, he sent him to work on the fisherman's ship as an apprentice. The boy was kind. He was not like the other men. Occasionally he would sneak me some food when night time came. He could not bear to see another child locked up like a dog. And so, one night, when we were relatively close to the merchant port, he freed me, unlocking the cage I lived in like a dog for weeks. We were so close to the shore and all the men were asleep. I could just jump into the sea and swim for the shore. But I didn't."

"Why not?"

"Because, Daisy, a fire built up inside of me. A rage so strong that I was unable to free myself before getting a proper revenge. This sense of vengeance raged through my veins. I wanted everyone to pay for what they had done to me and more importantly, to my father. So, I gathered the nearest steak knife, and I went into the room of one of the men who was sleeping peacefully in his cot. I covered his mouth and slit his throat. I watched the astonishment in his face as I continued to hold onto his mouth, feeling the blood as it oozed from his neck. I stared deep into his eyes until I could see the life disappear."

Daisy was horrified yet intrigued by this story. "Weren't you afraid?"

"No. I was angry. Any sort of fear was pushed aside by this anger that was far stronger than any other emotion. Seven more men I murdered in cold blood. But the captain, that was who I was after. The man who used his own fillet knife to slit my innocent father's throat. The man who took my father away from me. The man who destroyed my childhood. That was the man that I wanted dead most of all. But he somehow got away, quietly dropping his lifeboat into the ocean and rowing himself to the shore."

"So, you never found him?"

"No, not yet."

"And what of the bodies?"

"I left them as they were. Cold, lifeless and bloody. Then, I sailed the ship myself and retuned the boy to Virginia."

Daisy was astonished by this story. She looked down into her empty cup and realized how warm her entire body felt. Her mind was foggy, and yet she had never thought so clearly in her life.

"You have had a rough life," she began, "but you are so beautiful, Wilhelmina, and you need not allow your past to define who you are."

Willie shuddered at Daisy's use of her true name. She gazed admiringly at Daisy, no one had ever spoken such kind words to her, and no one had ever been courageous enough to ask her to share her past. She felt as if sharing her story was freeing. She felt as if it allowed her to relinquish some of her anger, allowing her to let a bit of love in, something she wasn't sure she could ever do.

Willie leaned in, closer to Daisy, and placed her hand on her soft cheek, a gesture that might signify friendship between two women. But then, she did something that was confusing to Daisy. She leaned in even closer and kissed her gently on the lips. Daisy pulled back abruptly and placed her hand on her lips in shock. She stared at Willie in utter disbelief, but she did not get up. Was this gesture also that of friendship, or was it something else? Daisy was frozen on the bed, sitting next to a beautiful woman, and she could not explain why she couldn't move; or was it that she wouldn't move?

Willie took another large swig of her rum and then placed it on the floor. She studied Daisy's face, and when Daisy did not rise to leave, she sensually grabbed the back of her head and kissed her on her luscious, pink lips even harder, allowing her silky tongue to slip into Daisy's mouth. Daisy did not understand why she accepted this.

Willie then proceeded to untie the back of her own corset and dropped it to the floor. She did the same with her trousers as she stood naked in front of Daisy. Again, Daisy was in absolute shock, yet was frozen in her place, feeling new emotions she could not understand.

Willie took hold of Daisy's hand and placed it between her thighs. Daisy felt the beads of liquid drip down her legs. She began to feel a throbbing sensation between her own thighs, with a strong desire to be touched. Willie came closer to Daisy and again kissed her on the lips, this time as she was fully nude. Daisy allowed Willie's moist tongue to enter her mouth. She reached around Willie and gently touched the skin on her back, stroking down until she reached her rounded buttocks. She liked how the cheeks on her bottom felt against her palms. She allowed Willie then to deliberately untie the back of her corset.

Willie drew Daisy's corset down below her breasts and began sucking on her nipples. Daisy felt confused but did not want it to stop. The pleasurable sensation of a woman's soft skin gently caressing her supple breasts made her shudder in pure bewilderment. She felt Willie's tongue glide in circles around her nipples as they immediately firmed. Willie pulled the dress to the floor and knelt down just below the bed as she placed her head between Daisy's thighs. She peered back up at Daisy, watching the desire burn in her eyes. She then used her tongue to moisten Daisy's already dampened labia, thrusting it inside of her. Daisy was unsure if she should feel ashamed to allow a woman to do this to her, but she surrendered to this new sexual reality that enlightened her soul.

Willie reached up and caressed both of Daisy's breasts as she pressed her mouth even tighter against Daisy's womanhood, thrusting her tongue in and out, lapping the sweet juices as they rushed out onto Willie's lips. Finally, Daisy lost control and screamed out in ecstasy. Her entire body shuddered as her pelvis contracted wildly against Willie's tongue. Willie then climbed on top of Daisy's naked body, thrusting her hips against hers and kissing her lips until her own body trembled in uncontrollable pleasure. Then, they lay still, holding their bare bodies against one another, breasts to breasts, drifting off to sleep to the rocking motion of the ocean's cradle.

DAISY AND THE CRIMSON ROSE

CHAPTER FIFTEEN

Soon after they fell asleep, Daisy and Willie were jerked from the bed and onto the floor. They quickly dressed and headed onto the main deck where some of the women were hastily struggling to find cover and run safety lines to stabilize the ship until the storm was over. Zenobia was holding on tightly to the mast pole as she attempted to climb down from the crow's nest.

Willie raced over to Zenobia to help her down the slippery pole. "What is happening?" Willie demanded to know. "And why had we not prepared the ship for this storm earlier?"

"The storm came from nowhere, Captain. Storm clouds never formed."

"Well, are we close to land?"

"No land is in sight, Captain," Zenobia replied.

Willie froze as her greatest fear, but anticipated feat, was in plain sight, yet invisible to their eyes.

"Stop!" She shouted. "Cease safeguarding this ship!"

The women looked at Willie as if she were insane. "Captain," Zenobia questioned, "what are you saying? We surrender our ship to the ocean's majestic strength and potentially commit ourselves to death?"

"No, Zenobia, we are here. We are at La Isla. We need to ride out this storm."

"But I have seen no land," Zenobia protested.

"But it is here, I can feel it. La Isla is close."

"La Isla?" Zanobia's eyes widened. "Where have you taken us?" she demanded to know.

"La Isla de las Sirenas," Willie whispered under her breath with a look of utter maliciousness spread across her face.

Daisy stood behind the two women, watching their encounter in even more confusion. Her honey-golden locks were now darkened and drenched from the torrential rains.

"You," Zenobia pointed at Daisy with anger in her voice. "Did you know of this destination?"

Daisy stuttered again, confused at what was happening.

"Don't answer that," Willie demand as she held her hand up to Daisy before she could answer.

"Aye, you did have knowledge." Zenobia suddenly grabbed Willie by the throat with her strong, masculine hand as a few other women raced toward the altercation.

Willie had one hand on Zenobia's wrist as an attempt to loosen the grip and another on her pistol that she had pointed upward towards Zenobia's chin. "Zenobia," she said through her gritted teeth,

"I demand thee let me go at once or I will murder you in cold blood and watch it drain from your skull."

Zenobia released Willie and shouted wildly under the torrential downpour, "It is she who is corrupting your soul!" She pointed directly at Daisy. "Word had it that she was a witch and yet you were convinced she was not. You chose to bring her wretched soul upon this ship, cursing us all. She must have cast a spell on you, altering your fair behavior."

Daisy interrupted, "Never was I a witch. My true spirit is kindhearted and never was corrupt."

"Then what is it?" Zenobia asked spitefully, "You needed a lackey who was so naïve that she would help you lead our entire crew into a suicide mission?"

"Zenobia, shut your mouth this instance! "You have no idea what you are saying."

"Yes, Captain, I do know what I am saying. You would never run your crew with such secrecy, such deceit."

"I had no choice. "You, apart from the rest of the crew, would never have gone for such a voyage."

"Precisely," Zenobia responded. "But is that not of the code for which we follow? All for one. If just one of the sisters is against it, then the whole crew is against it."

"I had to make this decision on my own, Zenobia, for the entirety of the crew, and you, amongst all the crew are one of the most essential members for this mission to work. Your strength and commitment to protect this crew are crucial. Zenobia. You must understand, this voyage will forever make us rulers of the maritime world, and we will prove ourselves not only as good as any man, but far superior. How could you think I would lead this crew to an escapade I did not think them capable of surviving?"

"What makes you so sure we could survive a feat no other man was ever capable of?"

"We are women, Zenobia. We are scorned, bitter, battered women; and this past that we all hold onto makes us stronger, more vicious, and more powerful than any man who has ever walked this land. Our strength together is that of one thousand men! We will, for sure, defeat this island and retrieve the most extensive treasure that stories claim it holds!"

Zenobia calmed down and replied, "What is your plan?"

Willie smiled, "The plan is not set in stone, but based off instinct. We shall use our feminine intuition to drive our mission. The Sirens are the main defense, and they shall have no power over us."

Zenobia nodded in agreement, "I will ready the warriors of the crew. We will gather all weaponry and prepare the gun deck for war."

Willie smiled wildly. She believed in the ferociousness of Zenobia. After all, she was the only woman on the ship with the ability to kill a man with her bare hands.

The storm was becoming unbearable, making the ship vulnerable to the vast ocean surrounding it. The three women who were up on the main deck had now removed the safety lines and were desperately attempting to dump barrels full of water overboard. The ocean was drowning the ship's deck. Daisy helped the women empty the water back into the ocean, yet the rain was so abundant the women could not keep up. Daisy feared the ship would sink.

"Captain!" Daisy shouted. "The ship will not make it. We need to anchor. We have no idea where this storm is taking us."

"Aye, that is where you are wrong," Willie shouted over the pounding sound of the downpour on the wooden deck. "This storm is taking us exactly where we need to be." Willie laughed wickedly as she left the women and raced to the bottom of the ship to secure their supplies. She needed to ensure little water damage would be done so their ship would be suitable for a safe departure from the island.

Hours went by, and the women struggled to maintain composure of the ship. Suddenly, and without warning, the torrential rains stopped. The women who were on the main deck, drenched from the storm looked upwards toward the heavens where the sun was radiant in the sky. No clouds were in sight and the sky was a rare, pinkish tone. The waves were quiet. A distant muffled sound of pouring rains surrounded the ship. They looked around to see sheets of grey sky and torrential rains encircling the area. The ship rocked gently with the calm current. To the east, a lush island lay in the center of the surrounding storm.

Willie raced up to the main deck. She removed the telescope from her satchel and peered over toward the island.

"Captain," Daisy questioned, "What do you see?"

"Shh," Willie shushed the entire crew who were now standing in awe underneath the pink, glowing sky. "Do you hear that?"

The women were silent and then responded in unison, "Aye, Captain."

Daisy shivered at the melodious tunes encircling the Crimson Rose. Willie touched her ears and brought her hand in front of her eyes. She smiled when she did not see blood dripping from her fingertips.

Zenobia mimicked Willie's gesture and laughed. "Aye Captain, you were right. The Sirens' songs are not affecting us. But you must explain to the women why you have brought us here without our consent."

Chattering amongst the women filled the ship's deck. "Yes, Captain. This is unlike how you have ever led our crew. Why have you not called for a vote?" One of the women questioned.

"She should be marooned!" Another woman bravely called from the crowd followed by an uproar of angry shouts.

"Hush down," Zenobia demanded, allowing Willie to speak.

"Legend has it that the fear from anticipation of what might come throws pirates into an early demise; even before they reach the land. The sense of fear migrating from a ship full of men is enough to alert the Sirens toward a possible attack. Remaining calm allows a crew to stay in control, at least until we set foot on land. Withholding the knowledge of the whereabouts of our destination ensured that your souls would stay calm, preventing the Sirens from gaining the upper hand in knowing the exact timing of our arrival."

"But how will we prepare ourselves with such an approach?" a woman argued.

"Preparation, my dear, you already have. You already possess the skills to demolish an army of men, the courageousness to encounter any feat, the sense of adventure that thrills your soul. Most importantly, you possess what no man can have, your womanly instinct will guide the entirety of our mission toward success," Willie professed encouragingly.

The women began smiling, sounds of chatter shifting from those in anger to those in understanding. Their confidence was built up; they were ready for war.

"Now," Willie continued, "you want a vote? All in favor of moving forward with the most challenging yet rewarding mission of your entire life, one that will grant you more treasure and more power than any man could ever have in a lifetime, say aye."

The word "aye" rung unanimously in the ears of all the women aboard the ship.

"So, what's next?" Daisy asked the question everyone was curious to know.

"We wait," Willie instructed. "We allow this slow current to quietly push the Crimson Rose close enough to the island where we will then be able to anchor and lower our lifeboats to row to the island."

***

After a couple hours, Willie determined that the ship was close enough for lifeboat departure. She ordered the anchoring of the ship and the lowering of the boats. The women lowered three lifeboats into the calm ocean below and seated six women in each. Then, they began to row.

Their confidence grew as the melodious tunes of the Sirens grew louder and no blood drained from their ears nor did deafness ensue. Daisy sat beside Willie in the leading boat. She eyed Willie admiringly, hoping for some sign that what they did the night before meant something to her. But her look was cold, uninviting, and strictly business-like. Daisy continued to row, trying desperately to erase the memory of her immoral sexual encounter from her mind so she could focus on the danger that lie ahead.

Suddenly, the current began to hasten. The boats rocked uncontrollably against the perilous waves. Land was in sight, but the boats were defenseless against the rough sea rocks that projected from the bottom of the now shallow waters.

"Try to evade the rocks!" Willie yelled over the now unbearably loud songs combined with the sounds of crashing waves into jagged rocks. But her instructions were no match to this highly protective island defense. The middle boat crashed into a jagged sea rock that destroyed the bottom of the wooden craft, causing it to flood and begin to sink.

"Captain!" the women shouted from behind. But Willie was unable to turn her boat around through the now extremely turbulent waves.

"Help them," Willie shouted to the boat in the rear. The women in the sunken boat tried to hold onto the jagged rocks, sitting within the small valley they created. When the third boat arrived, they were able to rescue five women from the tortuous ocean.

"Where is Mary?" a woman shouted from within the boat. A second woman responded by pointing to Mary's lifeless body impaled upon a sharp rock that jutted straight out of the sea, a wave of crimson waters surrounding her body.

"Mary!" the women shouted from the boat desperately hoping for an answer, although the gruesome sight was unpromising. They were able to manipulate the boat toward the woman, hoping for a better outcome. But just as they suspected, the tall, sharp rock made its way completely through Mary's abdomen.

A few women allowed some tears to form while the rest persistently rowed their way toward the island. As soon as they reached land, the atmosphere fell silent, the melodious tunes ceased to exist. Just two boats with now seventeen women arrived on the shore. Drenched and exhausted, they secured their boats on the land as they reported the death to their Captain.

Willie looked up toward the sky and sighed deeply. She removed her hat and asked the women to bow their heads in unity to pay respects to Mary for her bravery and sacrifice.

The silence was interrupted by Tabatha who shouted, "Aye, Captain, look over there!" She pointed to a cave that emitted a radiant green light from within. "Methinks the treasure may be hidden there."

Willie was unconvinced that the treasure would be buried with such easy access to the port of arrival, but she decided to have a look.

"There is no sense in all of us going. Daisy, Zenobia, let us go seek the nature of those strange lights. The rest of you look out for anything out of the ordinary. Alert us if you see any danger coming our way," Willie commanded.

The three women headed in the direction of the green lights emanating from the cave. Willie placed her hand on her pistol to ensure it was in its place secure on her hip. Zenobia wore her satchel loaded with a bow and poison-dipped arrows, her preferred weapon. Daisy carried a sword on which she was now highly trained as well as a loaded pistol in the holster adorning her dress.

When they reached the entrance to the cave, they listened to the continuous dripping of water from stalactites that hung from the ceiling of the cave. All else was silent. The green lights seemed to emanate from deep within the cave. Willie led the two women as she deliberately placed one foot in front of the other across the smoothed path along the edge of the cave. The ocean extended itself inside the cave.

After walking for a few minutes, the women came to a wall that blocked their path. The green light continued to glow from within, booming through a six-inch wide crack in the center of the wall.

"We must swim underneath the wall," Willie commanded.

Zenobia and Daisy nodded in agreement as they followed Willie's lead and dove underneath a solid rocky area, holding their breath for what seemed like four minutes until they came up at the other end of the thick wall, desperately gasping for air.

The cave now had a solid floor just above the pool of water they floated in. The women lifted themselves out of the water and stood erect within the depths of the cave. The green light was still there, even brighter than before. The women followed the light until they heard some splashing and gleeful laughter. Willie raised her hand as if to silently demand Zenobia and Daisy to stop. They peaked around the wall to see seven of the most beautiful creatures they had ever seen. The creatures had the faces of beautiful, angelic women and perfectly sculpted torsos with uncovered supple breasts. Their pink and taupe nipples exposed to the cool air of the cave. But these beautiful creatures were not human. They had no legs, but rather long, dolphin-like tails that fanned below their hips, glowing an iridescent green light that illuminated the entirety of the cave.

"We must confront them," Willie stated, "but it must be done by someone who matches their beauty, who matches their utter perfection. Someone with the face of a goddess." She stared at Daisy and smiled.

Daisy was taken aback by the compliments bestowed upon her. She believed Willie had forgotten about their passionate lovemaking the night before, but now she began to understand her role. All the women on the ship had a special purpose. They each had unique characteristics that contributed to the crew in a meaningful way. Willie was obviously a born leader, and her skills were prominent above the others. Zenobia was the warrior of the crew, aiding in profound protection. And while all the women on the crew were attractive, Daisy was the most beautiful of all. Beauty, a characteristic that she once allowed to be her weakness, was now to become advantageous to her and make her a valuable member of the crew.

Daisy nodded and smiled back. She then took a deep breath in and exhaled all her fear before making her way toward the frolicking Sirens. When she was close enough for the Sirens to recognize an intruder, they all stopped and stared at her in silence. Their radiating tails dimmed to darken the cave.

"Hello, fair maidens," Daisy curtsied in respect. "I have come in search of answers. I bring forth no harm."

One of the Sirens who appeared to be the leader examined Daisy closely. Daisy noticed as her eyes followed her curvaceous figure until they reached her sword that hung from below her waist.

"Come hither," the Siren demanded.

Daisy walked closer to the Sirens and bravely sat down on the edge of the pool where the seven of them had been frolicking. She allowed her legs to dangle into the water, just as the Sirens had done with their tails. The Siren leader peered at Daisy suspiciously, then gently caressed her thigh and onward down to her foot. Daisy remained still, accepting the odd gesture.

"You are human," she stated, "yet so remarkably beautiful."

Daisy responded confidently, "Yes, I am."

"And you see us well with no blurring of your vision? No burning of thine eyes or piercing needle-like pain?"

"No, I can see you all well," Daisy responded without a shudder in her voice.

"How is this possible?" the Siren leader asked, more so to herself.

"Her beauty is comparable to ours," another Siren responded as to offer a reason to Daisy's inability to be negatively affected by the Sirens.

"Ah, yes, so it seems," the leader responded. "So, what is it that you need from us?"

"Information," Daisy responded, this time more confidently then before.

"Information unto what?" the Siren asked.

"The whereabouts of Pharoah Mostafan's treasure."

The pool became filled with concerning chatter until the Siren leader placed her hand into the air to silence the rest. "Such a foolish human. That treasure has been untouched for centuries. What makes thee think we would assist thee in your endeavors?"

"Because you and your Sirens are desperate to be freed from this island," Daisy responded assuredly as if she knew the Sirens' true desires. "Your ties to the island remain solely due to your designated task to act as a primary defense to ward off men desperate to uncover a fortune. If we are unable to retrieve the loot, rest assured, there will be a time when some other courageous souls come along and retrieve it for themselves. And chances are, the next crew to come along will be men." Daisy paused to watch the expressions on the faces of the Sirens and then continued when she realized she had their full attention. "Legend has it that if you fail to protect the treasure from a man, all the Sirens will be doomed. Turned to stone to forever remain a symbol of the inferiority of women to men. However, no spell would be cast against the Sirens should a woman uncover the treasure. The Egyptians thought it completely absurd to believe a woman would be so courageous to attempt a journey, let alone succeed."

The Siren leader smiled and paused, seemingly in deep thought. "My name is Doyenea, and it is a pleasure to make your acquaintance." She paused to wait for a response from Daisy.

"I am Daisy."

"And are you alone, Daisy?" Doyenea asked.

"No, I am not."

"Please," Doyenea responded, "will you uncover the rest of your sisters?"

Daisy stood and retreated to where she entered the depth of the cave. She motioned to the two women to come with her. When they arrived at the pool, the Sirens were baffled by the sub-optimal aesthetic nature of the other two women, but they decided to accept their presence due to their newly found respect for Daisy.

"My name is Wilhelmina," Willie introduced herself.

"And I am Zenobia."

The Sirens all nodded and returned their names in exchange.

"So, it is my understanding that the three of you are attempting a journey that is unheard of in all of mankind?"

"That is correct," Willie responded.

"And will it be just the three of you?"

"No," Willie admitted, "we have a crew of seventeen waiting to proceed."

"Well I suggest you limit that number to seven."

"Seven?" Willie questioned.

"Seven is the number most appropriate for this island, anything above seven is more intimidating and alerts more danger."

"How do you mean?" Daisy asked.

"Anything over seven will be immediately eliminated once you reach the enchanted forest. The island has a way of sensing too much threat. Best to increase your chance for survival by eliminating the rest on your own."

Willie nodded and Doyenea continued, assured with her understanding. "After walking for some time, you will come across a temple. You will need to enter the temple and walk until you come to an atrium. The atrium will have seven doorways, one of which you should have come from. There, you will need to select the correct door. Within that room, will be yet another door. If it is the correct room, that door should be marked with the blood of a baboon. Beyond that door will be a hallway that will lead you to the tomb of Pharoah Mostafan, and where the grand treasure should be hidden."

The three women nodded in unison.

"You must be cautious, be alert. For the safeguarding of the tomb remains unknown as all previous journeys ended with us, or as you call it, the island's first defense. But I can assure you, our strength to ward off intruders is nothing compared to the curses placed upon a tomb by the Egyptians of ancient times."

The three pirates thanked Doyenea and departed from the cave with new insight on a journey that was not even near to the end. They walked in silence, contemplating the consequences of pursuing their feat. They departed the cave in silent understanding for the continuation of their journey.

DAISY AND THE CRIMSON ROSE

CHAPTER SIXTEEN

Willie approached the rest of the crew that congregated along the beach where their lifeboats were secured. She had a look of anguish across her face. She knew this journey would not be easy and she feared it may result in more casualties. Yet her decisions seemed to be guided by greed; greed not only of claiming the greatest loot known to man, but the hunger for recognition as the most feared, powerful captain of all the seven seas.

She quickly contemplated which members of their crew would be most suitable for this journey. Much time was not needed as she already had a strong perception of who were the strongest pirates aboard the Crimson Rose.

***

Maria Ortega was a Spaniard. She was strong, determined and manipulative. She grew up in a poor family on a coastal town in Spain. Her mother had died during childbirth and her father remained ill for most of her life. She and her twin sister, Juana, were his primary caregivers. They had an older brother who was killed in the

163

war. There came a time when money was running low, and they needed to afford the medicine their father needed to stay alive. Furthermore, they could no longer afford food. Maria had no choice but to find work. But for a young woman at that time, it would have been impossible. So, she did the only thing she knew would guarantee her enough money to support her ill father, sister and herself; she posed as a man and joined the Spanish military.

A year went by and Maria was sending money and food home to Juana and her father. Juana reported that her father was finally getting stronger, almost strong enough to return to work and allow Maria to return home. The sooner Maria could return, the better it would have been to avoid her exposure. But she was too late. One night, a soldier caught Maria undressing only to reveal a pair of finely seated breasts upon her chest. His excitement to uncover a woman during his year away from his wife prompted a strong desire he could not resist. He attacked Maria from behind and demanded she give herself unto him. When she refused, he forced himself unto her. She tried to be discreet as she fought back, but their altercation was not unnoticed. Four more soldiers along with the head officer burst into the room only to discover Maria standing disheveled in a corner and the man who attacked her sprawled out, unconscious, in the center of the floor.

The officer demanded Maria dress herself and grabbed her by the arm as he led her to the General's chamber. Flabbergasted by Maria's deception, he demanded she go to trial. The jury, compiled of a panel of all men, responded exactly as Maria expected and sentenced her to death for not only joining military forces as a woman, but for misleading the government as to who she truly was. She was locked in a jail cell pending her execution.

As she waited for her death to arrive, she pondered ways she could manipulate her way out of the situation, as she had manipulated her way into it. The guard on duty the night before her scheduled execution reeked of whiskey as he wobbled in to take his place at his desk. Maria knew this was her only hope, her only escape to freedom. She messed her short, dark hair until it fell seductively across her eye and allowed her bosoms to be free, emerging from the manly blouse she unbuttoned deliberately from the top. She called the man over to her cell and caressed his face through the bars. He embraced her touch as he fumbled to unlock the cell. She no sooner had his pistol in her hand as she smacked him with it across his temple, watching him fall to the floor.

Maria removed the keys from the hip of the unconscious man and let herself out of the jail house, racing through the town by foot until she could no longer run and had to rest. But after just a short rest, she continued on her way. Thirty-two hours, it took her until she was able to reach her family home on that coastal town in Spain. She intended to inform her sister of her plans to board a settlement ship and escape to Hispaniola, an island in the Caribbean that the Spanish had founded. They were beginning to transfer Spaniards to the land to create a life, a new life, one where she would be unknown and could take care of her family.

When she arrived at the home, she found her father lying in a pool of blood on the floor next to his bed, sobbing like a baby. "He took my child," he repeated over and over. When her father saw Maria and she was able to calm him, he explained to her that three men in uniform came to their home looking for her and shot her sister with a rifle. They mistook Juana for Maria as their appearances were identical. Her father informed her that they took her body and tossed it into a carriage before trotting off down the road.

Maria knew she couldn't risk staying, arguing that if they re-discovered her, they would kill her and her father as well, as he was now an accessory to harboring a criminal. He agreed, and they packed their few belongings and headed to the sea port late that night where they discreetly boarded a settlement ship and hid in the lower level of the ship, waiting for boarding and departure the next day.

Maria's father didn't make it. He was too weak to endure the eight-night-long trip without proper food, medicine or rest. He developed a fever and was dead within the next twenty-four hours.

Maria departed the ship in her military uniform, posing once again, and for the last time as a man. When she stepped foot onto the new land with lush vegetation, she wiped the tears from her eyes and inhaled the thick, humid air. Her guilt was strong, but her anger was stronger. And it was these emotions, along with her training as a soldier, that made her suitable for this difficult journey.

***

Margaret Baynes was intelligent, motivated and angry. She was raised in an English town that glorified masculinity. Her father was a prestigious doctor who performed surgeries on soldiers who needed amputations. Margaret worshipped her father, and he loved her very much as well. When she was old enough, she told her father than she wanted to go to school to learn medicine, as he did. She was unable to do so as women were forbidden to go to school, so he decided to teach her himself.

Margaret spent many nights studying with her father. The basis of her studies was with plants and herbs. She learned which plants were for healing, she learned which plants were poisonous and could lead to death with minimal consumption. Then, when Margaret was ready, her father used her in his practice. While he performed the surgeries, she was able to nurse the patients back to health and provide herbal concoctions that she discovered prevented infections and led to lower mortality rates than those who did not receive her care.

While the patients were truly grateful, word spread like rapidly growing wild fire. The king did not appreciate the news of a woman unlawfully working as a medical doctor, a job reserved for only a man. He ordered her detainment by the police where he sentenced her to seven years of jail time. Time enough, he determined, to cause her to forget all her teachings. Her father protested, but he too, was sentenced to jail time for treason.

The night she was to be relocated from the jail house to a dungeon where she was to remain for the next seven years of her life, her transfer was intercepted by Captain Willie Spade and her crew. Willie had heard of this intelligent, female doctor who was sentenced to prison and knew that she needed her expertise upon her ship. So, Margaret accompanied Willie and her crew and sailed away to a life where she would never have to hide who she was or what she knew.

While her physical strength was minimal, her intellect was enormous. Her time on the Crimson Rose allowed her level of knowledge to soar. She discovered different herbs and plants from other lands and learned how to create new remedies from witch doctors she encountered from different countries they travelled to. Her work was valuable on the ship. Not only did she treat the members of the crew when they fell ill or were injured, but she used her remedies as a war tactic to poison their enemies. Willie knew that she would continue to be needed on this journey.

***

Tabatha White was beautiful, intelligent, and fearless. She was a house slave. The light, caramel complexion of her skin and her soft, minimally coiled hair was what saved her from enduring tortuous work under the blazing rays of the Virginia summer sun. However, it brought upon the horrific misfortune of being the victim of nightly sexual assaults as her master forcefully entered her bed chambers and forced her into sexual submission. Envied by the other slaves for her seemingly more comfortably life, as she was the only slave allowed to sleep in the enormous plantation home, she often was faced with cold shoulders by the others. When she fed the slaves scraps from the dinner she cooked for their master, his wife, and their three young adult children, they made it known that they were displeased that she was treated better, or so they thought, than they.

So, Tabatha was alienated by everyone on the plantation. But despite her misfortunes, she decided not to let it ruin the hopes of a possible future as a free woman. So, night after night, after her master relieved his sexual tensions inside of her and left her room to sleep the rest of the night with his wife, she would remove a book she had hidden under her mattress and teach herself how to read. It was dark, yet her mastery of the English language and newly gained knowledge flourished. She read maps and even obtained newspapers where she was able to gain current information about slaves and where she would find sanctuary.

Tabatha studied until she had an escape plan memorized. Then, one night when the moon and stars were barely visible by the darkened storm clouds that draped the sky, she waited patiently, wearing nothing but her undergarments which had been routinely expected of her. This night, however, was different. This night, she decided, she would have the upper hand. This time, she was going to be sexually dominant.

She lay in her bed draped with soft, cotton sheets until she heard the squeaking of the oil-thirsty doorknob to her bed chamber. Then, she watched through the shadows as her master slowly crept into the room; the old, wooden panels of the floors creaking as they had done every night. He crept slowly as if to quiet his steps. An attempt not to wake his wife, although Tabatha knew that she was already aware of what was happening as she lay awake in the next room, listening to her husband fornicate with another woman. Then he reached her bed, as he had done every night and was shocked as

Tabatha spoke. "Master," she squeaked holding still the wavering of her voice. "Might I ask you a question?" The master was taken aback by her words as the deed was done typically in silence.

"What is it?" he asked seemingly annoyed.

"Well," she chose her words carefully, "you work every night to find yourself pleasure as you enter me. What if I put forth some effort and use my mouth to pleasure you instead?"

Intrigued by such a request, he found himself in agreement.

Tabatha remained clothed in her undergarments, as she had never done and waited until her master took a position lying flat on his back. He removed his trousers and waited eagerly; his face like that of a dog watching a piece of raw beef dangle before his eyes. Then, Tabatha tied her hair back with a ribbon; something she had never done before. Her master typically requested her hair flow freely so he could pull it violently as he watched her squirm. She opened her mouth and placed it around his member. She watched as his eyes rolled back in his head as he enjoyed the wet, hot sensation move back and forth, teeth gently grazing his shaft for a new, unique sensation. Then, when she felt his member engorge at the moment of release, she bit down with all of her might, castrating him with one, swift motion.

A pool of blood saturated the white, cotton sheets as her ears rang with the piercing scream of her master lying pathetically in a pool of blood between his legs. Her mind went blank as she leapt out of her second story bed chamber's window and hit the ground softened by a large pile of leaves she had raked up the day before. She heard her master's wife's panicked screams from the opened window. She heard the upstairs rushing footsteps of the guards who had left their posts at the entrance of the home to witness the event. She quickly rose out of the pile of leaves and ran as fast as her legs could take her. She entered the forest and raced beneath the darkened sky until she reached the sea port where she was greeted by a beautiful woman in trousers with fiery hair and a pistol on her hip. And so, the story goes, her bravery and other skills would be much needed on this journey.

***

Sarah Adamson was a typical, loving, caring wife. But her marriage was not typical of the times. She was white, and her husband was black. Her husband, Benjamin, had been a slave but was set free in Maryland when slavery was abolished in their state. Close to the Virginia line, however, they knew they needed to move northward as slavery was still legal in the south. However, while slavery was no longer legal in Maryland, interracial marriage was still very much frowned upon to say the least. Their relationship remained hidden in the small town in which they lived. However, their fear of the proximity to slave towns drove them to travel northward together.

They attempted the travel by night where they would go unnoticed. However, one night when they were nearing their destination, their horse collapsed, dragging their carriage along with it. The loud crashing of their vehicle drew the attention of some local townsmen as they lit lanterns and withdrew from their homes to find the cause of the commotion that flooded their road.

171

The men immediately caught site of a white woman helping a black man to his feet. She then rushed over to tend to the collapsed horse.

"What on earth is going on here?" One man shouted while four other men followed his lead.

"Well, I was merely just helping this man as his horse collapsed in the street," Sarah stuttered in an attempt to create a story that would justify her being there.

"I just don't see how a little lady like yourself would come out here alone, in the middle of the night. And yet, you managed to get here before us, fully clothed."

Sarah looked down at her day time attire under the bright glare of the moon. Unable to quickly think of an excuse, Benjamin blurted out the truth, knowing that punishment would be delivered unto him for their crime and she would remain innocent. "The truth is," he began, "this here is my wife and we are travelling through your town until we reach our destination a little further north."

"The hell you is!" the poorly educated man shouted. "This here is a sin. A black man and a white woman together in holy matrimony. Wait 'till we call the commissioner on this one."

Two of the men grabbed Benjamin by the arms, one on each side and escorted him down the road.

"Where are you taking him?" Sarah shouted with tears in her eyes.

"Why, he is going straight to jail, little lady. Don't you worry, we will get you a real husband here in this town. That is, if anyone would want you after you had been tainted by this negro."

"Take care of Penelope!" Benjamin shouted as he allowed the men to escort him down the road. He knew she would need proper transportation should anything happen to him. Sarah rushed over to a nearby pond and filled a bucket with water. She brought it back over to her horse, poured some over her body to cool her down and allowed her to drink the rest. After about thirty minutes, Penelope was back on her feet, and Sarah began working on lifting the carriage from its side and restacking their belongings within.

When dawn arrived, Sarah made her way to the jail house where she demanded to see her husband.

"That is absurd!" the constable shouted. "It is unlawful for a negro to wed a white woman. And to think you would come through our town in the middle of the night unnoticed! You will wait here until the judge decides what to do with you."

Sarah was handcuffed to an armchair next to the constable's desk. She watched Benjamin as he sat in agony with dark rings around his eyes and dried blood decorating his forehead. They were not allowed to speak. They just sat in silence until the judge arrived.

"Your honor," the constable spoke, "should I escort this man to trial?"

"No need," the judge responded, looking displeased. "His admittance to matrimony with this white woman is evidence enough.

He will be prosecuted to the fullest extent of the law; death by hanging."

"No!" Sarah rose from her seat shouting at the unsympathetic judge. "That is my husband. He is a good man, and our marriage is none of your business."

"You quiet yourself!" the judge shouted. "Normally, the woman affiliated in such a sin would get jail time as well. However, I couldn't imagine a pretty little thing such as yourself would intentionally find yourself wedded to a negro. Therefore, I find it within my heart to believe that you were manipulated by him, and therefore I am letting you go free."

Before Sarah was able to argue with the judge, Benjamin stood and demanded she silence herself. The judge, shocked by his warning, looked back at Benjamin but said nothing. He whispered something to the constable and walked out of the jailhouse. Sarah was then escorted out to the street where she was ordered to take her horse and leave the town.

But Sarah could not leave the love of her life. She needed a plan, a way to rescue him. Execution was planned for the morning, so she needed to move quickly. That night, she dressed in her husband's dark clothes and made her way to the jail house. But when she arrived, what she saw was horrific. She watched as two men shook hands with the constable as they left the jailhouse, her husband's limp body brutally beaten and left in a pool of blood. He was dead, and before the scheduled execution could take place.

Sarah felt her blood boiling. Her face was hot. Anger was ready to explode. Before she could allow herself to mourn her beloved's death, she swiftly followed behind the two men. She kept a careful distance and watched one disappear into a small brick house off the side of the road while the other continued on down the dirt path, stumbling in a drunken stupor. Before the man could reach his home, Sarah grabbed an axe that she found nearby and struck the man in the side of the head. She watched as he fell to his knees without a sound from his lips and fell forward in a puddle of blood pouring from the massive hole in the side of his skull. She stood above his lifeless body and spat on him in pure disgust. Then, she strolled back down the road from where she came, axe laid across her shoulder and quietly entered the door to the home she passed by earlier.

Soon after entering the house, she entered a smaller room where the other man she witnessed leaving her dead husband's body was found sprawled out on a mattress next to his sleeping wife. She stood above his bed and stared into his snoring face. Then, stared at his wife a while. She vaguely resembled Sarah. She seemed to be around the same age with soft blonde curls that rested gently against the smooth skin of her face. She considered leaving, but then cringed at the thought that this beautiful, young woman would get to live the rest of her life in pure wedded bliss. So, before she knew it, Sarah held the axe high over her head and chopped the man straight into his chest. A loud squeal came from the man, and then silence. The woman jerked awake and when she saw what had happened, she too began to scream. Sarah dropped the axe and climbed into the bed where she placed her hand over the woman's mouth.

"I lost the love of my life tonight to the hands of your pathetic excuse for a man. Did you think you would be able to keep yours?"

Sarah watched as the woman became wide eyed in recognition of this woman straddling her in her bed, wearing men's clothing. It was that moment that Sarah realized that the woman had prior knowledge of what was happening and was able to sleep like a baby. She then realized that she would have no regrets as this woman was just as cruel as the men who physically murdered her husband.

"Now you better keep your mouth shut," Sarah threatened, "or I will come back for you as well. Now you wait sixty minutes before contacting the authorities, do you hear me?"

When the woman nodded her head in agreement, Sarah fled with her horse and carriage until she reached the sea port where a ship was surprisingly readying itself mid-night to set sail. Sarah noticed a black flag with a skull and two crossed red roses underneath. Soon after, a beautiful woman with fiery red hair emerged on the top deck. She took one look at this blood-soaked woman in men's clothing before she gestured for her to come aboard.

***

Zenobia Iwu, the most powerful woman warrior on the planet. Zenobia was a princess warrior in her African country. She was trained from childhood to fight even the most vicious of men. Her father was very proud of her. He watched as she protected their tribe from enemies countless times over the years. But one night, their tribe

176

was raided by an enemy that was no match for Zenobia and her tribe. The army consisted of men they had never seen before, an army of white men with guns. Her tribe's lack of sophisticated armory fell short to these evil intruders. Zenobia's father was killed soon after the men arrived. He was old with greying hair. All the elders in their tribe were killed. They seemed to be targeted as their aging bodies would not allow them to work, which was what the white men came for: working slaves. Babies were stolen from the arms of their mothers, never to be seen again. The rest of the people were chained up and forced to board a ship with an unknown destination.

The ship was cramped with little room even to sit. The people were given just enough food and water to stay alive. Zenobia stood, exhausted, for two days before she decided she would no longer stand for this treatment. Miraculously, she was able to wiggle her arms out from the chains that rested heavily on her wrists. When dusk fell upon the rocking ship, Zenobia snuck into the captain's chambers where she silently killed him by breaking his neck with her bare hands. She stole the keys that were placed just next to the ship's wheel and slipped back under deck to release as many of the prisoners that she could.

Before the sun could rise, war broke out on the ship. The tribal people fought fierce, but they continued to fall short with the weapons they could find. The white men used their sophisticated pistols, killing a larger number of people more quickly than the tribal people were able to kill in the same amount of time.

Soon, another ship was approaching. Zenobia feared another army of white men would board the ship only to join the already stronger opposing army and defeat them. She believed at that point that her death was inevitable. Most of the tribal men were now dead. The women who were left behind under the deck were slowly being killed off by a few white men that stayed below the deck, raping and torturing the women, one by one.

Bullets began spraying from the newly approached ship, but they were not directed toward any of the few remaining tribal people. Rather, the target appeared to be the white men. Zenobia attempted to focus her eyes on the other ship. She wasn't able to see exactly who the army was, but she could see that they were white. The only possible reason Zenobia could think of was that the other ship wanted to steal the slaves for themselves. Nevertheless, she continued to fight, using any weapons she could find, evading the spraying bullets. She felt defeated as all her tribal brothers lay lifeless on the main deck of the ship. She rushed to the bottom of the ship where she was disgusted to see three white men raping and slaughtering the tribal women who desperately tried to unchain themselves and escape.

Zenobia immediately killed two of the men with kitchen knives she managed to obtain. The third man, she broke out into a sword fight with after she took the sword from the hip of the lifeless white man who lay beneath her. Another white man, or so Zenobia thought, appeared at the entrance to the room on the lower deck, pulled out a pistol from his hip and shot the white man that Zenobia was fighting. When the intruding enemy approached and removed his hat, Zenobia was shocked to see that it wasn't a man, but rather a beautiful woman with fiery-red hair in trousers and a corset. Willie smiled and said smugly, "You have the strength of one hundred men," then held out her hand waiting for Zenobia to shake it.

After returning twenty-three women to Africa aboard the Crimson Rose, Zenobia decided to stay with Willie, stating, "Your women are smart and know how to use your fancy weapons, but where is your strength? Where are your warriors?"

CHAPTER SEVENTEEN

The women stood when Willie approached out of respect for their beloved captain. They said nothing, awaiting orders. "Maria Ortega, Margaret Baynes, Tabatha White, Sarah Adamson, please step forward. As for the rest of you, seven of you return to the ship, the remaining three should stay on the beach, compose a shelter and watch guard of the last lifeboat. You may take turns day by day returning to the ship should we not return in good time. Just be cautious when returning the boats. We only have one more life boat on the ship and we need for the three to remain intact."

As she motioned the four women to follow her toward the jungle, another woman shouted, "But why must the rest of us stay here? Surely more pirates would be better than just the seven of you."

Willie turned and stared coldly at the woman who undermined her authority. "You will do as I say and nothing more, no explanation shall be warranted."

The woman looked flabbergasted to hear such a response, yet she turned to retreat with the rest of the crew. The newly formed sub-crew stopped at the entrance of the jungle for a briefing. Willie said, "Ladies, you have been chosen to join our small crew for your strength, your power, your intellect, and your courageousness far superior to that of the other women on the crew. Together, you are representative of what the Crimson Rose stands for. Your safe return will be necessary to maintain our high standards. Yet it will not be an easy feat. We are facing many great dangers as we enter this jungle. Your support and performance above what you normally do is prudent to our survival. Do you all feel you will be able to handle such an endeavor? You must speak now or forever remain silent."

The six women glanced at Willie and smiled. They responded in unison, "Aye aye, Captain," as they mentally prepared themselves for what was to come.

Willie pulled out a map from her satchel and stared at it a while. She then looked at her compass and pointed northeast into the vast jungle that lay before them.

"Where did you get that map?" Daisy questioned.

"Do you think I would spend a night with Santiago without snooping around?" she replied smugly. "Here is the temple that Doyenea informed us of." She pointed to a spot on the map. "We just need to avoid any dangers in the jungle, for there are surely Egyptian safeguards upon the temple that holds the tomb."

***

After trudging through the thick brush for hours, the crew finally came to a marked path.

"Which way, Captain?" Tabatha asked.

181

Willie looked down at her map that was now in hand and pointed, again, northeast. The path was relatively clear, as if people had dwelled there and created a road. The women walked carefully, deliberately, attentive to any danger that may come their way. Two and a half hours later, and still nothing.

"Captain?" Daisy questioned. "Are you certain we are headed on the right path? It seems awfully easy compared to the many stories we have heard."

"Perhaps that was just what they were, stories."

"But the Sirens exist, there must be more danger ahead."

"Perhaps, but it seems to me nothing we cannot handle," Willie responded matter-of-factly.

Suddenly, the forest darkened. An enormous storm cloud was forming overhead.

"Take shelter!" Willie shouted as the women entered a nearby cave.

Torrential rains began to fall from the sky. Lightening was striking close by, setting a few trees on fire. The cave began to flood.

"We need to move to higher ground, Captain!" Zenobia shouted.

"Indeed," Willie agreed.

They began to move into the cave which seemed to rise on an incline. The space was small. They had to crawl occasionally until they arrived in an area that seemed to be very opened. It was dark aside from a small blue gas flame that resided on the opposite wall of the cave. Willie took a large shaft and lit it upon the flame. It grew into a large, orange ball of fire that lit the cave within. As soon as the light engaged, a swarm of bats, angry that they had been awoken by the light, frantically flew in circles around the women. The women fought the bats with swatting motions, using their satchels as weapons.

"I've been bit!" Sarah shouted as she held tightly onto her neck that was now saturated in crimson blood.

Willie took out her pistol and shot one of the bats, watching it fall clumsily to the ground. The rest of the bats, fearful from the loud noise, fled deeper into the cave. Sarah lay on the ground grasping her neck.

"What do you think, Margaret?" Willie questioned.

Margaret knelt beside Sarah and examined her neck. It was quickly turning black and expanding into a bubble.

"Gangrene!" she shouted. "And none of which I have ever before seen. It's spreading so rapidly."

"What on earth does that mean?" Willie demanded to know.

"It means that if she doesn't receive treatment soon, she will die."

"Well how on earth will we find treatment?"

"Let me go scavenge for some herbs and see what I can find. Daisy, will you come with me?"

"Of course," Daisy replied, knowing that her floral expertise might be beneficial to their search.

They exited the cave from where they came. The rain had slowed to a drizzle and the bottom of the cave was still flooded up to their knees.

"Wet ground is good for finding mushrooms," Margaret stated. "I will look for some that have specific healing properties. Can you look for lotus, honeysuckle and snapdragon?"

Familiar with the flowers, Daisy said, "but snapdragon does not help with healing."

"It is a mild sedative. Sarah will need something to relax. With the rate that her gangrene is spreading, it will likely cause some serious stress. Oh, and we will also need some black root if you can find it. Just be careful when picking it."

"But black root is toxic," Daisy protested.

"Yes, in large doses it is. But in very small doses, it will help kill the bacteria that is on the surface of Sarah's skin."

Daisy nodded in agreement and then separated from Margaret in search of the requested florae. She was not gone long before coming across a rapidly-flowing river. Across the river appeared to be an extensive garden with colorful flowers she had never seen. "I must get to the other side, quickly," she thought to herself as she contemplated ways to cross safely. She noticed a monkey vine that hung from the branch of a large tree that draped the river just a little further south.

She raced to the vine and took hold of it without thinking. She swung across the river but when she reached the other side, a large tiger magically appeared in her landing space. The tiger swatted

184

its claws at Daisy causing her to grasp back onto the vine, but her hands slipped, and she plummeted into the rapid waves of the river.

Her body was carried swiftly down the river. The tiger followed the current upon the land, watching Daisy hungrily as he tried to maintain sight of her. She tried rigorously to grab hold of any vines, branches, or rocks that jutted out from the river bend on the opposite side of the tiger. The river moved too swiftly. The tiger could not keep up with Daisy's whereabouts and soon gave up his hunt. Daisy was unsuccessful in her attempt to evacuate the river until her body smashed into some jagged rocks that sent a piercing needle-like sensation through her spine as it tore through the skin of her leg, the same leg that was gashed just a few months earlier when she fled Yorkston. She grabbed onto the tall, elongated rock and managed to climb out onto the grassy beach.

After choking up what seemed like a liter of water, Daisy caught her breath and sat up to gather her boundaries. She was carried quite far from where she started. Her leg was bleeding profusely. She found a couple of stones and some nearby dried brush where she was able to spark a flame. She watched the fire grow as she took the dagger from her waistband and let it saturate under the hot flames. She placed the bottom portion of her dress into her mouth and bit down tightly. Then, she placed the scorching blade of the knife onto the long laceration and moaned deeply into the fabric between her teeth.

When she was certain the bleeding had stopped, she looked around for something she could use as a protective dressing. A bunch of bananas adorned a nearby tree. She stood to retrieve the large leaves and tied a few tightly around her leg. Then, she sighed and ate two bananas before placing the rest into a homemade bag she had draped across her back. She stood and began to make her way back upstream.

She walked attentively back toward the cave, carrying the dagger in her hand. This time, she would be prepared should any fierce creatures cross her path. When she finally came back across the luscious garden, she was relieved to see the tiger had gone. Had she imaged it? Was it ever really there? She sat down next to the garden and closed her eyes. She hung her neck backward and inhaled deeply, reminiscing back to an easier yet more degrading life. A life where she could live simply, tending to her vast garden, cooking and cleaning. But then, she remembered the abuse. The nightly run-ins with Mr. Clark as he entered her delicate flower and beat her down with shame.

She sighed again. She contemplated staying there, in that moment, forever. Alone. To do what she wanted. Uncontrolled by Mr. Clark and without the responsibilities of being a first mate of a notorious pirate crew. Yes, this new life was crazy, almost entirely against her upbringing. Her mother would be disappointed. She was leading a life as a vagrant, an unethical pirate. But she knew that despite all of that, she was strong, loyal and beautiful. All the qualities she had never known until she met Captain Willie Spade. Wilhelmina. The beautiful, authoritative, strong, demanding, enchantress of a woman. One that Daisy had come to realize, she would do anything for, just as the other women on the crew would. She thought back to that beautiful, strange night when all her inhibitions were set free under one sexual euphoria. What was it that made her do those things unknown to her demeaner? Did she love Willie, or did she love her new life as a strong, independent, feared woman?

Daisy settled her thoughts and remembered why she was there. Lotus, honeysuckle, snapdragon and black root. To her surprise, every single flower she could possibly imagine was there. She located all the flowers she needed and separated them, placing them into the banana leaf pouches she created. She gathered some other flowers she thought might be advantageous at some point. Then, she took a deep breath in and crossed back to the other side of the river using the same monkey vine she had swung on initially.

When she arrived back at the entrance of the cave, the water had now diminished. Zenobia was standing guard at the bottom. "Where have you been? And what has happened to your leg?" she asked as she noticed Daisy limping on a leg wrapped in banana leaves.

"How long have I been gone?" Daisy questioned.

"Four hours!" Zenobia responded.

"I have the florae," Daisy said, ignoring Zenobia's previous questioning of her whereabouts.

"Good, let me take you back to the others, they have moved deeper into the cave, in a safer spot."

When they arrived deep within the cave, Margaret was using a blade to cut the infection out of Sarah's neck. Yellow and black pus drained from the gaping hole.

"The infection has gone very deep and she has developed a fever. Do you have the flowers?"

"Yes," Daisy responded as she removed the individually wrapped flowers from her bag. I also brought some food." She handed each of the women two bananas from her bag, watching the woman gratefully consume the fresh fruit.

Margaret laid the two bananas next to Sarah's head. "She shouldn't eat just yet. She needs the medicine and water first, so she does not vomit." Margaret gave Daisy some instructions for mixing the medicine. She created two separate medicines, one in the form of a hot tea for Sarah to drink, the other a thick paste made from the black root. Margaret used the banana leaf to spread the paste onto Sarah's neck. She cut a piece of her dress and drenched it in water. Then she draped it across Sarah's forehead to help cool her down.

Willie emerged from a different section of the cave. "How is she doing?" she asked walking toward the sickly woman.

"Not well," Margaret responded, "but we just gave her the medication. We will need to give it to her every four hours and allow her to rest. We should stay here overnight."

Willie agreed but decided she needed to investigate the island a little more. "We need to scope the island out a little better. Daisy, will you come with me? Zenobia and Maria, stand guard at the entrance of the cave to ensure no intruders will come. Tabatha and Margaret, stay here and take care of Sarah."

The women all nodded in agreement and dispersed into their designated roles. Daisy walked alongside Willie as they exited the cave. She studied the map, looking around the now darkened island underneath the dusk-filled sky.

"It's cooler now. We can determine where our route is while we wait for Sarah to recover. We all need good health to get through this journey."

The two women walked in silence for about an hour until Daisy could not control her curiosity and blurted out, "I'm confused about your behavior. You have said nothing to me since the other night. You treat me as nothing more than another member of the crew. What we did the other night, was that something special between the two of us? Are we more than crew mates or is that just something you do with everyone, taking advantage of their initial vulnerability?"

Willie looked at Daisy, annoyed. "You shut your mouth! I would never take advantage of any of the women on this ship. All of us were taken advantage of, sexually manipulated, and torn apart. Myself included. Why would I engage in the same nightmare we are all trying to escape?"

"Then why me?" Daisy questioned. "Why would you engage in such a sensual experience with me and then act as if nothing had happened?"

"Daisy, you mustn't get caught up in feelings of the heart. What we had, what we have, is special. Our relationship is unlike my relationship with any other women of my crew. However, I have to treat everyone fairly. I cannot show you more attention than the rest of the women. That would not be fair, and that is not how I run my crew. Furthermore, there is a time for business and a time for pleasure. I take the business of piracy extremely seriously. Now let's just keep moving. We need to be cautious of anything to come."

Daisy could not argue with Willie. However, the feelings she felt overwhelmed her, and she would not be a true pirate if she did not express her desires. She grabbed Willie by the arm and turned her back to face her. She placed her hand on Willie's face and pulled her closer until she was starting into her eyes.

"The business of piracy is to take what you desire. Is that not what you taught me?" Daisy whispered seductively into Willie's ear.

She then pressed her mouth tightly against Willie's and allowed her tongue to glide attentively, entangled with hers. Willie stroked her back as Daisy strung her fingers through Willie's long, fiery-red hair. Their rapid inhales and exhales were in sync until they became just one breath. Then, the two women lowered their bodies to the jungle floor, lying side by side. Willie untied the back of Daisy's dress and lowered it to expose her large, succulent breasts. She placed her whole mouth on her pink nipple and began to slide her wet tongue, encircling her nipple until it became erect. She pulled the rest of her dress down, exposing her naked body to the perilous jungle before untying the strings to her own corset and tugging her trousers below her ankles.

The two, beautiful, naked women grasped tightly onto each other as they grinded their pelvises together. A throbbing sensation rushed within the lips between their hips. Warm, soft liquid flowed between their thighs, dripping sensually amid their intertwined legs. Willie grasped tightly onto Daisy's head with her fingers entangled in her long, honey-golden locks. She placed her mouth on Daisy's neck and bit down tenderly, eliciting a gentle squeal from Daisy's opened mouth. They continued grinding into one another until both of their bodies clenched like a fist and released their muscles in the purest form of ecstasy, together. Then, the two women lay holding each other tenderly for just a few moments, listening to the heavy breathing they shared as one.

After a few moments, the two women rose and redressed. Willie smiled, grabbed Daisy by the back of the head and pecked her gently on the lips. They said nothing as they continued to walk in the dark.

Finally, they reached a foot bridge. Across the bridge in the distance, they could see portions of a large temple. Willie looked down at her map, illuminated by the moon in the sky.

"That's it!" she whispered loudly. "Now we must retreat back to the cave and wait for dawn until the others are well rested and ready to move on."

Daisy and Willie walked back to the cave, again in silence. Daisy contemplated their relationship, wondering if it could ever be more than just hidden sexual escapades. But she was concerned with the monstrosity that this type of relationship was; how inappropriate, how society would never accept it. Surely, she could never live a normal life with a woman in her bed. Raising children? Out of the question! What would her mother think? Her behavior was unspeakable, unthinkable! But then, she rested her thoughts and realized, she is no longer a normal member of society. She is no longer a kind-hearted, decent, appropriate woman. She is a pirate. And she could do whatever her heart desired, always and forever.

CHAPTER EIGHTEEN

Once back at the cave, Willie instructed Daisy to get some rest. She also took over for Zenobia and Maria and allowed them to rest as well. Willie didn't sleep much. She attributed it to her days trapped in a cage, staying awake to prepare herself for the sexual abuse that rushed her into adulthood. When a few hours were left until dawn, she traded places with Maria and slept a few hours until the sun rose.

When the sun was crossing over the horizon in the east, Willie rose and made her way to the secluded area in which Sarah was sleeping. She still looked very ill. Her head was hot. "What's happening?" Willie asked.

"I'm not sure the medicine is working," Margaret answered. "She may just need a little more time. Thirteen hours is not enough to heal such a large infection." Sarah had a gaping wound on her neck. The necrotic skin had been cleared away and only pink, healthy tissue remained. However, it was a large hole nonetheless and needed time to heal.

"Okay, we cannot wait any longer. It may take days before she is even feeling better. Margaret, I need you to stay here with Sarah. The rest of us will go to the temple. We will return as soon as we have found the treasure."

Margaret smiled and nodded in agreement. The rest of the women stood, gathered their belongings, and began marching toward the entrance of the cave. The five of them tread by foot until they came to the foot bridge that Daisy and Willie had found soon after their seductive experience the night before. The bridge was attached to either side of a large mountain. Below was an aggressive, rapidly flowing river that submerged the most jagged of rocks.

Willie stepped onto the wooden plank. It cracked, but not all the way through. She sighed and continued.

"Wait, Captain," Tabatha urged. "It is not sturdy."

"Well the way I see it," Willie continued, "there is no other way to get to that temple. So, we walk!"

The four women looked at each other. They watched Willie slowly glide across the wobbly foot bridge and began to slowly follow one by one behind her. When they reached the middle, the bridge swayed violently with a large gust of wind. They grabbed hold of the rope rails tightly and crouched down to force their weight to hold the bottom of the bridge rather than flipping it over. When the gust disappeared, they continued until they reached the opposite side.

"Well, that wasn't so bad," Willie joked.

The rest of the women laughed in relief that the bridge did not break, causing them to plummet fifty feet to their deaths. They continued to walk. The temple was vaguely in sight. Swarms of mosquitos molested the women as they continued to travel through the humid jungle. When they neared the entrance to the temple, a hazy fog encircled them. The fog was so thick that they could barely see their own feet.

"Stay close," Willie urged.

The women followed her lead and trudged slowly in a line behind Willie as she led the way to the entrance of the temple. When they arrived, there was nothing but a wall. No door, no gate, no window.

"How do we enter?" Zenobia questioned.

"There must be some sort of a code," Willie responded as she placed her hands on the wall, gliding them until she felt a loose brick. She pressed the brick and it fell off the wall, shattering on the jungle floor. The women jumped back, startled.

"Seven," Willie continued. "There must be seven bricks to open the wall."

"What makes you think of this number, Captain?" Tabatha questioned.

"Seven is the number of the island," Willie continued. "Seven Sirens, seven intruders, seven bricks."

The women looked at each other and then got to work, pressing at the wall until one by one, each of the women found a brick that displaced from the wall and crashed to the ground, shattering as it landed.

"Only six," Willie concluded. "We must get higher."

Zenobia and Maria got down on their hands and knees. Willie did the same, placing one knee on Zenobia's back and one on Maria's. Finally, Daisy climbed the human ladder and stood atop Willie's back, feeling gracefully around the upper portion of the wall until she felt a loose brick, pressed it hard, and watched it collapse to the ground.

Suddenly, the women felt the ground rumble and heard a growling sound emanating from the wall. The human ladder fell apart as the women stood back at a distance close enough to see through the fog. A six by six-foot portion of the wall began to crumble and landed on the ground with an explosion of dust. The women waved their arms to disperse the dust, covering their mouths and noses with their other arm until the dust cleared and they could vaguely see inside a deep, dark hole. A soft, yellow glow was seen in the far back corner of the room.

"Amazing," Daisy proclaimed.

Willie smirked and began to enter the temple, pistol drawn. Suddenly, she felt the ground below her feet soften, followed by a loud hissing. She quickly stepped back out into the fog.

"I need a flame," Willie requested.

Maria picked up two pieces of brick that now laid at the bottom of the wall in a pile and stroked them together over a pile of brush until she elicited a spark. Willie lit the top of her shaft on fire and stretched her arm into the temple.

When she peered into the temple, she saw thousands of snakes now standing alert with their elongated necks high in the air. Their tails were rattling in warning.

"Well, there is no way we are getting through all those snakes without getting bit. We need a plan," Willie said.

"A potion," Daisy interjected. "I will concoct a potion to kill them. I'm just unsure how we will get them to drink it."

Willie smiled, "Well, do you have anything to concoct a potion?"

"Of course," Daisy pulled out her banana leaf pouches and carefully placed the black root and snapdragon in a bowl she had made from a coconut. "The snapdragon will sedate them while the black root will slowly kill them, in large enough doses of course."

"What if we make it into a gas?" Tabatha asked. "That way they would not need to drink it, but rather it would kill them by inhalation."

"Good thinking," Willie complimented Tabatha.

"We will need something hot enough to turn the liquid into a vapor and spread it throughout the air. Perhaps in an explosion."

"What about gun powder?" Tabatha questioned again.

"That might work," Daisy proclaimed. "Do we have enough?

"Of course," Willie smiled as she pulled a small bag of gunpowder from her satchel.

"I can use my rifle to cause the explosion," Maria added.

"That would work," Daisy continued.

When Daisy was finished mixing the ingredients, Maria took the concoction and mashed it into her rifle with the gun powder. She heated it with the flame of Willie's torch just to be sure the potion grew hot enough to vaporize. Then, she covered her mouth and nose with a portion of her dress. The other four women did the same, awaiting the blast from the rifle. When Maria shot the rifle into the temple, they felt the walls shake. An echoing "boom" followed the explosion. The hissing grew louder, the snakes were upset. Slowly, however, the hissing grew quieter and eventually stopped. They peered into the temple entrance to see lifeless bodies of thousands of snakes sprawled out onto the temple floor.

"It worked!" Willie celebrated. "Let's keep going."

The women walked through the temple, pushing the snakes aside with their feet. When they reached a door, they opened it and entered a large atrium. The ceilings were high and there were multiple doorways, each marked with a symbol at the top. The door they came from was marked with a yellow pendent engraved with a snake. The women walked together, shuffling about as they encompassed the room, necks cocked back as they studied the symbols above each doorway. A red tiger, a green bear, a gold lion, a silver tortoise, a purple elephant and a blue baboon. Seven pendants. Seven doors. Seven rooms.

"We should use the doorway with the baboon," Daisy insisted.

"But why?" Maria questioned.

"From the direction of the Sirens," Zenobia continued. "We must enter a room marked with the blood of a baboon."

"But there is no blood on this door," Tabatha protested.

"But there may be another door within," Willie clarified.

Willie slowly opened the door that creaked loudly and entered first. The women followed closely behind. Down a narrow hallway they walked. The flame from Willie's torch began to fade, making it more difficult to see. The room became colder the further they walked. Suddenly, the women heard the sound of a wooden board shifting followed by a high-pitched yelp. They turned quickly to see that Tabatha had disappeared from the back of their line.

"Tabatha!" Maria yelled.

"I'm here!" Tabatha replied desperately. "Help me, please."

They soon discovered that a panel was missing from the floor where they just emerged. Tabatha was dangling upside down below the ground into a dark cellar below. Her dress had caught on a spike that was jutting out from the floor.

Maria quickly kneeled on the ground and reached down into the hole, grabbing Tabatha by the hand. Suddenly, they heard a loud, hoarse screech, and Tabatha felt the back of her dress being violently tugged back through the hole. Zenobia grabbed hold of her other hand as she squeezed next to Maria in the narrow hallway, desperately attempting to pull Tabatha back through the hole.

Willie held her flame over the abyss to where she witnessed Tabatha being pulled violently downward by a large primate with a bright red face.

"Baboon!" Willie whispered loudly, wide-eyed, staring in awe at the danger that lay just below them.

Tabatha shrieked, "It bit me!" Suddenly, the rest of the floor opened up and the women fell nine feet to a solid ground. The women were surrounded by fifteen baboons bouncing and squealing, eagerly awaiting a much-needed snack.

The women removed daggers from their belts and began swaying their arms fiercely at the baboons. The primates showed their large, yellowing canines as they rushed toward the women. Blood sprayed from some of the baboons as the women dug their daggers deep within their necks. Suddenly, the baboons' squealing shifted from that of anger to that of fear. They swiftly moved away from the women and into the dim background, tails between their legs. The women stood in a circle, backs to one another facing out into nothing but darkness. Willie's flame, flickering mildly through the ceiling where it was left behind when the women fell through the ground, was powerless against the darkness below.

Willie felt a hot, humid mist come across her face. The smell of rotting fish etched in the air. She turned her head to the left only to be face to face with a six-foot tall, angry baboon. The ape opened its throat and let out the most ferocious, deafening roar with a breath so powerful it knocked Willie off her feet.

"Ruuuun!!!!" Willie shouted as Zenobia and Maria dragged Willie to her feet and began running with all their might in the opposite direction. Willie, running in the rear, wind whipping through her hair, turned to face the large ape that was now chasing them, she shot her pistol in its direction. She missed the baboon but hit a large rock that fell from the ceiling, knocking the baboon briefly off track. She continued to shoot, with no particular aim as she ran backward through the temple halls. Falling wooden panels and loose bricks slowed the ape down. Finally, they came to a wall that was slowly closing them into the baboon's den. Daisy and Tabatha had already made their way behind the wall. Zenobia and Maria had to duck to get under the wall that was coming down from the ceiling. It was closing quickly, Willie was a few feet behind. Zenobia and Maria used their masculine strength to hold the wall from fully closing, their biceps bulging as they struggled to lift the closing wall. They were able to slow it just enough for Willie to get through as she dove underneath, sliding on her belly until the wall closed an inch away from her foot that freed itself beneath the wall. They heard a loud thump and the whining of a large animal. Willie sat with her back against the closed wall, hand on her head, catching her breath.

"Are you alright, Captain?" Tabatha asked.

Willie looked up, a smile drawing across her face. "What a rush!" she proclaimed.

Zenobia shook her head. "You are mad, woman. You almost lost your life."

"And what a way to go," Willie joked. "Relax, we are invincible. We are women, remember?"

Zenobia smiled and held out her hand for Willie to take. She pulled herself to her feet and brushed off her trousers. Then, she straightened her corset, bosom almost fully protruded from the top.

"What's next, ladies?" Willie asked.

Daisy turned and pointed to a door at the end of the hallway. It was clearly marked in a maroon-colored blood that had obviously been dried for some time. Blue flames lined the walls of the hallway.

"Well then, let's go," Willie instructed.

The women walked steadily toward the door, more alert toward the walls and the ground. Suddenly, they heard another sliding sound and instinctively jumped their feet to the side of the walls, holding on as if to prevent from falling through the ground again. But the floors did not open. Instead, daggers fell from the ceiling.

Maria screamed. The women turned to look at her. She was bent over, removing a dagger from the center of her foot.

"It's fine," Maria said as she pulled the dagger from her foot and placed it into her satchel.

"Now, how do we open this door?" Willie questioned. She looked around. There was an odd-shaped hole where a doorknob should be. "It looks like some sort of key."

"It looks like the shape of the baboon's canine," Daisy said.

"So, we must obtain a tooth from the baboons we just encountered?" Zenobia asked seemingly irritated.

"Aw, bloody hell!" Willie shouted as she placed her hand on her forehead in a frustrated manner.

"Wait a minute!" Tabatha shouted. "That devilish monkey bit me on the leg." She reached down and pulled out a large, yellowish tooth that was jutting through the bottom of her dress and into her calf. Her adrenaline had been so high that she hardly felt the foreign object implanted into her leg.

Willie smiled and grabbed the tooth. She placed it into the socket and watched as the door lit up with a blue, glowing light and began to open. The women stepped back and watched the door open on its own. They walked into the large room with high ceilings. A radiant glow emerged from within the room. Seven shrines were meticulously placed within the room. Each shrine was surrounded by clay pots painted in Egyptian writing that were filled with gold, silver, and shimmering jewels of all colors.

The women shouted gleeful cheers and raced to the treasure so extensive that they would be able to feed and shelter all the colonies in America. They began to fill their bags and satchels with as much treasure as they could. They wore necklaces and bracelets made of jewels they had never seen before. They each topped their skulls with the most radiant crowns, dubbing each other princess of the Crimson Rose. Then, they each bowed down to Willie and placed the largest of the crowns atop her head and praised her for her instinct, her courageousness and her manipulation of the crew to lead them to a treasure they only imagined in their wildest dreams.

As the women continued to frolic around the room, filling their satchels and adorning their bodies, Willie strolled off to explore the rest of the tomb. She walked behind a wall that lay behind the shrines. It partially closed off the room, leaving a three-foot-wide space from floor to the ceiling, leading into another room. Behind the wall lay a golden coffin engraved with the seven animals that were etched into the pendants.

Willie studied the engravings, tracing her finger over each one. Then, she slowly opened the casket. A blue light radiated from within, blasting toward the ceiling. The mummy that rested peacefully within the coffin had a blue medallion engraved with a baboon that penetrated his forehead. Willie used her dagger to pry it out of the skull. She examined it closely, unable to peer into its blasting blue rays without having to squint. Then, she placed it in her satchel and removed two red roses. She placed the roses, crossed at the stems on the chest of the mummy.

Suddenly, the ground began to rumble, silencing the women's gleeful cheers. The ceiling began to break apart as wooden boards fell to the ground. Dust filled the air, dimming the radiance of the treasure.

"The temple is self-destructing!" Willie shouted as she rushed back from behind the wall. "Take what you can and let's flee!"

The women finished filling their bags with all they could carry and began running toward the door in which they came. Wooden planks and bricks fell from the ceiling and blocked their entrance. They looked around for another way out.

"There!" Maria shouted as she pointed to the top of the high ceiling where a small opening seemed to lead to some type of duct. They climbed the pile of bricks until they were able to touch the ceiling. Zenobia pulled herself up first, then Maria. The two of them helped the other three women into the hole.

The path was hardly large enough for them to crawl, so they had to stay low. They crawled through the pathway, listening to the thunder behind them. Finally, the pathway stopped, leading to another room. They hopped down and landed on the floor below. There were red markings along the top of the room. A glowing red light emanated from the corner, dimmed by a large, shadowy figure. Willie's eyes narrowed as an attempt to make out what the creature was.

"Tiger," Willie whispered as she contemplated the pendants that lined the atrium walls. Before she could turn around, she heard an aggressive, low growl escalate to an impatient roar as a large tiger rose from his sleeping spot and approached the women. They turned and ran down the long, narrow hallway to the right of the room. Maria was in the rear. They heard her scream followed by a horrific crunch. Then, silence. They looked back and saw the tiger tearing Maria apart with his teeth. The flesh from her face torn off, leaving nothing but a bloody mush and exposed white bone beneath. Willie started to move back toward the tiger, drawing her sword, but Zenobia grabbed her by the arm.

"It's too late, Captain. We must go."

Willie turned back and followed the rest of the women as they continued to race down the pathway. Bricks continued falling from the ceiling; the room with the tiger was now completely enclosed. They exited through a door and back into the large atrium. Then, they raced through the door adorned with a yellow pendant and re-entered the room with the deceased snakes. The wall where they entered was almost entirely closed off by wooden panels and bricks.

They raced to the wall and began tirelessly pulling the debris away, dodging more bricks as they fell from the ceiling.

"We are going to get stuck in here!" Daisy shouted. "We are going to die."

The women continued to try to pull the bricks away, but it was hopeless as the building continued to collapse. The wall remained closed off while the rest of the temple fell apart around them. Miraculously, the bricks from the wall began to tumble outside, leaving a narrow opening at the top. The women climbed to the top of the rubble and one by one, crawled through, grabbing hold of an unknown hand that was reaching in and helping to pull them out.

When they reached the outside, Margaret and Sarah were standing outside of the temple, seemingly amazed to see the women emerge.

Margaret peered into the small spaces between the boulders, "Where's Maria?" she asked, eagerly awaiting her to emerge from the rubble. But the women fell silent, bowing their heads, and Margaret knew she had perished.

When the commotion fell silent, Margaret and Sarah squealed wildly at the amount of gold and jewels the women were carrying.

"You were right," Margaret said.

"Of course I was," Willie stated adamantly. "Did you think I would risk my life along with the lives of my sisters on some mythical story?"

The women smiled and threw their arms around Willie.

"Now let's get out of here before any more danger can present itself."

The women turned and followed their brave captain out of the jungle and back to the oceanside beach from where they came.

CHAPTER NINETEEN

Willie and her crew reached the seaside shore hours after dragging heavy jewels through the scorching jungle in perspiration-soaked clothing. Two other pirates were seated under the shade of a large palm tree, attempting to evade the blasting sunshine rays. When they saw the women approach, they rose to their feet and clumsily walked through the white sand to greet them.

"Captain, we're so happy to see you safe, and even happier to see such a treasure," said one of the women, staring greedily at the jewels that bedazzled Willie and her crew.

"But where is Maria?" the second woman interjected.

"Maria is no longer with us," Willie said solemnly.

Without any more procrastination, the crew helped push the lifeboat through the jagged rocks along the shore. Once they entered open waters, they climbed in and rowed to the Crimson Rose that sat proudly atop the vast ocean that surrounded them.

When they embarked the ship, they were welcomed by celebratory shouts and stares of awe and wonderment. Willie and her sub-crew were greeted with bottles of rum and wine, spilling over their glasses with healthy pours.

"Before the celebration continues," Willie raised her hand to silence the crew, "I am asking that we all have a moment of silence for the brave, strong Maria Ortega who lost her life so you all could have a better one."

The ship fell silent, and all the women held their heads down low.

"We lost two good women to this difficult journey," Willie continued, "but in the heart of a pirate, we must know in good faith that they would not want us to spend another moment of our lives in mourning, but rather in celebration of what is to come. Tonight, we celebrate like queens!"

"Here, here!" The women shouted as they hurried along to start cooking for their celebratory dinner.

***

That night, the dining hall was filled with the aroma of a savory roasted pig, a vast array of succulent vegetables and the sweet scent of warm apple pie.

"Before we eat," Willie said, standing at the head of the table with a large wine goblet in her hand, "Let us have a toast to the most courageous pirate crew in the history of mankind. To the Crimson Rose!

The words "to the Crimson Rose" echoed throughout the deck followed by the clinking of glasses that chimed through the air. The room was filled with gleeful chatter and laughter from the women who were now seated and feasting on a dinner meant for queens. Daisy, sitting to the left of Willie subtly touched her on the top of her hand and smiled. Zenobia, who was now across from Daisy, peered up from her food to get a glimpse of the intimate moment and then quickly looked back down at her plate to avoid being noticed.

The evening continued until all the food was gone and the last drop of wine had diminished from the final bottle.

Later that evening, Daisy lay alone in her sleeping chamber until she was interrupted by a knock on her door. "Come in," she called from behind the closed door.

When the door opened, Willie appeared, gazing admiringly at Daisy who was now in a white, cotton night gown that draped low upon her breasts.

"How's that wound healing up?" Willie asked as she glanced across the room at the stitched-up wound on Daisy's leg.

"It's healing much more nicely than the first gash I had some time ago," Daisy replied as she also looked down at her leg.

"Did you stitch it up yourself?"

"I did," Daisy admitted.

"You're strong, Daisy, stronger than you know."

Daisy smiled. She pulled an ointment she made down from the table by her bedside.

"Let me help," Willie grabbed the ointment from Daisy and began slowly rubbing it onto her leg. When she was finished, she wiped her hand on a cotton rag.

"You are so beautiful," Willie continued, gazing into Daisy's eyes. She pulled her closer and kissed her tenderly on her lips, allowing her tongue to slip in and dance within her mouth. Daisy allowed tears to drip from her eyes.

"What is the matter?" Willie asked.

"It's just," Daisy responded, "there was only one person in my life, who sees me the way you do, and I'm embarrassed to say that our lovemaking is causing me to feel guilty, as if I am betraying him somehow."

Willie sat back, still holding the back of Daisy's neck, "Were you married to him, Ms. Flynn?"

Daisy looked taken aback by Willie's use of her surname. "Well, no, but."

"But what then?" Willie interrupted.

"You see, he was the only man that allowed me to step outside of my comfort zone, to leave my life behind. He tried to save me, he said he would have a ship waiting to take me away from Virginia, but then you came instead."

"So, you think he tried but failed to save you?"

"Well, in a sense." Daisy responded.

"But he did save you, Daisy." Willie stared at Daisy, searching her face.

"No, you saved me, Wilhelmina. You and the brave women of The Crimson Rose"

"I was merely answering the call of a friend."

"A friend? What are you talking about?"

"I received a message, from Sir Nathaniel Alexander, about a strong, beautiful damsel in distress being abused by a terrible man and needing a way out. He knew I would be that way out. He knew I couldn't refuse that type of request, especially for him."

"But how?" Daisy looked perplexed.

"How do I know Mr. Alexander?" Willie asked.

"Yes, I mean, I don't understand how a governor's son, and strong supporter of the law would ever allow the love of his life to turn over her life to piracy, let alone befriend a pirate in the first place."

Willie laughed. "Mr. Alexander and I have a strong understanding. In fact, I owe him my life." Daisy again looked confused, so Willie continued. "Do you remember when I told you the story of how I became a pirate in the first place?"

"Yes."

"Well, do you remember when I told you that night after night, I was brutally, sexually tortured by countless large, ale-drenched men and locked in a cage like an animal? And remember when I told you the only way I was able to escape was by the sweet, innocent cabin boy who was beside himself in horror to know of the terrible things the men did to me?"

"Nathaniel?" Daisy whispered.

"Yes, Nathaniel saved my life."

"But why on earth was he working as a cabin boy in the first place? He was fortunate to be born into a rich, powerful family."

"Nathaniel's father understood the value of hard work. He didn't want Nathaniel growing up a privileged child without the experience of a day of labor. So, every summer, he was sent to work on a fisherman's ship to work as a cabin boy, you know, get the feel of what it was like to be a real man."

"So, he really did save me?" Daisy asked in an attempt to clarify the situation.

"Yes, my dear, yes he did."

"Well that seems to make things worse." Daisy continued.

"How so?" Willie asked.

"Because now I'm torn. I had such strong, lustful feelings for Nathaniel and now, I have strong feelings of similar sorts toward you, but I'm afraid they might be displaced."

"Why do you say that?"

"Because, you are a woman, and so am I. And women are not meant to carry on such an unethical, inappropriate relationship."

"Does it feel right to you, Daisy? Pretend that Nathaniel and the rest of the world do not exist. Does it feel right then when we are together?"

"Absolutely, when we are together, it feels like nothing else in the world matters."

"Well then, I don't see the issue here."

"The issue," Daisy continued, "is that we are not here on this land, alone. We are encompassed by a whole world of people and what's right is a man and a woman, not a man and a man and surely never a woman and a woman."

Willie laughed, "Daisy, you are forgetting, you are not just a common person anymore. You are a pirate. We do not think with our minds, we think with our hearts. We do what we desire and respond to the consequences later."

Daisy smiled and sat in silence contemplating what was just said. Then, she leaned in closely and kissed Willie on the lips. She closed her eyes and shut down her thoughts. She let go of the thoughts that were imprisoning her soul, conforming her to a set of standards. And she felt, right. She felt unjudged. She felt beautiful. She felt strong. And she felt loved.

CHAPTER TWENTY

The next morning, Willie instructed the crew to prepare the ship to sail off to sea. The dark storm that remained intact for days surrounding the ship had now dissipated and the island was quiet. No melodious songs, no attempts at luring sailors to their deaths. Willie touched the gem-strung necklace that draped her neck to ensure their journey was real. She smiled mischievously knowing that she, the only female captain with the only all-female pirate crew in history conquered La Isla De Las Sirenas. Even after the doubts of others, she still managed to get it done.

Suddenly, a streak of green lights illuminated the sea just below their ship and swam further and further away into the ocean. Joyful laughter filled the air. Daisy approached Willie at the bow of the ship, watching the creatures swim away. "The Sirens," she proclaimed. "They're free." Willie smiled.

Sailing through the sea had never been easier. The waves were calm. No storm was in sight. "Where to, Captain?" Zenobia questioned as she stood high above the ship in the crow's nest, holding a telescope to her eye.

"I have business in Virginia," she stated. "We shall stop there and load up the ship with goods then travel back to Port Royal for a much needed rest."

Zenobia nodded, "Aye aye, Captain."

They hadn't sailed long before another ship in the distance appeared to be approaching.

"Another ship, Captain. Shall we change course?" Zenobia shouted from the crow's nest.

"Can you identify who it is? Is it militia?" Willie questioned.

"Pirates," Zenobia proclaimed.

"Then no, we mustn't change course."

"But why, Wilhelmina?" Daisy asked, standing next to Willie at the bow of the ship, peering out across the sea with her telescope.

"We must send a message, to all the pirates in the seven seas. We, the only crew in the history of time, we as women, have set forth and conquered La Isla De Las Sirenas. Daisy, take hold of the wheel."

Willie left Daisy to sail the ship while she spread orders to the rest of the crew. "Zenobia, prepare the warriors for combat. Tabatha, man the crow's nest."

Tabatha took Zenobia's place atop the crow's nest, feeding bullets into her pistol in preparation of the approaching intruders. Zenobia left for the armory deck of the ship and equipped all her warriors. Six women remained below deck filling the cannons in preparation for the nearing ship. The rest of the women headed to the top deck with shields and weapons as they readied themselves for war.

When the rival ship arrived adjacent to the Crimson Rose, Willie laughed in disgust at who the leader was upon that ship.

"Captain Johnny Snakehead White. To what do I owe the pleasure of seeing your striking face?" Willie shouted, sarcastically, across the ocean.

Snakehead smiled and allowed his tongue to evade his lips, wiggling it back and forth. He had split his tongue in half so that it would resemble a snake's tongue. Snakehead was mentally insane. He retained his name by biting off the heads of snakes and sucking the blood from their bodies. He swore it made him immortal.

He was a large man, disheveled and always reeked of rum. His eyes were beady, and his face was grayed with dirt. His long, gray, disheveled hair was dreaded into his beard. He was an unpleasant sight to say the least.

"A little birdy told me that you and your repulsive crew of whores were trying to make a name for yourself stealing the treasure from Pharoah Mostafan's tomb. But I just couldn't believe that a ship full of useless, tainted women could overcome a feat such that no man ever could."

"Now now, Captain White," Willie continued. "Don't you know that women are smarter and stronger than men, especially my beautiful, powerful crew? La Isla De Las Sirenas has been conquered by the Crimson Rose. By women." Willie stood proud, staring coldly at Snakehead while the rest of his crew stood atop the deck, waiting for a signal from him.

"Prove it!" He shouted across the sea.

Willie reached in her satchel and retrieved the pendent with the face of a baboon that she removed from Pharoah Mostafan's skull. The stone glimmered brightly in blue as she held it high above her head. Its iridescence pierced the eyes of Snakehead, and he was forced to look away. When she placed it back in her bag, Snakehead peered back at her with a look of disbelief but shouted back, "So you must have the massive treasure that legend proclaimed he had buried down in the tomb with him."

Willie smiled and without warning, shot her pistol in the direction of Snakehead. She misaimed and ran to take cover. The ship was now in full-on war. Arrows were flying aimlessly through the air. Pistols sounding like thunderclaps interrupted the peaceful breathing of the waves. Gun smoke hazed the sky around them.

Before the fighting could go on too long, Willie watched a small, Hispanic man emerge from the deck below, holding tightly onto a small woman with long, flowing red curls. Another man appeared with a dark-skinned woman with long rope-like hair. Their faces were covered, hidden beneath burlap potato sacks.

"Cease fire!" Willie shouted. She watched as the other crew looked to their Captain for orders. Captain White raised his hand in the air and lowered it repetitively. The crew followed his orders and lowered their weapons. Willie's crew stared at her in silence, searching for answers.

Willie gulped, "What do you want?"

She heard whispers emerge from the women behind her. They were confused. Why was she surrendering? She had never done that before. They noticed two women held hostage aboard Captain White's ship. But again, surrendering had never been an option in the past. They would always fight first and rescue the captured women later. But this time was different. For some reason that was unknown to her crew, Willie was unwilling to take the risk of harming these two unfamiliar women.

Snakehead laughed evilly. "So, it is possible. They told me I was wrong. They told me it couldn't be done. The infamous Captain Willie Spade cannot be bribed, they said. She cares of nothing, she cares of no one. Ha! What a preposterous thought that a mother would ever put her child in danger. Even a whore like you wouldn't be so stupid!"

Whispers from the women surrounding Willie grew louder.

Willie stood strong and asked again, "What the fuck do you want, Snakehead?"

"Oh, we are using informalities now, are we?" Snakehead questioned sarcastically. "Well then, whore, I want all of the treasure you have retrieved from Pharoah Mostafan's tomb. And more importantly, I want you."

"Don't do it, Wilhelmina," Daisy urged. "We will fight, and we will get them safely back."

Willie looked back at Daisy, ashen in the face. "This man is crazy, Daisy. He will kill them for sure, no questions asked. I cannot take that risk."

Willie peered back at her crew who now had the most confused looks across their faces, then back at Snakehead. He now had the potato sack off Ella's head, his filthy hand tightly grasping the back of her neck and his slithering tongue wiggling inside Ella's ear. Ella scrunched up her face with a look of disgust but stayed strong and made no attempt to move nor sob. Marisha remained covered up. Her arms were tied with a rope behind her back. Her dress was torn, dried blood adorned the bottom of her trembling legs.

"Deal," Willie shouted for fear of hesitating too long. "But you must not harm a single woman in my crew."

"Don't touch one of your whores?" Snakehead asked mockingly. "Not a problem. We can find better whores elsewhere." He laughed again, evilly.

The women watched as Snakehead's crew lowered the plank from their ship to Willie's. "I will send the negro over first, then you will come, then I will send the young tramp," Snakehead informed Willie of the plan.

The small, Hispanic man removed the sack from Marisha's head and pushed her toward the plank. She had a look of fear across her face yet maintained her composure. Willie watched as she slowly walked the plank. When she made it to the other side, Willie cut the ropes from behind her back and wrapped her arms around her in support. Marisha left her arms dangling at her sides, flat affect to her face.

"Okay, okay, enough of that sappy whore nonsense," Snakehead demanded. "Now, move!"

Willie quickly walked across the plank and when she reached the other side, she grabbed her daughter by the face and whispered, "You are my child, you have the blood of a pirate within your veins. You have the blood of a captain within your veins. Use your instincts." Then she kissed her on the forehead, the first time she had ever placed her lips upon her child, and strolled slowly, yet confidently to stand next to Snakehead. Snakehead sniffed Willie's head and left his face buried in her fiery-red hair.

Willie groaned, "Have you heard of the word 'bath'?"

Snakehead appeared irritated. "Tie her up," he snorted.

Two men rushed alongside Willie and tied her arms behind her back with some rope. She watched her daughter gracefully walk the plank until she reached the other side. Marisha pulled her back in toward her chest and stepped back as eight men boarded the Crimson Rose.

"You will not touch them!" Willie shouted from across the sea.

"Shut up!" Snakehead commanded.

The men tied the women to a few poles, five of them together with their backs to the pole. Zenobia spat at a man who slyly brushed his arm across her bosom. A few other men descended the wooden stairs in search of any treasure they could find. They managed to emerge with all the treasure the women obtained on their difficult journey to La Isla. Two other men chopped down the ship's wheel with an axe, laughing and skipping around like school children.

When their tasks were complete, they all left the ship and re-boarded their own. The women remained tied to the various mast poles while the other crew set sail in the opposite direction. The women watched as their beloved captain stood tall, strong and brave surrounded by a ship full of enemies; her fiery-red hair flowing elegantly through the wind as the ship sailed away. And in that moment, the pirates of the Crimson Rose unanimously understood their captain to be the most important woman in each of their lives.

CHAPTER TWENTY-ONE

As Snakehead's ship disappeared on the horizon, with her small waist, Ella was able to crouch down under the rope that tied the women to the mast pole together. She then untied the ropes to free the other women.

Daisy took Ella by the hands and welcomed her. She then introduced herself and the rest of the crew to Marisha, who was standing barefoot with dried blood adorning her feet. Tabatha held Marisha by the shoulders and guided her to the washroom to allow her to clean herself. No one said anything to Marisha, for they understood the horror of being victim to sexual assault, and the shame the initial insult brings. No one cares to speak of it at first, just hold it in like a time-released poison, slowly killing one on the inside.

"Did those men hurt you?" Daisy asked Ella once Marisha disappeared down the steps.

"No," Ella confessed, "but they did hurt poor Marisha."

"I'm very sorry to hear that, Ella. Are you afraid?"

"No, just angry."

"That is very understandable," Daisy continued. "Can I get you anything?"

"We need to get Wilhelmina."

Daisy was taken aback by the utterance of Wilhelmina's full name. She did not verbally address her as her mother, but somehow her eyes did.

"Yes, of course," Daisy continued.

Zenobia approached the two women, "I cannot fix the ship, Daisy."

"There is nothing we can do?" Daisy asked.

"Not without the proper tools. She will sail, but in no particular direction without the wheel."

"Well then we need to think of another way. Surely, we cannot row the lifeboats throughout the entirety of the ocean. There is no land in sight." Daisy looked distressed. "The longer we wait, the further they will get away. And the less likely we will find where Snakehead is taking her."

Zenobia nodded.

***

That evening, the women sat at the dinner table in soft discussion. Their words were filled with apprehension as the ship rocked gently in a directionless way. The loud, gleeful chatter that usually filled the dining hall had vanished. Not even a bottle of rum nor wine sat upon the table. The women used their time to focus on business-like discussion on how to retrieve their captain.

"What can we do? Surely one of us has some experience fixing ships." Daisy started.

"We do not have a carpenter," Tabatha interjected. "Josephine, the previous first mate possessed more carpentry skills than the rest of the crew."

Daisy sighed, feeling a sense of obligation as first mate, yet she was never taught how to use tools. The only tools she was taught to use was a shovel, a broom, and a pot.

"I can do it," a soft, hoarse voice unknown to the crew spoke up from the middle of the table. The women looked up from their food and saw Marisha, who had been silent the entirety of her time there, staring down at her plate of untouched food.

"You know how to repair a ship's wheel?" Zenobia asked.

"Yes," Marisha continued. "When my father was alive in Jamaica, that's what he did. We lived in a fishermen's town. Many merchants or fishermen would find themselves stranded on our island when their ships would break down. My father was a carpenter, mostly mending broken ships. He taught me all he knew."

The women smiled. "I can take you to the tool deck," Sarah stated as she was responsible for obtaining tools when they raided towns and organizing them below deck. When her husband, Benjamin was alive, he was a skillful handyman, and Sarah was able to learn the purpose of different tools, although she never physically did any of the work. She learned how to clean and polish them to ensure they did not rust. That became an important role for her upon the Crimson Rose.

After dinner, Sarah and Marisha excused themselves so they could get started on the wheel. A few women began to clear the table. Daisy took Ella to Willie's sleeping chambers.

"No one goes in here," Daisy explained, "except for the Captain."

Ella smiled.

"I think she would be happy that you could stay here."

The two entered the room. It was much larger than Daisy's. A dozen dried roses rested limply in a golden vase on a table next to the bed. A small bookshelf lined the western wall, compacted with books of all shapes and sizes.

"Wilhelmina reads?" Ella asked.

Daisy shrugged her shoulders, "I did not know."

"I like to read, too," Ella said. "Marisha taught me."

Daisy smiled as she pulled a few books from the library. All the books were of maritime tales, except for one. William Shakespeare's *A Midsummer-night's Dream*. Daisy smiled at the irony. A story of love triangles, similar to what she believed that she, Willie and Nathaniel were in. A written note fell out from the center of the book. Daisy looked at Ella and then opened it. "I think it's from your grandfather. It says: *To my darling daughter. Believe in the power of magic, for it shall set you free.*"

Daisy and Ella sat in silence for a moment. Daisy thought back to the story of Willie's horrific childhood. She was just Ella's age when she was battered and bruised sexually by a ship-full of drunken men, caged like an animal, destined for a life of despair. Yet she turned it around. Had she believed in the concept of magic? Did she turn her life around, living off this notion?

Daisy never believed in magic until she set foot on La Isla De Las Sirenas. Ironically, her death sentence was placed on her for the suspicion that she, herself, was casting magical spells only a witch would know.

"Do you believe in magic?" Daisy asked Ella.

"I don't know," Ella responded.

"Well you should. Believe in it. Magic is real. I have seen it with my very own eyes. It truly does exist."

"Then can we use it to find Wilhelmina?"

"I fear I am not sure how," Daisy responded disappointedly.

"You will," Ella smiled as if she was confident that Daisy was the one to discover a way to find her mother. It was almost as if Ella could sense the special bond that Daisy and Willie had.

Daisy nodded her head and left Ella to sleep, quietly exiting the room and shutting the door behind her.

***

Daisy emerged atop the main deck to supervise the work that was being done.

"How is everything going?" Daisy asked as Marisha was engaged in physical labor while Sarah handed her tools.

"Well," Marisha responded. "The wheel should be repaired within the hour."

Daisy let out a sigh of relief.

When she was finished, Daisy accompanied her to the dining hall for a cup of tea.

"Are you alright?" Daisy asked.

"I am fine," Marisha responded, studying Daisy's face to determine whether she could be trusted. "You know, I always feared this day would come, but my fear eased over the years. That fear returned when I saw Wilhelmina this last time.

"How's that?"

"She had this glow in her eyes, a glow I had never before seen. One that concerned me. I know her life, I know what she does. I live just near the edge of the city of Port Royal and I have seen pirates come and go for years. As a child, I lived with my father in the center of town. It was there where he gained the most business for his work. But when I grew older, and my father passed away, the fear of being so close to pirates forced me to move a bit outside the town. Not directly engaged but close enough to know what was going on. You see, I have always been intrigued by the activities pirates involve themselves with, but never curious enough to involve mine own self."

"Then how, if you don't mind me asking, did you get so involved with Wilhelmina?"

"She was lost. She was vulnerable. A very pregnant fifteen-year-old woman managing a ship all on her own. Could you imagine? She feared getting caught for commandeering the fisherman's ship, and somehow she was given knowledge of Port Royal. She said that someone told her she could go there and hide, that no one would go looking for her there because no sane-minded person would step foot in such a wicked town. And so, she came. And child, I cannot begin to express the amount of fear that raged from her eyes, although the rest of her body remained courageous. She has always been good at hiding her true feelings, but she could never hide them from me. Her eyes told it all."

"I cannot understand how such fear could turn into such courage."

Marisha laughed. "She stayed with me until she went into labor. She left her ship docked alongside other famous pirate ships led by much older, much more experienced captains than she. It was a miracle her ship was not looted or commandeered."

"So, what happened with her daughter?"

"Well, she absolutely refused to hold her baby. Instead, she clutched onto a letter that she read over and over again. The next day, she walked into the kitchen where I was preparing a meal and said to me that she was seeking freedom from this world and that magic would lead her to it. She said that a baby did not belong on that journey."

"And so, she left her daughter with you?"

"Yes. But trust me, Ms. Flynn. It was nothing more than a blessing for me. You see, I had tried and failed to have a baby of my own. My own husband left me because I could not give him a child. I was very much alone. So, I was more than happy to take on the responsibility of a child."

"And what of Wilhelmina?"

"I did not see her for a whole year. When she returned, she brought me a pouch full of gold coins, but she did not want to see her child. For years, she returned in the same way, bringing forth a fortune without any explanation and leaving without mention of her child. I knew she turned her life over to piracy, and I believed that to be the magic she sought out to find. And her words seemed to come true. She was free. She found happiness. And she was protected. Year after year, this young, beautiful female leading a ship full of other vulnerable women was protected by the danger that lurked in the night, in the grand seas, in the world of piracy. How could it be? How could these women withstand so many dangers? Magic. It must be. Wilhelmina is completely protected by magic, and that I believe to be true."

"So why were you concerned this time, when she came in the same manner as always?"

"She asked to see her child, something she had never done before. It was as if she wanted her child to know who she was before it was too late. But because she has always lived with the belief that she is invincible, I knew that she knew in her heart that all the magic in the world couldn't protect her this time."

"Are you afraid of what can happen to her now?"

"I am trying not to live in fear any longer, just praying and hoping for a little more magic to be sent her way."

Daisy smiled at Marisha's words. Then, she walked her over to a small bed that sat in a room with four others.

"This was Maria's bed. She is no longer with us," Daisy said.

Marisha nodded and sat down. The other women were fast asleep and snoring loudly. Then she said to Daisy, "Wilhelmina has never spoken of a fellow pirate by name to me before, at least not until you came along. You are valuable, Ms. Flynn."

"Please, call me Daisy."

"Good night Ms. Daisy."

"Good night Marisha."

With that, Daisy left the room and went back to her sleeping chambers. She lay down on her bed and stared at the ceiling. Her thoughts were racing. She needed to find Willie. The whole crew needed to find her. She was what kept the crew together, what kept the crew strong. She lived her life knowing her value and helped other women find theirs. She found the most tainted, battered, worthless women and turned them into soldiers, goddesses, queens. Wilhelmina was the Crimson Rose. It would not sail without her.

CHAPTER TWENTY-TWO

It wasn't long before Ella came rushing into Daisy's room. "I cannot sleep!" she shouted.

"It's alright, you're just a little frightened."

"I'm not afraid!" Ella shouted adamantly. "When I close my eyes, I see things."

"What kinds of things?" Daisy questioned.

"I'm not quite sure. It's a little hazy, but I can see shadowy figures. It looks as if they are men. I can see them when I close my eyes like they are right in front of me, touching me. It looks as if they are laughing. Then, another man. He is pointing, and the other shadowy men flee. Almost like he is giving orders. He is wearing a captain's hat."

"Surely the image is just stuck in your head. It must have been traumatizing what you went through."

"No, this is different. This is not a dream, or a nightmare, or my imagination. This is real. The image keeps changing as if I am moving through someone else's life, like I am seeing with someone else's eyes."

"Tell me, what do you see now?"

Ella closed her eyes. "The man with the captain's hat is standing in front of me. His lips are moving. He is saying something, but I cannot hear."

Daisy thought a moment, then she placed her hands over Ella's ears and held tight. Ella's eyes flashed open in shock.

"I hear something now. It's muffled though."

"Concentrate," Daisy urged.

Ella closed her eyes again and concentrated. "He's asking for the pendant. Then, a woman's voice is saying she must have left it on the ship. I cannot see any women, though. The man, he sounds angry."

"Is he harming her?"

"No, just scolding it sounds like. What do you think this image is? Who are the voices?"

"It must be Captain White, the man you are seeing. And the woman's voice must be Wilhelmina's. Only, you cannot see her because you are seeing from her eyes," Daisy suggested.

"Oh my goodness! How could this be possible?" Ella questioned in awe.

"Magic." Daisy responded collectedly. "Can you see where they are, where they are headed?"

"No, I can just see the horizon rocking as the ship moves."

"So, they are still sailing. What does he want with this pendant?" Daisy asked, mostly to herself. "We need more information."

Zenobia entered the room and said, "Daisy, we have fixed the ship's wheel. Where shall we go from here?" With Willie gone, as the first mate, Daisy was logically the one in charge. She was the one to make all the decisions, the one to give all the orders. She was acting captain.

Daisy pondered for a while, studying her options. Then she decided, "We must redirect the ship and head to Spain."

"Spain? What for?" Zenobia asked quizzically.

"Do you know the typical whereabouts of Captain Santiago de la Cruz?"

"Yes," Zenobia responded. "But it is not quite in Spain. When he is not at sea, he lives in a lavish, hidden home in the Canary Islands, just off the coast of Africa."

"Then we shall travel there."

"But why?"

"Because he will have answers that will help us determine Wilhelmina's whereabouts."

Zenobia nodded her head and then raced off to inform the rest of the crew. Daisy headed to the bow of the ship and took hold of the wheel where she sailed in the direction of the Canary Islands.

***

When they arrived, Daisy, Zenobia, Marisha, Ella and Tabatha disembarked together and headed into the luscious jungle of the small, tropical island.

"Follow me," Zenobia stated as she led the women behind a tall, narrow waterfall adorning the front of a cave. Within the cave, there was surprisingly a wooden door. Two pirates sat in rocking chairs with a half-drunk bottle of rum that they appeared to be passing amongst one another. When they noticed the approaching intruders, they stood up abruptly and drew their swords. Zenobia, Daisy and Tabatha instinctively drew theirs as well. Marisha held Ella close to her chest behind the other women.

"Who the hell are you?" one disgruntled man asked.

"I am Zenobia of the Crimson Rose. We have come in search of your captain."

The man scrunched his face as if he did not recognize her name or the name of the Crimson Rose. The second man offered an explanation.

"You mean that pirate ship with the lady captain?"

"Yes, that is the one. Now will you kindly take us to him?"

The man seemed to ponder the notion for a moment, looking to the other man for an answer. "He does seem to be fond of the lady. Let me go check." He disappeared into the house, leaving the other man still standing out by the door, still with his sword drawn.

When the man emerged, he stated, "All is well. They may enter."

The man opened the door widely and scrolled his eyes adamantly over each woman as they walked through the door. The women placed their swords back into their sheaths as they attempted a less threatening approach. When they entered, the room was surprisingly large. The natural rocky cave walls were aligned with lanterns that were all lit, allowing the lighting in the makeshift cavern home to be dim yet sufficient. There was a large dining table near the back wall where a few men were seated. The home housed fourteen men, all of whom seemed to be excited rather than concerned by the intrusion.

"Well, well, well. Now what is your name, beautiful?" one apparently drunken man appeared from the kitchen holding a mug full of brown liquid as he approached Daisy. Another man pinched Tabatha on the rear causing her to grab tightly onto her sword in preparation for a possible fight. Daisy touched Tabatha with her hand, attempting to calm her. They did not want to stir up any animosity.

Another two men approached Marisha and Zenobia. "I like the dark ones," one of the more obviously drunken men grumbled. Zenobia looked annoyed and had to stop herself from grabbing him by the throat. Marisha appeared to be mildly nervous as tremors developed in her hands.

"I am Ms. Daisy Flynn. We must speak to your captain at once," Daisy stated boldly.

"You mean, you're not here to have a little fun with us?" the first man asked. The rest of the men laughed.

DAISY AND THE CRIMSON ROSE

"We're not in the market for drunken little boys," Tabatha responded smugly.

Daisy and Zenobia squinted at Tabatha with surprise. Then they smirked at her courageousness.

"Captain de la Cruz, boys. Where is he?" Tabatha continued with more of a directness in her voice.

"Who's asking?" a tall, muscular man appeared from the top of the wooden steps that led into a separate lair. The women stared and admired his looks that were far superior to any of the men in his crew. A closely shaven, dark beard adorned his masculine face, and his olive complexion contrasted nicely against the red vest that he wore over his white blouse.

The women curtsied in respect. "We have come to discuss some business, regarding Captain Willie Spade," Daisy began.

Before allowing her to go any further, he motioned them to follow him up the steps for some privacy away from his crew. In the lair that lay at the top of the cavern, there was a large, wooden desk adorned with feather pens and papers. A dark-skinned man rose from the desk when the women arrived. "Elijah, these women are part of Captain Spade's crew. They come forth with a need for our assistance." Elijah shook hands with each of the women. He seemed to hold a little longer onto Marisha's hand as he gazed admiringly into her eyes. Uncomfortable, she swiftly jerked her hand away.

"So how can I help you?" Santiago began. "Is Wilhelmina in danger?"

"Yes, she may very well be," Daisy replied.

"Has something happened to her on her voyage to La Isla de las Sirenas?" Santiago appeared stricken with grief.

"No, nothing of the sort. Fortunately, we made it to the island and back, just as Wilhelmina proclaimed we would."

Santiago exhaled, seemingly relieved. "So, what exactly is the trouble?"

"She has been taken," Zenobia interjected, "by Captain Snakehead White."

Santiago tensed again. "What does he want from her?"

"He took the treasure that we uncovered on the island, and he seems to want some blue pendant that Wilhelmina took from the temple of Pharoah Mostafan. Do you know what he would want with that pendant or where he might be taking her?"

"The pendant of the blue baboon?" Santiago asked.

"It seems so," Tabatha responded.

"Did she have any other pendants?"

"No, it seems she had just the one," Daisy replied.

"Then, he is going to take her back to the island."

"How can you be so sure?"

"Because she only has one pendant." Santiago shook his head and snickered subtly. "That bull-headed woman. She has many strengths, but her weakness lies in her eagerness to get ahead and her failure to listen to the whole story."

"What are you saying?" Daisy asked. "What story?"

"There are more pendants, am I correct?"

Zenobia's eyes widened. "Yes. The pendants shone brightly and were placed atop separate entrances into the temple. The blue baboon led us to the treasure. There were seven of them."

"A red tiger, a green bear, a yellow snake, a purple elephant, a gold lion, a silver tortoise, and a blue baboon." Santiago said.

"Yes, that is correct," Zenobia muttered.

"But what does he want with them, and what do they do?"

"Ladies, the massive treasure within Pharoah Mostafan's tomb is not what pirates seek to find. It is those stones, the pendants that guide the greed to attempt such a journey. The stones are magical. Legend tells that those pendants were given their power by a combination of Greek and Egyptian curses. They each possess a separate power. However, if just one soul possesses all the pendants together, the results would be detrimental."

"Detrimental?" Daisy asked. "How so?"

"That one soul would become the most powerful person on this land, unable to be stopped by anyone. In the wrong hands, the power of all the stones may lead to the end of our lives as we know it."

"So, what is the power that each stone possesses?" Daisy asked.

"The red tiger is protection. Legend has it that if one possesses that pendant, they cannot be harmed but by only one peril, and that peril is individually tailored to that person's weakness. The green bear is strength. Anyone who possesses that pendant will gain the strength of one thousand men. The purple elephant is wisdom. It almost opens a key to their mind, allowing them to remember and understand any piece of information they had ever learned. The yellow snake is heightened senses. It allows anyone who possesses the pendent to hear, see and smell miles away. The gold lion is for healing and the silver tortoise is for patience. Allowing one to feel no sense of discomfort should waiting become a necessity."

"Wilhelmina has the blue baboon, what power does that possess?" Daisy asked.

"The power of connection. It allows one to connect with anyone whose blood runs in their veins."

Ella, who had been silently listening, gasped. "'Tis why I can see what she sees and hear what she hears."

Santiago looked bewildered as he gazed over at Ella. His eyes widened once he realized the resemblance. Her fiery-red hair, slightly more coiled then Willie's. Her powder-white skin complexion. Her gazing, big green eyes. "You're," he hesitated, "her daughter?"

"It seems that way," Ella giggled.

Santiago was silent. He had never known that the woman he loved had produced a child, and with another man no less. While the notion sickened him to think of his lover with another man, he could not help but be happy. For the blood of the woman he loved ran through the veins of the one standing before him.

"Well then," he continued, "we must do everything in our power to get your mother back."

Ella smiled and hugged Marisha.

"Will you accompany us?" Daisy requested.

"I fear I could not, the Sirens are far too powerful for any man."

"But the Sirens have gone away. We freed them."

"How so?"

"It seems removing one pendent broke the curse of their servitude."

"I see," Santiago continued. "Then we must go together. I will ready my crew at once."

Before they set sail, Daisy returned to the Crimson Rose and instructed the women to stay docked in the port of the Canary Island. Then, she boarded Santiago's ship with the others. After the ship was at sea, the crew invited the five women to dine with them. Their meal was no less then what they were accustomed too. A lavish array of fine meats, succulent vegetables and bottles and bottles of the finest rum. The women, including Ella, had only one glass of rum. They intended to keep their wits about them until they were able to find and free their captain. Marisha did not drink, she believed it to be the drink of the devil. She found comfort in having control and feared what the poisons of alcohol might do to her mind.

While the men continued to attempt to court the beautiful women, they otherwise were not fortunate to meet on a regular basis, they were a bit more respectful at the direction of Captain de la Cruz.

"So, all of you ladies are pirates?" one man questioned.

"I am not," Marisha responded boldly.

Elijah looked up from his food and glanced over at her, a bit surprised, but at the same time relieved.

"We three, are indeed pirates of the seven seas," Zenobia interjected proudly.

"And who's the little one," another man questioned in a drunken state.

"Why must we be so quizzical," Santiago interrupted in an attempt to keep that question unanswered.

"I just don't understand how a woman could be a pirate. Surely she could not possess the strength of a man."

Offended by the bigoted statement, Zenobia reached across the table and grabbed the man by his wrist, squeezing tightly as her large bicep bulged. They watched as his hand turned from a peachy flesh color, to red, to whitish-purple. His face reddening from pain. The man tugged his arm back. Zenobia released him, watching his skin return to the complexion of the rest of his arm.

Santiago laughed, "Are you all finished asking ridiculous questions? We have more important business to attend to."

The men vaguely knew how Santiago lusted after Willie. They did not, however, realize how deep his love ran. They thought him insane for leaving the comfort of their joyous home for none other than a rescue mission. To make matters worse, it was a rescue mission of a woman. But just as most pirates, they obeyed their captain's orders.

After dinner, the women were led to cots they could rest on. Marisha did not rest. Instead, she ascended the steps to the main deck. The black sky ran deep above her, speckled with billions of tiny stars.

She breathed in the salty air, smiling at the wind that brushed gently against her face.

"Beautiful," she heard a man approaching and jumped to face him.

"Pardon?" she asked as she saw Elijah approaching her from behind.

"The night sky, opened upon the sea. Almost as if they run together as one. It is a beautiful sight to see." Elijah smiled.

Marisha stared into the night sky. "Yes, 'tis very beautiful."

"You said you were not a pirate, yet you have arrived with the others?" Elijah questioned.

"I was kidnapped." Marisha stated unmannerly.

"Kidnapped? By those women?" Elijah questioned.

"No, no. I was kidnapped by Captain White and his pirate crew. These women saved me and Ella from their ship, or rather, we were traded for Wilhelmina."

"Captain Spade?" Elijah asked for clarity.

"Yes, Captain Spade."

"Have you ever sailed on a ship?"

"No," Marisha replied. "My father used to work as a carpenter on ships, and I often accompanied him. But we were never fortunate enough to own one. I did have a small boat, but nothing like this."

"Where are you from?"

"Port Royal, Jamaica."

"Oh," Elijah seemed surprised.

"Have you been?"

"Yes of course, you must know it is the home away from home for all pirates."

"Yes, I am aware."

"But I have never seen you there."

"The town tends to be crowded, I only go into town when I need to buy food and supplies. Otherwise, I live in my cottage deep within the jungle."

"You live alone?" Elijah questioned.

"If you are asking, sir, if I am wedded, no I am not."

"How could a beautiful queen such as yourself have no man to call her own?"

"I had a husband, but no longer am I wedded. Finding a new husband has been difficult. I live in a secluded area, as I mentioned. I tend to stay away from the town. The opportunity to find a man who is not a," Marisha hesitated.

"A what? A pirate?" Elijah asked.

"Yes, a pirate. Well, that opportunity is limited."

"And what's wrong with a pirate?"

"Pirates are evil, they are thoughtless, they are cold-hearted. I cannot be with a man who steals from others, harms or even kills another man."

"But what if that other man is evil as well, but in other ways and deserves to have their belongings stolen, or deserves to be harmed?"

Marisha said nothing.

"A pirate can give you the world and be more loyal to you than any man you may ever meet."

Marisha fell silent for a moment. Then responded, "You seem different, not like the rest of those drunken bastards."

Elijah laughed. "I am different, I am the first mate and must conduct myself professionally. Furthermore, I am here for different reasons."

"You mean you are not in the business of piracy for the greed, the maliciousness?" Marisha responded sarcastically.

"I would not call it greed. I take only what I need from people who deserve to lose, and I don't aim to be malicious. If it happens, it is because the world made me so."

"So how did someone like you end up on this pirate ship?"

"I was a slave, for many years. I was taken from my home in Africa and forced to work for the white man. I was stripped of all my belongings and brought to a land I knew not of. Then, I was forced to work. I was beaten, punished if I did not work. My wife was miraculously sent to the same plantation as I, just six months later. Apparently, she was sold elsewhere at the beginning but was resold later to my master. It was like we were destined to be together. Then, one day, I was finally able to speak to her. She told me that the master was raping her, every night. I was beside myself. The anger built up inside of me. So, I tried to kill him. But I failed."

Tears began to form in the corners of Elijah's eyes. "He slit my wife's throat in front of me and made me watch as she bled out, the life draining from her eyes. They locked me up in a shed in the yard and didn't feed me for days. He said his plan was for me to die of heat stroke and starvation, every day re-living the image of my wife's limp body in his arms. He said if he killed me right away, it would be too easy."

"So how did you escape?" Marisha asked.

"One night, there was a thunder storm and lightning struck the shed I was in. I felt a jolt through my veins, but it was more empowering than painful. The shed wall broke open. I crept into the master's sleeping chambers and shot him and his sleeping wife with his very own pistol. So, did I kill a man? Yes, I did. But I ask you to think long and hard. Do you not think he was deserving?" he asked rhetorically.

Marisha sat in silence a moment and then spoke, "How long has it been?"

"Ten years."

"Do you miss her?"

"Every day. But that does not mean I will never let love back into my heart," Elijah smiled subtly.

Marisha peered at him in the eyes, searching for answers. Wondering if she should let this man into her heart. He leaned over. She pulled away. He stopped, watching her, studying her face, waiting for her to come back to him. She thought another moment, then leaned in until their lips met. He caressed her back as he pulled her closer. They remained that way for what seemed like hours, glistening in euphoria under the moonlit sky.

CHAPTER TWENTY-THREE

The sun was high in the sky, no clouds were in sight. The sea was quiet, other than the gentle waves created by the ship itself as it sailed smoothly through the calm, open waters. Daisy stayed by Santiago's side as Elijah was off courting Marisha. She acted in his place. Her leadership skills flourished since joining the Crimson Rose.

Daisy studied Santiago's strong, masculine face. His face looked rough with course, black hair laid upon his jawline. It was not like Nathaniel's. For his face was smooth. His hair was dark and shaggy but somehow was appealing to her. She felt her eyes follow the curves of his shoulders to his large, boulder-like biceps. Again, different from Nathaniel who was slender with smaller muscles lining his arms.

She couldn't help but feel a slight sense of jealousy when watching this man. She thought about how he made love to Willie, how his strong arms caressed her, protected her. She knew she couldn't offer Willie that much sense of security when she held her, for her physical strength was miniscule compared to his. She cringed

247

at the idea of Santiago entering Willie; she knew she would never be able to do that, and it upset her, the idea that she could never give Willie what Santiago could. But then she thought of Nathaniel, and how he entered her. How amazing it felt. How absolutely secure she felt in his arms. And then, quickly, her mind went back onto Willie. Her supple, soft breasts gliding gently across her own. Her feminine hands caressing Daisy's entire body. Her luscious lips attentively kissing every ounce of her skin.

"You have come a long way," Santiago spoke, interrupting her chaotic thoughts.

"How do you mean?" Daisy asked.

"Your demeaner, you are far more outspoken than when we first met."

"So, what is the problem with that?"

"Nothing, nothing at all. You seem stronger, that's a good thing."

Daisy smiled, "I like to think Wilhelmina had something to do with that."

Santiago looked at Daisy, "She is a strong woman, empowering. That's what I love the most about her. You know she has taken each one of these women and empowered them into becoming the most feared women in all the lands?"

Daisy nodded but said nothing. She almost felt as if she was not more important to Willie as the rest of her crew, that they were all equals, including Daisy, in the eyes of the great Captain Willie Spade.

"It was interesting, though. She spoke most about you. I had never heard her speak of another woman as much as she spoke of you. Even her previous first mate. Actually, she loathed her. Had a sense she was conniving but needed to prove it." Santiago peered at Daisy suspiciously to see her response. Daisy did not respond, for she felt Santiago's eyes wandering all over her, attempting to find reason not to like her.

Suddenly, Ella came rushing to the bow of the ship where Santiago was steering the ship's wheel. "Ms. Daisy!" she shouted. "There's something you must know."

"What is happening?"

"They have already made it to an island, it appears. It looks like they are walking upon a sandy beach and straight toward a jungle."

"How many men are with them?" Santiago asked.

"I am not quite sure," Ella responded. "I can only see the back of Captain White's head. It appears she has not yet turned to face who is behind her. Wait! It looks as though he is grabbing her by the neck and turning her around for some reason. I can see now, behind her is," she paused to count the men, "at least a dozen men more."

"Then we must go in with at least a dozen of our men," Santiago proclaimed.

"No, we mustn't," Daisy interjected. "Only seven, we shall gather a crew of seven only."

"That makes no sense."

"The island runs on sevens. Seven Sirens. Seven pendants. Seven bricks it took to open the temple's wall. Seven shrines within the tomb."

"I do not see your point why we cannot have more than seven men?"

"Doyonea, the Siren leader, informed us that any more than seven men is a threat to the island and will be eliminated immediately. Wilhelmina knows that, she is using that to her advantage."

Ella held onto her ears, "Men are screaming."

"What's happening now?" Daisy questioned.

Ella closed her eyes, "Men are sinking, not all but many of them. They are drowning in the mud."

"How many are not drowning?" Santiago asked.

"It's hard to tell, the scene is frantic."

"Let's give it some time," Daisy suggested.

After a few minutes, Ella could see more clearly who was left. "Six men," she reported, "including Captain White."

"And Wilhelmina makes seven," Daisy smirked, satisfied that she was correct. "As I said, we need a crew of seven."

Santiago nodded.

***

A few hours later, the bright sun that was high in the sky suddenly turned gray. Torrential rains were relentless, flooding the ship's top deck. The men that were resting comfortably below deck raced to the top floor of the ship after being knocked off their cots by the angry

250

waves. Bucket after bucket, the men attempted to unflood the ship, just as the women had done when they approached Le Isla de Las Sirenas.

"The weather has changed so suddenly," Santiago said. Then, he began giving orders to change course.

"No! Cease orders!" Daisy demanded. "We are near La Isla, the storm is taking us to it."

Santiago followed Daisy's instructions and ordered his crew not to change course and to stop safeguarding the ship. He allowed the ship to direct their route.

Finally, the ship entered into a new realm, swallowed by pink sunshine. Again, the torrential rains encircled the ship, allowing calmness to remain within. Just as before, La Isla lie just east in the distance, but this time, all was silent. The melodious tunes of the beautiful Sirens were now extinct, forgotten. La Isla was defenseless, allowing all who wanted to enter its majestic home, to do so effortlessly.

Closer to La Isla, the pirate ship of Captain Snakehead White sat calmly atop the vast ocean. Santiago used his telescope to help him see the ship. It was vacant, the whole crew appeared to leave it behind, anchored, while they headed for the island.

"We need to anchor the ship away from the island," Daisy instructed, "the island is surrounded by jagged rocks that will damage it."

Santiago nodded as he ordered his crew to anchor the ship and bring down the lifeboats. He instructed all but three members of his crew to stay behind. Elijah, his first mate, along with two of his strongest men, Francisco and Julio, were instructed to disembark with Santiago. Daisy, Zenobia and Tabatha joined their sub-crew. Before they disembarked, Elijah wrapped his arms around Marisha and promised he would return safely. Marisha dropped a few tears from her eyes before bidding him adieu. Ella stayed behind with Marisha.

As the crew rowed the life boat gently toward the island, they were careful to evade the jagged rocks that lay near to the beach. When they safely arrived, they followed Daisy into the luscious jungle that lay ahead. Daisy led the crew past the cave where they took shelter and past the river where she encountered the ferocious tiger. She led them up to the foot bridge where she had an intimate moment with her beloved Wilhelmina. They stopped at the bridge, peering down as it rocked heavily above the long drop to the white-water river that lay below.

"This is the bridge we must cross?" Santiago questioned.

"Yes, and the temple is just at the other side," Daisy answered.

When they crossed the bridge and walked the short distance to the temple, they realized that the temple was only half constructed. The rest of it, a pile of rubble. Daisy noticed where the entrance had been now had a pathway through the large bricks and wooden planks that fell, blocking its path.

"There is the entrance. It appears they have made a way to enter into it," Daisy suggested.

"Then we shall enter as well," Santiago instructed.

One by one, following Santiago, the crew entered the small opening leading into the temple. A strong, rancid odor emerged from the temple floor where thousands of decaying snakes remained. They covered their noses and continued onward; slowly, quietly, deliberately. When they finally reached the large atrium with various doorways, the pendants remained at the top, labeling the entrance of each room.

"The blue baboon pendant is still intact. How is that possible if Wilhelmina has it?" Daisy questioned.

"I do not believe those are the actual pendants," Santiago responded. "It seems that would be far too easy. The pendants should be guarded."

"We went through the room with the baboons," Zenobia stated. "Captain must have retrieved the pendant from there. The red room, if you remember, had a live tiger within. That tiger must be guarding the pendant, and therefore all the rest of the rooms must have beasts guarding their pendant as well."

"We need to gather the pendants and have them destroyed before one person could obtain them," Santiago instructed.

Daisy peered at Santiago whose greed was far inferior to any other pirate. It was then that she realized that Santiago and his crew were not like the others. They were good. They stole from those who were deserving and only fought if they needed to. Santiago knew what greed could do to a person and therefore he only took what he needed, enough to be able to live comfortably. He did not obsess over extravagance. That was why, she realized, he was so concerned for

Willie when she came requesting the coordinates. He admired her courageousness but despised her greed. But because he still loved her, he gave her the coordinates hoping that once she got the treasure she was looking for, she would be able to settle down with him and live the rest of their lives, alone on a deserted tropical island.

While he understood her desire for fortune and fame, he could not allow her to obtain the most powerful magic known to mankind. He wouldn't allow anyone to be in possession of it. So, he knew that this rescue plan would not be just to free Willie from her captor, but to destroy a powerful magic encrypted with both Egyptian and Greek curses that would redistribute all the power in the world to just one person, ultimately leading to the end of days.

It was then that Daisy realized that she, too, could have what she truly desired. This life of piracy could be different than the tales she heard of as a child. She could still be a pirate but remain good. She knew her goodness had not faded away, she just needed evidence that it was possible to have goodness while living a life of piracy. She saw that in Santiago; her proof.

"We must go back to the snake room. The yellow pendant must have been guarded there by the snakes when they were alive," Zenobia said.

"Let us split up," Francisco recommended. "There are six more rooms we need to enter to search for the pendants. I will go with Zenobia."

"Very well," Santiago replied. "Tabatha, Julio and Elijah will go together, and I will go with Daisy."

The seven of them split up. Zenobia and Francisco headed back toward the snake room from which they came. They searched the room, kicking away at dead snakes that lined the ground, some of them decaying into the temple floor.

"I don't see it anywhere," Francisco declared.

"Snakehead must have gotten to it first. We need to look for the rest of the pendants. Let us go to the room of the green bear."

Francisco nodded and the two of them exited the snake room, swords drawn, deliberately stepping into the main atrium which would lead them through the next door.

Meanwhile. Daisy and Santiago were entering the tiger room. Daisy's breath ceased as she saw human bones scattered along the temple floor. She thought back to how their brave Maria was left behind, face torn off by the vicious tiger that lived in the room. They were quiet, walking on their tip toes as an attempt not to wake the sleeping tiger that was now in the corner of the room. A bright red light radiated from behind him.

Suddenly, the tiger's eyes flew open and he immediately lunged onto Daisy. She pressed her hands into his throat and dug her nails as deeply as she could. The tiger's face dangled over her head, salivating into her face. A musty, hot odor was exhaled from the tiger's mouth. Suddenly, a loud thunder-clap sound emanated from within the room and the tiger was distracted from his current prey. He looked up and saw Santiago standing with a pistol pointed at his head. He climbed off Daisy and lunged at Santiago. Santiago shot his pistol again, but it misfired, and the tiger swiped it out of his hand, leaving a bloody gash on the outside of Santiago's large arm.

The tiger stood on his hind legs with his paws on Santiago's shoulders, he attempted tirelessly to sink his elongated canines into Santiago's face. Santiago was strong, almost as powerful as the tiger, he pushed back. The tiger's back hit the wall, but it did not seem to trouble him. Daisy rose and reached for the pistol. She aimed at the tiger and shot it in the head. The tiger fell to the floor, blood draining from the fresh hole deep within his skull. She ran over to the corner where the tiger was lying and picked up a radiating, red pendant.

"I've got it!" she yelled as she placed it into her satchel, then raced back over to Santiago to tend to his wound. "Let me fix it."

"I'm fine, we need to keep moving."

"You will not be fine if you continue to lose blood. Let me wrap it for you, the pressure will stop the flow of blood from seeping out."

Santiago nodded his head, and Daisy ripped a portion of the bottom of her dress. She then proceeded to dress the wound tightly until the blood flow slowed.

"Now, let's go!" Daisy shouted.

The two of them left the room and headed to the next one. A purple gem was placed elegantly above the doorway. They entered the room. A thick stench hung in the air. They covered their mouths and noses. Inside the room lay a large elephant, drenched in its own blood.

"Smells as if it has been dead for hours," Santiago said.

"You're right, and the pendant is gone. Snakehead must have already gotten to it. We should keep moving. Let's see if the others need help."

They exited the room into the main atrium that was surrounded by doorways. The rest of the crew were there waiting.

"The yellow and the green pendants are gone," Zenobia reported.

"The gold pendant is gone as well," Elijah added, "the lion was already dead when we entered."

"The only one we were able to find was the silver pendent, but we need your help," Tabatha requested.

The rest of the crew followed Tabatha into the silver room where she pointed out the whereabouts of the gem. The tortoise was enormous, filling the majority of the room from wall to wall, floor to ceiling.

"The pendent is underneath," Tabatha pointed out as a silver glow emanated from the belly of the large beast.

The tortoise was timid. He tucked his head and his arms into his shell when they approached.

"We need the men to lift the tortoise. Tabatha, you are the smallest, you need to slip underneath and grab the stone," Daisy instructed.

They all nodded their heads in agreement and the men began to lift. The tortoise removed his head and arms from his shell and began flailing his enormous arms, knocking the men off their feet. Then, Daisy thought a moment. She remembered long ago when a tortoise made its way for a visit in her garden. She remembered stroking the tortoise on the back of its rounded shell as it kept moving about. But when she gently tickled its arms, it pulled them back inside.

"They don't like being tickled," Daisy said. "Try it again."

The men lifted the enormous tortoise off his belly and again, he flailed his arms. Daisy walked over and stroked his right arm, and he pulled it inward gently. Zenobia followed and did the same to his left. He pulled it in as well. The men were able to lift the tortoise enough for Tabatha to crawl underneath. Once the pendant was retrieved, they carefully placed the tortoise back down. He remained inside his shell until everyone had left.

"We only have the red and the silver pendants," Santiago proclaimed as he took the glowing silver stone from Tabatha. "They must have left with the rest of them."

"I don't think so," Daisy responded, "Snakehead is a slithering snake. He has come for everything."

"How do you mean?" Elijah asked.

"We were not able to carry all of Pharoah Mostafan's treasure with us. He must have gone back for it, I'm sure."

"Then let us go to the tomb," Zenobia instructed as she led them down a narrow hallway to a pathway that was created through the bricks that had once fallen and blocked the entrance to the tomb.

They heard voices within. Six men, including Snakehead were scooping buckets of gold and jewels into their satchels. Willie's arms were tied up behind her back.

"After this, we need to go back and get the last two pendants, and of course, you will have to give up your hiding spot for the blue one before I slit your neck from ear to ear," Snakehead threatened as he breathed into Willie's face.

"Do it and you will never get your stone," Willie laughed.

Snakehead smacked her across the cheek. Willie spat blood from the side of her mouth.

From outside the tomb, Santiago and the crew began discussing their approach. When the plan was formed, Daisy quietly snuck into the room and crouched behind a large pile of bricks until she was directly behind the shrines. Then, when the men had their backs to her, she silently walked over to Willie and placed her hand over her mouth. Willie looked back to see who it was and allowed Daisy to cut her lose. She kept her hands hidden behind her back, and Daisy slipped back in her hiding spot behind the pile of bricks.

Suddenly and intentionally, Daisy came out from the other side, kicking a small pebble that alerted the men. They all drew their swords and faced the intruder.

"I have come for our captain," Daisy stated proudly.

Snakehead laughed, "Are you out of your mind, woman? Did you really think you could come in here with demands? You must be more insane then your idiotic whore of a captain."

"Leave the pendants and walk away, Snakehead," Daisy stammered.

"What's with all this disrespect? It's Captain White to you. You and your crew of whores have been disrespecting me far too much. I've had enough of this." Snakehead pulled out his pistol and aimed straight at Daisy's head. A loud thunderclap rang through the room, prompting the rest of Daisy's crew to rush in, swords drawn, and began fighting Snakehead's crew.

Willie fought the tears from pouring out of her eyes, but she could not help it and a few escaped. She struggled to allow herself to look and see the love of her life, likely lying in a pool of blood with a gunshot wound to her head. But to her surprise, Daisy was still erect, encircled by a red aura glowing around her body. The bullet was spinning directly in front of her face. Daisy's eyes were wide as she stared directly into the tip of its silver head. Then, it dropped to the ground.

"You have the red pendant!" Snakehead shouted as he rushed over to retrieve it from Daisy.

With the rest of the crew in direct combat with Snakehead's men, the sound of swords clanging together rang throughout the tomb. Willie chased Snakehead and grabbed him by the arm, pulling him off balance. She then pulled his sword from his sheath and sliced him across the arm. Snakehead turned and looked surprised to see her standing directly in front of him.

"How did you get loose?" He asked rhetorically.

He quickly grabbed his other sword and engaged Willie in direct combat. Willie sliced through his satchel, and the treasure along with the other four pendants fell from his bag. The green, yellow, purple and gold rays shot up and burst into the ceiling. Daisy, still glowing, raced over and collected the remaining stones. She suddenly felt a surge of power rush through her veins. Her senses became more vivid. She rushed over to where Willie was still fighting Snakehead, now glowing in a green aura, and grabbed him by the back. With the immortal strength the green pendant bestowed upon her, she lifted Snakehead above her head and threw him into the wall. He grabbed his side in pain as he stumbled to his feet. He pulled the pistol from his hip and aimed directly at Willie.

"Do not come any closer," he shouted, "or I swear I will shoot your beloved captain."

Just then, Daisy tossed the red stone in the direction of Willie. She caught it with one hand. The red aura left Daisy and encircled Willie's body. Snakehead looked back at Daisy, astounded. She rushed toward Snakehead, without any weapons. The strength building up within her like a loaded cannon. Her body emanating a bright green glow. Snakehead moved his pistol from Willie's direction into that of Daisy's. He pulled the trigger. This time, the bullet did not stop but protruded directly through Daisy's skull. Daisy's legs flew upward as she fell backward and landed on her back, a pool of crimson blood forming around her skull.

Enraged, Willie ran over to Snakehead who was now dumping bullets from his pistol in Willie's direction as quickly as he could reload, the red aura beaming as it slowed and stopped each bullet from entering her aura. He turned to run but Willie shoved her sword directly through the middle of his back and into his beating heart. She pulled it back as she watched Snakehead fall to the ground, clutching his chest as his eyes turned grey.

261

She raced over to Daisy and held her close as she allowed a pool of her own tears to drown Daisy's lifeless body. With the rest of Snakehead's crew now dead or having run away, Santiago was left without a battle and slowly walked over to see the two women seated at the base of a shrine, one very much alive and the other, lifeless. He watched as the love of his life rocked this woman in her arms as she cried like an infant above her, an image he had never seen before, nor even thought possible. A woman so strong, even he thought she was incapable of shedding tears. He watched as she rested her lips upon Daisy's forehead, slowly caressing her soft, honey-golden curls.

Suddenly, a golden glow lifted out of Daisy like she was a goddess. The blood that pooled around her skull moved backward into the bullet hole that was left in her head, and Willie watched as it slowly closed. A gold, shimmering aura projected through her lifeless body. The golden lion pendant engaged as it was healing her. Daisy then fluttered her eye lids until they were opened and staring at the most beautiful woman she had ever seen. Her lungs expanded with a deep, sensational breath, and a smile grew across her face.

Willie wiped the tears from her eyes and whispered, "Daisy?"

Daisy acknowledged her greeting with a whimper. Willie leaned down and kissed her passionately on the lips. Santiago watched the intimate moment in silence. Tabatha and Elijah smiled, lovingly. Zenobia looked toward her feet, allowing the moment to be private. Julio and Francisco watched desirably, salivating like dogs at the seductive scene.

When the moment was over, Willie helped Daisy to her feet and walked back over to the crew to thank them for the bravery and perseverance involved in her rescue. All were seemingly happy to see Willie alive, to see that their mission was worthwhile. All, that is, except for Santiago, who stood with a look of envy and disbelief saturated across his face.

CHAPTER TWENTY-FOUR

Still standing in the room of the temple that hosted the tomb of Pharoah Mostafan, Santiago urged Willie to destroy the stones.

"Are you mad? These stone will change the world," Willie proclaimed.

"Yes, but in what way?" Santiago asked. "These pendants will destroy the world. The maritime world will break out in the most brutal war in all history. No, the treasure, you may keep, but the pendants must go."

"I don't think so, de la Cruz. We have come too far, sacrificed too many to leave without the most important piece of our journey."

"You had no knowledge of their power until you were kidnapped by Snakehead."

"Well, now I know, and there is no way you can strip me of these stones."

"But Wilhelmina," Daisy interjected, "Santiago is right. Who knows what the stones are capable of when put all together in the hands of one person. We have enough, don't let your greed get in the way of your reason."

"Greed," Wilhelmina laughed, "now you call it greed? You are a pirate! You, you and you! All of you, pirates! Start acting like one."

Willie turned her back and started walking slowly out of the temple, still holding onto the red pendant. The blue stone remained uncovered, but everyone was sure that Willie had it. When she reached the doorway, Elijah appeared from outside and placed his sword horizontally across it, blocking Willie's path.

Willie stopped and peered back at Santiago, "Is this a jest? Surely you cannot think you are all going to stop me."

"Wilhelmina," Daisy urged.

"No. No. This is not happening. You all work for me!" Willie yelled as she pointed to Daisy, Zenobia and Tabatha who were all staring at Willie in disbelief. "You all answer to me. I am the captain. I made you. Each of you. You would be nothing without me."

The three women stood in silence, discomfort written across their faces. Then Willie strolled toward the women and spoke condescendingly to each one.

"Tabatha, without me, there is no doubt in my mind that you would have been caught by one of your master's prestigious guards. Is it not true they were trained by the military? They would have found you and when they did, they would have taken you back and destroyed you, every night, over and over just as your master had."

Tabatha gasped at such a disturbing thought.

"And Zenobia. Yes, you are very strong, and very violent. I do not doubt that for one moment. But you had no skills outside of your warrior training. Not knowing how to sail the ship on your own, not knowing where you were or what direction to travel to. You would have died at sea."

Zenobia inhaled and exhaled deeply, holding her sword by her side. Still, however, she remained silent.

"And Daisy." Daisy looked up at Willie, hoping her words for her would not be so harsh. "You were the weakest, most vulnerable woman I have ever met. While your strength and independence has developed nicely, it never would have without me. You allowed men to treat you like the dirt you walk on. You were blind to your own beauty, you didn't know how to take advantage of the gifts that god hath given upon you. Instead, you lay in the mud and let a man ram into you night after night while you cooked and cleaned and took care of his daughters like his whore of a wife. You, out of every woman I have ever met would have amounted to absolutely nothing had it not been for me, molding you into the woman you are now. You did not see it, Daisy, just could not see your worth. I gave you that power. And now, you are going to take this power away from me?"

Santiago shook his head, then spoke as he approached Willie. "Your words are dangerous. Do not think they will not get you killed some day. These women are loyal to you, I am loyal to you. Yes, you are the captain, but that does not mean you will always be right. You must listen to others who may be just as wise as you, who may know some things you don't."

Willie sighed heavily. Daisy approached her and handed her the pendant that bore the purple elephant. "Use it," she demanded.

Willie took hold of the pendant and closed her eyes. Her aura emitted a radiant lavender glow. The power of the elephant gave her wisdom. She saw what the pendants would do, how they would destroy the universe, ultimately leading to her early demise. She saw how her possession of all the stones would lead to her self-destruction. She tried to find another way, searching the depths of her brain. But every alternate version led to her death, and the death of all of those she loved.

She then realized that Santiago was right. They did need to be destroyed, but how? She remained in meditation, her mind filled with knowledge she was pulling from every corner of her brain. Finally, she opened her eyes and blurted out, "Peru. We must go to Peru to destroy the stones."

Santiago had a look of relief flash across his face, "Why Peru? What's there?"

"They need to be destroyed within a volcano."

"A volcano?" Zenobia asked rhetorically.

"Yes, a volcano, along with an animal sacrifice."

"Well then, let's go," Santiago instructed.

***

It wasn't long before they reached the ship. They were greeted by a very relieved Ella and Marisha, as their time surrounded by an army of pirates wasn't what they were accustomed to. Willie hugged Marisha and held her tightly. Then, for the first time, she stood in front of Ella, stroked her long, curly red hair and smiled. Santiago stared, impressed by the resemblance. Willie took Ella by the hand and walked with her to a private area on the ship.

"Look who you have grown to be," Willie said. "You are absolutely beautiful."

Ella smiled, "Just like you," she replied timidly. "You know I could see and hear everything you did. It was like I have been closer to you than I ever have been."

Willie removed the blue pendant from her satchel and held it in front of Ella. "You hold onto it."

When she released the stone to her precious daughter, Willie felt a sudden surge shift within her. Ella watched the pendant glow as she took it into her own hands. She fell silent for a few moments, then asked, "Why did you leave me in the first place?"

Willie sighed, "I was just your age when you came along. I was unwedded. There was no place for a young, unwedded girl with a child in this world. And I was angry. Not at you. Of course not. How could I be? You were beautiful. But I was ashamed. And scared. And angry. So much anger built up inside of me, and I had to do something. Then, I met Marisha. She had been yearning for a child for years but because she was unable to bear children, her husband left her. She was alone, so I gave her a gift. I gave her you. And she gave me freedom."

"So, you were better off without me."

"Yes, but that does not mean I didn't think of you. I thought of you all the time. Life is difficult, my dear. That you will soon learn. Society teaches us that men are stronger than women and that we cannot do everything a man does. But I will tell you for certain, that is very untrue. You can be just as strong, if not stronger, than any man. You can do whatever your heart desires. You can live your life like the princess you are."

Ella sat and thought a moment. "I don't think I could be a pirate, like you."

"That is fine. Be anything you want. Just don't be broken. Don't be weak. Don't be worthless."

***

Days later, the ship finally arrived at Peru. Willie, Santiago, Zenobia, Daisy and Elijah set off by foot toward Huaynaputina, the most active volcano in all the lands. The trek was long and mountainous. They climbed rocks in places where no path was laid until they saw a thick cloud of smoke rising from a mountain in the near distance.

"There is the volcano!" Willie said as she pointed at the smoky rocks in the distance. The crew trekked through the rocky land and snow topped hills for near to an hour before coming to the top of the volcano. They covered their faces with cloth as they arrived at the smoky crater. Elijah dropped the tusked boar he had over his shoulder, limbs tied together by rope. The boar squealed and flailed its arms and legs about as it touched the ground, attempting to be freed.

"The sacrifice must be made first," Willie said.

269

Elijah picked the boar back up and threw it into the pit of fire. Molten rock smothered the hog as it disappeared into the orange flow of the burning rocks.

"Now, for the stones," Willie continued as she tossed the red one in, which blended seamlessly with the raging redness in the pit. She then dropped the purple one in after it. They watched as the radiating lavender color quickly disappeared. Daisy went second and tossed in the green, gold and yellow stones. Santiago tossed in the silver one and watched its metallic shine dissipate within the golden flow of the molten rocks.

"What about the blue stone?" Santiago asked.

"I tossed it with the lavender one," Willie declared.

"I didn't see it."

"It must have blended with the purple, you know how similar those colors were. What's wrong, Santiago? Do you not trust me?"

"No, as a matter of fact I do not. It would not be the first secret you hid," Santiago scolded as he subtly peered at Daisy, then quickly back at Willie."

"Fine, search me if you must."

Santiago approached Willie and searched her belongings. Daisy watched in anticipation as he slowly caressed her arms, to her abdomen, to her breasts, then down between her thighs. She wanted so badly to tell him to stop but she remained still, quiet.

"Satisfied?" Willie asked when nothing was uncovered.

"Yes."

"Very well then, let's head back to the ship."

The crew headed back to the ship in silence. All the while, Willie smiled, knowing she would forever be connected to her daughter, no matter where her journey would take her.

CHAPTER TWENTY-FIVE

Back at the ship, Santiago requested Willie to accompany him in his sleeping quarters. When she entered the room, he fell silent and stared at her lustfully.

"So, you retrieved the treasure, just as you wanted," Santiago began. "Now what?"

"How do you mean?"

"Don't think I forgot the night I gave you the coordinates. We spoke of what would happen after, what would happen with us."

Willie stayed silent.

"Or has something changed?" Santiago continued.

"Nothing has changed, but I cannot leave this life. I cannot abandon my women. They need me."

"Do they? Or do you need them? Or, one of them, rather."

"One of them?

"Do you think me an imbecile? Do you think I am a blind man? I can see the love between you and Ms. Flynn."

"What are you saying, Santiago? If I have her then I cannot have you?"

"Of course not."

"But why?"

"Because love should be shared between one man and one woman. You and I and no one else."

"Who says that's how it should be?"

"The world, Wilhelmina. That's how it works in the world in which you live."

"Well, I'm sorry for you that you live in this world with such rules. But I don't live in that world. I am a pirate, you are a pirate, these rules do not exist for us. We can do whatever we desire, take whatever we want, love whoever we lust for. How can you not see that is the way of the maritime world? There are no rules. Half the time, we are lost at sea: a vast, underexplored, mysterious world that keeps all sin hidden. It quiets screams and darkens what should be seen by the day. But you wouldn't know this. No. You claim to be the captain of this infamous Spaniard pirate ship, yet you are no pirate. Santiago, you are kind. You live by good morals. You take only what you need and only from people who are bad. That's not what a pirate does. We act with no good morals, no conscious thought that what we do might be evil. Because there is no good or evil in our world. There is just piracy. We take it to mean whatever we want. We do not obey the law of the common world. We obey the law of the sea."

Santiago was silent for a moment, then spoke, "Wilhelmina, I know that you have been hurt in the past. Deep down, you know you want to find love, but you will not allow me to love you. What is it that you need? Do you need more time? I will give you that. But I will only wait for so long. I cannot wait for you forever."

"Then if that is how you feel, you must move on. Santiago, this is my life. I am a pirate. I chose this life. I gave up love when I sold my soul to the god of the sea."

"Why must you choose to dwell on this idea that there can be no love if you are a pirate? There can be no good if you are a pirate? You said it yourself, there are no rules in piracy. You can do as you choose. If you choose to have love, you can have that also."

Willie turned to face the door to leave. Santiago grabbed her by the arm and pulled her in toward him, her backside against his groin. He began kissing her neck, and she felt her body surrender. She felt his erection grow into the cheeks of her buttocks. She felt weak at the knees. He held her up and spun her around, tipping her backward, supporting her with his forearm as her neck lengthened. He started moving his kisses down her neck and onto the top of her bosoms. She groaned loudly. He untied her corset from the back and placed her gently down on his bed. He grabbed her by the hair as he tugged gently, watching the desire rage in her eyes. He pulled the corset away to expose her large breasts and pulled her trousers to the floor. He climbed on top of her, his own trousers down, but leaving his blouse intact. She grabbed at his shirt as he entered her; her warm, moist insides engulfing his manhood. He thrusted his hips like the gentle current of the ocean into hers, holding her tightly with his arm underneath her waist. She licked her lips to taste the salty flavor of

Santiago's perspiration that dripped from his forehead and bit down just before an orgasmic explosion caused her mouth to open wide and let out a sensual moan. The increased wetness and contractions around his manhood caused Santiago to soon scream out in ecstasy and drop to his belly on top of Willie. She lay, defeated, with her arms to the side as Santiago stroked her hair, his shaft still inside her, slowly deflating in repetitious throbs.

***

When she left the room, Daisy was hidden behind a wall, watching, angry and green with envy. She tried to fight her feelings but was unable to and followed Willie to the top deck where she stood at the stern of the ship under the starry night, her fiery-red hair flowing gently in the wind. She was holding a small bottle filled with brown liquid that sloshed around as the ship rocked. When Daisy approached, she frightened Willie as she was deep in thought, lost to the world.

She stared at Willie, wanting to reach out and touch her but feeling as though the moment wasn't right. She studied her face, tried to find answers in her eyes. She wanted so badly to ask what she was doing in Santiago's room, but she didn't. She wanted so badly to ask why she was with Santiago and not with her. But she didn't ask that either. Instead, she decided it was best to just live in the moment and discuss the future.

"So, what's next?" Daisy asked.

"How do you mean?" Willie asked, already shaken up by the sensual time she just had with Santiago, not in the mood for more uncomfortable conversation.

"Where are we off to? What is our next adventure in the crazy life we live?"

"We can do whatever we want. We can go wherever we want. We have more than enough loot to last us a lifetime." She paused and thought a moment. "Where would you like to go?"

Daisy hesitated. She knew there was one place she wanted to go. She had business she needed to tend to. A man that she was starting to miss now that she felt Willie was fading away from her at the hands of Santiago. "I want to go to Yorkston."

Willie was taken aback. "You want to go back to the place you came from? The place where you had nothing but a non-deserving pseudo-family to take care of?"

"Right. I still need to take care of that family, but in a different way."

Willie smiled, "And how is that?"

"I need to give them what they deserve."

Willie did not dig deeper. That was Daisy's business. She needed to do what she felt she had to. She could only offer some advice. "The man who killed my father, he's still out there." She took a swig of her rum. "I felt that I sent a strong message by brutally murdering his entire crew of fishermen. But not a day goes by that I don't think how badly I want him to be dead."

"So why don't you go after him, I'm sure you are fully capable."

"Because it just doesn't seem like punishment enough, allowing him to quickly be put into the dark. No. He needs to suffer. For what he did." Willie took another swig of her rum and then offered the bottle to Daisy. "But to each his own."

Daisy took the bottle and pressed it against her lips. She felt the warm, brown liquid slide down her throat, a feeling she had begun to grow accustomed to. She smiled then said, "I still would like to go to Yorkston."

Willie took the bottle back from Daisy and replied, "Then it is off to Yorkston we go."

CHAPTER TWENTY-SIX

Willie reclaimed the Crimson Rose that was docked at the Canary Islands and sailed toward Virginia at Daisy's request. It was winter time. The mild temperature in the Canary Islands was now dissipating as they approached Virginia. The blue skies slowly faded to gray as they headed northwest across the Atlantic. Birds were scarce as the weather shifted from mild to harsh across the open ocean.

When they docked at the sea port in Yorkston, Daisy stood at the bow, taking it all in. Her home. Her prior life. All her past that she hoped had simply vanished, was now back in plain sight. But her past, she decided, would not depict her future. One year of life as a pirate. One year of life on the sea. One year, a changed woman.

Daisy remembered the days when she was silenced. Silenced by society for being a woman. Silenced by Helen. And silenced by Mr. Abner Clark with his rough, filthy hand. She quivered at the thought of Mr. Clark and his heaviness upon her fragile, adolescent body. She was sickened by the thought of the stench in his breath of ale and rotting teeth as he breathed deeply into her child-like face. The mere images haunted her existence, and she wanted it to end.

Nightfall was among the Crimson Rose as it docked in the sea port cast in dark shadows of the night. Willie and Zenobia accompanied Daisy at the bow of the ship, as they knew this excursion was for her.

"Second thoughts, Ms. Flynn?" Willie offered.

Daisy flinched at the sound of her surname. She hated when Willie called her that, as that was the name she used when they first met and knew nothing of one another. She felt their relationship was far too evolved for the salutations to be formal at that point.

"No," Daisy responded, "nothing has changed. This is what needs to be done."

Zenobia, always ready for a good fight, nodded. "Then we will be with you as long as you need us."

"But this is my fight," Daisy protested, "You need not accompany me if you wish not to."

Willie laughed, "Have you learned nothing in this year with us?"

Zenobia interjected, "You must now know that this is the way of the sisterhood of the Crimson Rose."

Willie began reciting the chant she had created when the first few women she recruited joined her crew. "We are sisters upon this ship."

Zenobia and Daisy joined in.

"Drink of the devil upon our lips

279

For hell on earth has brought us home

To our righteous place in which we roam

The seven seas in all its might

Should evil call, then we will fight

To secure the safety of one, of all

For hell shall rage if one should fall

And so, we live in this glorious tale

In dangerous waters, once we set sail

To stand strong and feared as the story goes

Aboard the ship of the Crimson Rose."

The women looked at one another and held hands in a circle. "You are one of us, Daisy," Willie said. "You transitioned from a weak, silenced, scorned woman who did not understand her true beauty to one who is strong, fierce and unrelenting. You have found your true beauty. You have found your worth. You have found your strength. And you will never let anyone take your voice away again."

Daisy nodded in agreement.

"This is your chance for revenge," Zenobia added. "You spent your life fearing a man who truly had no power over you, had you not given it to him. You need to take back your power, prove your strength, your worth, yourself."

Daisy inhaled deeply and let it out slowly. "I'm ready," she proclaimed.

As the three women disembarked the ship, walking into the Virginia night, Daisy dwelled in the familiarity of the land. A frosty white snow dusted the ground, contrasting against the darkness that lurked in the sky. Daisy watched her breath form ghostly swirls in the cold, dark air.

The women commandeered three horses that were resting peacefully near a small cottage. They traveled up the dirt roads surrounding the great forest that Daisy had travelled through in her initial attempt to escape. As her horse galloped upon the open road, Daisy felt strong. She no longer needed to hide as she had done before, racing through the brush of the forest, trying to camouflage herself from anyone trying to capture her. No. This time was different. She was strong. She was brave. She was feared.

She led them to the edge of the road where she used to reside. They climbed off their horses and traveled the rest of the way by foot. They stopped at her old home, where she had once lived with her mother and father. Daisy walked up to the door and opened it. Willie and Zenobia stood outside the doorway as Daisy peered inside. A coldness rushed through her veins. She tried to picture her mother, but she couldn't. She feared the memories were disappearing. Or was the guilt of who she had become gotten so great that she could not allow her thoughts to taint her mother's resting soul?

But then, she thought a little longer. She was wrong. Yes, she had become a pirate, but that did not mean she had lost who she was. Her mother taught her to be kind and to be loyal and to love. And that hadn't changed. She was kind to those who were kind to her, she was loyal to her sisters, and she loved, hard. Her mother wanted her to be strong and to be brave, and those qualities were those that she did not have before, not until she met Willie. Her strength grew, and her bravery flourished once she joined the sisterhood of the Crimson Rose. Her mother would understand that. She should understand that. Daisy's life, after her mother had passed away, was unlivable. Yes, since then she had done some horrible things, had some horrible thoughts. But she was still a good person.

Daisy struggled with this concept. The concept of being good versus bad. The notion of holding onto her goodness while living the life of a pirate. She desired both, yet she constantly fought with her conscience over what was right and what was wrong. Nevertheless, revenge was a high priority on her mind, and she felt she could not rest until she accomplished what she came to do.

She stepped out of the old, wooden home that was now vacant and led the women next door to the Clark family home. She quivered at the sight of the small, white-paneled, two-story home where she had spent her adolescent years as a maid, living in constant fear of "being punished" by a man who claimed to be helping her.

She inhaled deeply, gathering courage. She could not smell the sweet aromas of her vast garden as the frigid air had put them all to rest. She walked to the house.

"Wait out here," Daisy whispered.

"But surely you will need some help?" Zenobia protested.

"I will need your help when it comes to Mr. Clark, but he is not inside, I can assure you of that."

Zenobia and Willie nodded as Daisy quietly opened the unlocked door and peered inside. The house was lit up and being warmed by the fire within their stove. Daisy could see sheets of dust spread across all the shelves and furniture in the home, as if her leaving truly impacted the cleanliness of their life. She crept up the old, wooden staircase to the second level of the house. She steadied herself as the floor creaked. She did not want to wake the girls.

When she entered her old bedroom, she saw Elizabeth sleeping peacefully in her bed. A precious smile rested upon her face between the chubbiness of her cheeks. She cuddled gracefully with the blankets that draped over her body. She looked like a large pumpkin in the center of the bed. Helen, on the other hand, seemed to disappear under the covers with her long, lanky body. Her face looked older, even though it had only been one year. She looked over at her bed. It was still there. Empty. Not even a pillow or a blanket decorated it. She sighed in reminiscence of all the nights she lay awake, fearing the moment Mr. Clark came stumbling into the room.

She walked over to Elizabeth and stood smiling above her face. She pulled a golden necklace adorned with emeralds, rubies and diamonds from her satchel and placed it in Elizabeth's opened hand. Elizabeth groaned and clenched the necklace in her hand. She remained asleep as she turned over. Daisy silently walked out of the room and back down the stairs.

Outside, Willie and Zenobia were patiently waiting in the icy Virginia air.

"'Tis time," Daisy proclaimed as she led the women toward the courtyard. The same courtyard that day after day, as just a young child, she was dragged through the mud, thrown on the ground, and violently sexually assaulted by a man who had been trusted to act as her father. Just as she suspected, Mr. Clark was sleeping on a pile of hay that lined the ground of the barn. A lantern with a lit candle sat on a table nearby, flickering quickly as it was reaching its end. Daisy nodded at the two women. Zenobia stood at Mr. Clark's head while Willie stood at his feet. He was lying on his back, arms and legs sprawled out.

Daisy stood for a moment, studying his face. Remembering how close it came to hers, his disheveled beard invading her face and neck as he thrusted the heaviness of his weight back and forth on top of her fragile body. Her breathing became heavier as the rage built up inside of her.

When her breathing steadied, she forced herself to speak, "Abner, wake up you pathetic drunk." The harshness in her voice stung.

Mr. Clark's eyes twitched open and when they fell upon Daisy's face, he jumped into a sitting position, only to be overwhelmed by the hands of a stronger person pressing down on his shoulders. He blinked a few times to make sense of the situation. He saw three beautiful women with swords standing above him, his dream and his nightmare all at the same time.

"How, how? What? You're not, you can't be real!" Mr. Clark stuttered in pure bewilderment. "You are supposed to be dead. You were hanged!"

"Was I?" Daisy asked in a demeaning tone.

"Yes, your death was confirmed by the governor himself, after the men came. Those men came and killed the executioner. Then, you were hanged, that's what the governor said."

"Did he?" Daisy laughed.

"Witch!"

"If only I were a witch, this might be far easier for you!" Daisy laughed.

"What are you going to do to me?" Mr. Clark gulped.

"What do you think I'm going to do to you?"

"Are you going to kill me?"

"Now why would I do such a thing."

Mr. Clark gulped again. Now he was confused, fearful. He didn't want to answer, afraid he might say the wrong thing.

"Because," he stuttered, "because I turned you in."

"Turned me in?"

"Yes, I, I, I turned you in for being a witch."

"But was I a witch? How could I be a witch? Do you think a witch would stay in your home, cook and clean for you, be your sex slave for thirteen years?"

"No, but you must be, you survived being hanged."

Daisy laughed once again. "But I am not a witch."

Mr. Clark relaxed, almost relieved to hear that she wasn't a witch.

"I am a pirate," Daisy whispered in Mr. Clarks ear.

Mr. Clark's eyes grew wide. He opened his mouth and tried to scream but Zenobia stuffed a rag inside. She flipped him over onto his stomach, pushing on his back to hold him down while Willie held down his legs. He squirmed and tried to flail his arms, screaming through the rag in his mouth. Daisy got down on her knees and whispered in his ear, "what is the matter? Are you trying to scream? Do you remember when you put your rough, filthy hand over my mouth? I could not scream either."

With that, Daisy rose to her feet and pulled a dagger from her side. She cut Mr. Clark's trousers from the back and ripped them until his large, hairy behind was exposed to the frigid air. She grabbed a nearby broom and sighed deeply as she fought her conscience. The good in her wanted to let it go. But the revenge, it was far too overwhelming, and she was unable to live with it.

She knelt down by his flailing side and shoved the end of the broomstick deep inside his rectum. She heard him squeal through the rag that burrowed into his mouth. She pulled it out and continued this repetitive motion, in and out, in an out, watching blood leak from between his cheeks and drip down his legs. She stopped, shortly after, convinced he had enough. She threw the broom on the ground and instructed Willie and Zenobia to turn him over.

They let go when he was on his back. He lay helplessly, tearful and begging as the three women stood, swords drawn above his body.

"I am so sorry," he pouted. "Please don't kill me. Please, please."

Daisy hesitated, listening to his pleads. She looked at Zenobia, ready for anything, the numb rage constantly flowing through her veins. She looked at Willie, her face was solemn, she offered no advise in her expression. This was up to Daisy, this was her decision. Her revenge. Her tragic beginning. Her ending. Daisy thought back to her conversation with Willie on the ship. The fact that death might be an easy way out. No. She did not want that for Mr. Clark. She wanted him to remember this, forever. She wanted him to live with feelings of betrayal, worthlessness, weakness. She wanted him to fear her, just as she feared him for years and years. She wanted him to remember, just as she had. The tragic events to be burned into his brain, just as it had for her. He needed to remember.

Daisy put her sword back in its sheath that rested at her hip and without saying a word, walked out of the barn and into the dark night. Willie and Zenobia followed, replacing their swords and stepping over Mr. Clark's pathetic body as he lay bottomless in the blood-saturated hay on the cool ground of the Clark family barn.

CHAPTER TWENTY-SEVEN

The women returned to the ship to sleep the rest of the night. Daisy did not sleep. She was conflicted with so many emotions. When the sun crept over the horizon offering slight relief to the frigid air of the night, Daisy quietly disembarked the ship and headed alone through the market square of the town. Her bravery still at its peak, she took the horse and rode through the town, wondering if anyone would recognize her. Wondering if anyone would remember her as the witch that, one year ago, they all stood below the lynching stage, chanting and celebrating the event of her hanging. But no one recognized her. She received nothing but admiring looks as she passed proudly through their town.

She rode until she came to the enormous brick house surrounded by a wrought-iron gate. Two guards stood with rifles. When Daisy approached, they put their rifles into position.

"Good day, madam," one of the guards began. "How may we help you?"

"I am here to see the governor's son."

The men looked baffled at one another.

"I am sorry, Miss, the governor does not have a son."

Alarmed, with nothing but horrid thoughts racing through her mind, Daisy contemplated what could had happened to Nathaniel. Did his father have him killed after their incident? Did he simply leave the town?

"Well, what has happened to Sir Nathaniel Alexander?" Daisy asked more directly.

Again, baffled looks sprawled across the faces of the men. "Why, Sir Nathaniel Alexander is the governor himself; he has no son."

Daisy sighed in relief. "What happened to the previous governor? His father?"

"I'm sorry to report he passed away nearly six months ago. What business do you have with the governor?" he questioned.

"Please, just inform him that Miss Daisy Flynn is here to see him."

The guards looked as if the name sounded familiar, as if they were deep in thought, trying to pull a memory through. Daisy was concerned that they would remember who she was, but she sat bravely atop her beautiful, white horse.

"I will go see if he is available," the other guard left his post and entered the home.

Soon after, Nathaniel appeared breathlessly at the door. He raced down the long gravel path from his home to the gate as he yelled wildly at the other guard, "Let her in!"

No sooner had the guard opened the gate that Daisy leapt off her horse and ran toward Nathaniel to be welcomed into his arms. He grabbed her by the back of her head, his fingers interlacing into her long, flowing, honey-golden locks as he pressed his lips tightly against hers, inhaling her sweetness. Her cold skin warming against his as he engulfed her into him. She surrendered. Everything about her surrendered. Her body, her heart, her soul.

"You are alive!" he yelled astonished, laughing gleefully. "And you are more beautiful than I can remember!"

The guards stood patiently, waiting for an explanation, but he offered none. Instead, he ordered the men to tie up her horse as he guided her into his home. Nathaniel brought Daisy into his den and instructed her to sit down in a large armchair that sat comfortably next to a fire burning in the hearth.

Nathaniel knelt below Daisy and placed his head in her lap. She stroked his soft, blonde hair, allowing a salty tear to drop onto his scalp. "This is unbelievable. I am so pleased to know that you are alive. My father informed me that you had been hanged."

"So I've heard," Daisy responded.

"Tell me, what happened?"

"Well," Daisy began, "you saved me."

"How did I save you? You never made it to the sea port. Your execution was scheduled."

"That ship you sent me, they came."

Nathaniel smiled, "And you have been with them ever since?"

"Yes," Daisy hesitated. "I'm different now, Nathaniel, not as I was before."

"Yes," Nathaniel winked, "she has a way of doing that to women. But is your love for me different?"

"Absolutely not!" Daisy confirmed. "I have missed you more than you could know!"

Nathaniel looked at Daisy, happy to hear that. He placed his hands on her soft, porcelain-like face and stared deeply into her chocolate-colored eyes. "You are so beautiful," he stated again. And with that, he kissed her more passionately than before. "I never want you to leave me again."

Daisy was silent, again, conflicted.

"I've done something, something bad. If you knew, I don't think you could forgive me."

Nathaniel stood and sat in the chair across from her. He took her by the hand. "What? What is it?"

"I did something to Mr. Clark."

"Did you kill him?"

"No, but I hurt him, badly."

Nathaniel looked at Daisy in disbelief, uncertain at how such a delicate, beautiful flower such as herself could inflict pain upon anyone. But he knew Wilhelmina, and he knew it might be true.

He thought back to the previous year when Mr. Clark divulged Daisy's whereabouts. How his father, accompanied by two constables, invaded the privacy of his sleeping quarters to search for the woman he loved who was alleged by Mr. Clark to be a witch. He remembered the lies, the deceit. And he didn't care. He also knew that Mr. Clark wouldn't report the incident knowing that Nathaniel was now in charge, and his father was gone.

"We will overcome that, Daisy. What is important is that you are back here, with me."

Again, Daisy was silent. She just smiled daintily as he admired her beauty.

"What about you?" Daisy finally spoke. "You are the governor now?"

"Yes, it happened six months ago after the passing of my father."

"I'm very sorry to hear about that."

"It's fine. Our relationship shifted after I met you. He was convinced that you were a witch, and he was disappointed that my love for you would not fade."

"But do you think I am a witch?"

"Not at all. I never thought such a thing."

Daisy smiled.

That night, Daisy gave herself unto Nathaniel. She lay by his side, conflicted with her new life. Never had she dealt with such feelings or needed to make decisions so important. But at that moment, she felt that she needed to be with Nathaniel. She chose to stay with him. She chose not to inform Willie of her whereabouts. She did not let her know she was safe. Instead, she lay lovingly next to Nathaniel as he warmed her naked body with his, draping her body with sensual kisses throughout the entirety of the night.

The next morning, an urgent rapping came at the door. Daisy stood in the doorway to the upstairs bedroom as she watched Nathaniel open the front door to the home. She heard the guard whispering, informing him that there was yet another woman at the gate. Daisy disappeared from the doorway as she heard Nathaniel agree to let her in.

Willie stood in the openness of the grand entrance to the home. The ceiling was high, adorned with a large, crystal chandelier. When they spoke, the echoes traveled through the air and into the bedroom where Daisy stood.

"Wilhelmina, what a pleasant surprise!"

"Is it?" Willie responded sarcastically.

"Well, I had an inkling you would come."

Willie smiled tensely. Then, Nathaniel continued, "I wanted to thank you for rescuing Daisy. She means the world to me."

"I'm sure she does. Where is she?"

"What do you mean? She has been gone for a year, surely you don't think she is going back with you."

"Oh, but she must. She is a pirate now. There is no place for someone like her here."

"Wilhelmina, I know what you do for these women, I know how you help them. But I also know how you change them, make them into something they are not. But Daisy, she's different. I understand she has done some things that may be unspeakable, but she has a good heart, I can see that."

"Yes, she does have a good heart, but that heart now belongs to the sea."

"You're not taking her, and don't even think of threatening her, because I am the law now. There is no way I will allow you to touch her. I will protect her no matter what."

"So, your plan is to force her to stay here with you? That would be taking away her freedom, the very freedom I have opened her eyes too. I'm sure she would not appreciate that very much."

"No, that would not be my intention at all."

"Then let her make the decision. Let her decide if she wants to stay here with you, or come back to sea with me."

"Fine," Nathanial agreed.

Nathaniel instructed his servant to prepare lunch and set the table for three. When everything was ready, the two women sat adjacent to Nathaniel.

"Daisy," Willie began, "you have to decide what you are going to do. You cannot live two lives. Either you are a pirate; a strong, brave, liberated woman joined by a sisterhood that will always protect you, provide you with adventure and happiness, or you will be the wife of a governor in this simple life that will imprison your soul."

Nathaniel rolled his eyes and looked over at Willie, "Don't make it sound like that. Daisy, you know you will never be a prisoner with me. I love you, with all my heart, and I would never be disloyal to you or threaten you with a lack of freedom."

Daisy watched, amused, at the two defending their points, trying desperately to get Daisy to make a life-changing decision.

"I have to think about it," Daisy said simply as she stood and excused herself from the table.

***

Daisy contemplated long and hard about her decision. She wondered for so long what it would be like to be back in Nathaniel's arms. How she yearned for his warm, tender, manly touch. The comfort in having a man that would always protect her, a man that loved her the way a woman never could. While she truly appreciated everything that Willie had done for her; the rescue, the freedom, the empowerment, the loving, sensual bliss, she was angered by her being with Santiago. She knew that she could never compete with the love of a man. For she, too, was able to feel that, with Nathaniel. The love of a man and a woman would be stronger than any other bond. If she went back with Willie, surely she would lose that feeling, that companionship she desired.

That evening, when Daisy finally emerged, Willie and Nathaniel both stood from the dining room table.

"Wilhelmina," Daisy began, "you have encouraged me to be strong and brave. You shined a light on my true beauty, allowing me to see what I always should have seen before. You empowered me to be independent, be my own woman, be free. So as a free, empowered woman, I must decline the offer to continue to live a life of piracy. I want to be free, but I believe I could be free and happy here with Nathaniel, even more so than living on the Crimson Rose. You see,

295

day after day, I am faced with danger and fear, and while yes, I feel protected and supported by you and all the other women, I would not have to live in the fear on the unknown if I choose to be here with Nathaniel."

Nathaniel smiled, feeling as if he had won. But he said nothing, allowing the women to have their moment.

"I understand," Willie said, "but if you ever change your mind, we will be waiting."

Daisy hugged Willie and kissed her on the cheek. Willie took off her hat and tipped it in Nathaniel's direction. Daisy and Nathaniel stood, hand in hand, at the doorway to his enormous, brick abode as they watched Willie gallop away on her black horse, disappearing through the draping trees on the long dirt road toward the sea.

CHAPTER TWENTY-EIGHT

Daisy waited anxiously, wondering if a constable would come to the door and try to take her away for what she did to Mr. Clark. Wondering if he gained enough courage to report her actions. And what if he did? Could Nathaniel truly protect her? He did protect her before, she thought, but only indirectly. He did not actually remove her from harm's way, Willie did. She pondered the thought a moment. Then she reconsidered. It was merely his father who had all the power to make it happen that interfered with Nathaniel's ability to protect her. Nathaniel had all the power now. Surely, he could use it to protect her.

She paced the hallway to the large, brick home. Nathaniel was working in his den. She admired all the paintings that lined the walls of the home. Most of them large portraits of war generals and previous governors. All white men wearing large, white wigs that adorned the tops of their skulls, curls draping at their necks. She stopped pacing and studied the portraits closer. All the men had distinguished faces, like Nathaniel's. Clean. Neat. None of them were scruffy, masculine, like Santiago's face. All the men in the portraits were slender, charming. Not strong, muscular, masculine. They looked as though they lacked adventure. Nathaniel looked as though he lacked adventure.

But she loved Nathaniel, she felt it deep down to her core. The first man to truly look at her. The first man to take her away from her reality and allow her to see that there was more to life than what she knew to be.

She was content, in her previous life. Never knowing that there was more. Never knowing that life existed outside of Yorkston, Virginia, outside of the Clark home. She lived in fear, day to day, wondering if she would ever be "punished" by Mr. Clark again. And that fear caused her silence. It created a woman that was weak, subordinate. But nevertheless, she was content. It wasn't until she met Nathaniel who showed her that there could be more to life than simply living in obedience. He believed in her. He showed her the way.

But Wilhelmina, Daisy thought, it was truly Wilhelmina who molded her into a new woman, nay, the woman she was meant to become. Daisy pondered the thought, she always had it in her to become this new, strong woman, just didn't know the way to get there. Wilhelmina was the one who truly showed her that way.

Daisy wandered into Nathaniel's den where he was working diligently. He placed his fountain pen down atop various papers that were scattered about his desk and stared lovingly at Daisy, unable to take his eyes off her. "You truly are the most beautiful woman I have ever seen."

Daisy said nothing in response. "What will my life be like here, with you?"

"Well," Nathaniel began, "I would like nothing more than to make you my wife. Then, your only job would be to care for the children."

"The children?" she asked unsurely.

"Why yes, of course. I would like to have three children, myself. My father always wanted to have three children, but my mother died during childbirth, and my father never remarried. Therefore, I lived a life as an only child, just my father and me. It was rather lonely. I would have enjoyed the company of siblings." He looked up at Daisy who now appeared to be searching her thoughts. "But don't worry, dear. You wouldn't have to do too much work, we have servants that would cook and clean and do all the things that nasty man used to make you do. You are far too beautiful to lift a hand to do any of that house work anyway."

Daisy considered the words carefully. It sounded like, again, she would not be free. "So, I would be stuck here?" she asked deliberately.

Nathaniel laughed, "Of course not. You can come and go as you please. There will be plenty of time for you to go to the market to make purchases and babble with your friends."

"What friends?" Daisy remembered that the only friends she had ever made were the women on the Crimson Rose. "I do not have any friends here."

"Well, you will make some."

"How?"

"I host galas here all the time. In fact, I am having one tonight, to announce our engagement."

"Engagement?"

"But of course."

"But I didn't hear a proposal."

Nathaniel shook his head smugly, "My apologies. Where are my manners?" He stood up from his desk and walked over in front of Daisy. He got down on one knee and took her soft hand into his. "Daisy, my love. Will you make me the happiest man in the world and be my wife?"

Daisy appeared utterly shocked, but the look on Nathaniel's face, pleading for her "yes," was unrelenting. She pulled the words deep down as they seemed not to want to escape her lips. "Yes, Nathaniel, I will marry you." She faked a smile as he grasped onto her hair and drew her face closer to his, kissing her with all his might.

***

That evening, Alice, Nathaniel's main servant was in the room with Daisy. She laid out the most beautiful gown Daisy had ever seen. A clean, white dress adorned with swirls of lavender in a floral pattern. The dress clung tightly onto her waist and expanded like an umbrella below her hips to accentuate her hour-glass figure. Her neck was

300

adorned with a silver necklace with an ornament in the shape of a daisy holding one, large canary yellow diamond in the center.

Alice helped Daisy pin her hair up into an array of curls that draped her skull like a hat and placed a daisy on the right side of her head, entangled in her honey-golden hair. "Mr. Alexander suggested the flower," Alice stated, pleased.

Daisy smiled at the bizarre play on her name.

When she was fully dressed, she exited her room and stood on top of the stairs. Music from violins, pianos and cellos filled the home. Chatter from various people flourished in the house. When Daisy appeared at the top of the stairs, chatter ceased. Only the sounds of the melodious tunes remained. Daisy held in her breath as she walked down the stairs. She watched smiling faces staring admiringly in her direction, mostly from men and older women. She could see the looks of envy flush across the face of some of the younger women in the room.

Daisy was greeted at the bottom of the steps by Nathaniel who took her by the hand and kissed it gently, bowing as he did so. "My love," he began, "you look even more beautiful tonight. How do you like your necklace? I had it made specially for you."

Daisy took the charm in her hand and studied it. Now familiar with the looks of a grand treasure, this one did not impress her much. But again, she forced herself to smile and said, "Yes, I like it very much, thank you."

Nathaniel introduced Daisy to an array of people. From military generals, to judges and constables, to the wealthiest merchants in the state. Daisy shook hands with everyone and curtsied as she did, showing her respect to the various people who joined their gala to celebrate her and her engagement to Nathaniel.

Daisy was relieved by the fact that no one recognized her from the year before. She was also disgusted at their treatment, treating her like a princess, when only a year before they were chanting cheers of excitement at her execution. She wondered, if they remembered who she was, would they still be treating her as they were? She did not recognize anyone as the judge who had sentenced her to death. Apparently, Nathaniel removed him from office when he became governor.

Daisy spent hours chatting with the people of the gala, all the while feeling overwhelmed, manipulated, molded into a false pretense of herself. She forced herself to remain seemingly happy with a pseudo-smile upon her face.

Later in the evening, after men had been consuming wine for some time, she noticed conversation was getting less inhibited. She walked into a conversation between a judge, a general and their wives. There was also another woman involved who admitted that she was single. The men were discussing the role of a woman, noting that there is no circumstance when a woman should even touch a firearm. The women simply giggled and nodded their heads in agreement, sipping the red wine that sloshed around in their glasses.

Daisy could not stand for it any longer. She stepped into the conversation and said, "I think you are mistaken, general. I believe that a woman can be just as efficient if not better at using a firearm than any man."

The women became silenced and looked at Daisy in awe. The men chuckled and looked around for Nathaniel. "Mr. Alexander," the judge shouted across the room. When Nathaniel approached, he continued, "Your lovely, soon-to-be wife here believes that women should have the opportunity to use a firearm." His voice was demeaning, almost as if he was alerting Nathaniel to keep his woman in her place.

"Yes, I am so sorry, perhaps she has had a little too much to drink," he laughed as he turned Daisy around by the waist and walked her away from the conversing group.

"I've had nothing to drink," Daisy protested.

"I know, my love. And I know what you have been through the past year. But you need to unlearn all that nonsense and uphold a more appropriate status as the governor's wife here in Virginia. My wife cannot speak of such things, especially not in a gala of this sort."

Daisy was infuriated. He was already trying to silence her, and they had not even been wedded yet.

***

That night, after everyone had gone home, Daisy lay in bed with Nathaniel holding her tightly into his groin. She turned to study his face. He slept with a grin, seemingly happy, even in his sleep. She could not understand her feelings. She was getting everything she ever wanted. She was being treated like a princess, and not like a slave or a whore as she once had been. Yet life as a princess, she

303

realized, may be similar to life as a whore. In either life, she would be desired, but she also was not free. Even as a princess, she realized, she was being silenced.

Nathaniel silenced her, just as Mr. Clark had. While her treatment by each man was different, her independence was still being taken away. She was to remain subordinate, follow the rules. Her mind was racing. What had she done? Had she made the wrong decision?

Life as a pirate was dangerous, cruel and sometimes lonely during the times when she yearned for the touch of a man. But it was also adventurous, uplifting, and free. She lived her whole life being contained by a man. She lived her whole life silenced, imprisoned. She would not live the rest of her life that way.

She could feel her chest begin to tighten, her breathing become heavy, her thinking erratic. She slightly lifted Nathaniel's arm off her abdomen and slowly slid out of the bed. She watched as he repositioned himself but remained asleep. She quickly dressed in the white gown adorned with lavender swirls, but instead of pumps, found her masculine boots and pressed her feet securely into them.

When she left the house, her heart was racing. The guards were snoring loudly, sitting upright on the cold ground, backs against the wrought-iron gate that surrounded the enormous, brick home. The gate screeched mildly as she opened it slowly. The men moved but did not wake. Daisy un-roped her white horse and hopped on, galloping away as fast as she could get her horse to go into the dark, silent, frigid night.

Daisy was not affected by the cold air that flowed past her as her horse galloped down the road. Her entire body was reacting. She could finally see clearly. She knew what she wanted and knew where she belonged. Her life was finally in her hands, and only she had the power to decide how she would live it.

She rode through the market square and around the jail house. She couldn't relax until she finally smelled the salty aroma of the sea port air. Finally, her eyes were upon the sea, blackened from the night. She could see the Crimson Rose illuminated by the radiation of the moon, full in the sky, surrounded but not covered by milky clouds. She hopped off her horse and began screaming, louder than she ever thought she was capable of. She began jumping up and down like a child, waving her arms in desperation. Her heart thumping inside her chest. Her soul begging for another chance. Hoping, praying, willing the ship to turn around. She felt heat rushing through her veins, warming her insides as her skin was exposed to the frigid Virginia air. She watched, desperately waiting for the ship to turn around. Waiting, hoping, praying. Watching her freedom sail away.